"Was that...?" Willow asked, swallowing hard. Her heart rate kicked into overdrive.

"Gunshots. We've got to get out of here, now. Go," Rey shouted, pointing back toward home.

"What on earth happened?" she asked, her voice shaky. "Were they shooting at us because we were on their land?"

"Apparently so."

"Which means they either had some sort of shelter close by where we pitched the tent or they were out in the dust storm," she said. "Which makes no sense."

"Unless they were some sort of patrol, guarding the perimeter of the land."

"Out in the middle of nowhere?" she scoffed. "What would they even be guarding against? They had to have heard us coming. These things aren't exactly quiet."

"I don't know," he replied, his voice as grim as his expression. "But we need to tell Rayna anyway."

She nodded. By mutual agreement, they headed back toward the ranch.

Once they reached the storage building and drove the four-wheelers inside, Willow handed Rey her key. "You know, the fact that someone shot at us makes me even more curious as to what they might be trying to hide."

Dear Reader,

I love my little fictional town of Getaway, Texas. The people have become like family to me and it makes me happy to give them brief appearances in every book I set there.

In this story, Willow Allen couldn't wait to get out of small-town west Texas life. She moved to California after college and only returns from time to time to visit her grandmother Isla, who raised her. Rey Johnson also left after high school to join the military. Unlike Willow, he returned to help his father, Carl, run the family ranch along with his younger brother, Sam. He loves his life and can't imagine living anywhere else.

When both Isla and Carl (who have been dating) go missing, Willow rushes home. Rey had been on the road picking up livestock and is concerned to find his father has disappeared. His brother, Sam, claims to have no idea where Carl might have gone.

As Willow and Rey team up to find their missing family members, more and more older people from town are vanishing, and no one seems to know why or where they've gone. The mystery deepens, and Willow and Rey grow closer as they continue to search for clues. Willow knows she cannot return to California until her grandmother is found, and even then, she has her doubts. She hadn't realized how much she'd missed Getaway and her grandmother. Plus, the thought of leaving Rey has become physically painful.

I hope you enjoy reading this suspenseful love story as much as I enjoyed writing it!

Karen Whiddon

VANISHED
IN TEXAS

KAREN WHIDDON

ROMANTIC SUSPENSE

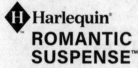

H Harlequin®
ROMANTIC SUSPENSE™

Recycling programs
for this product may
not exist in your area.

ISBN-13: 978-1-335-50250-6

Vanished in Texas

Copyright © 2024 by Karen Whiddon

For questions and comments about the quality of this book, please contact us at CustomerService@Harlequin.com.

TM and ® are trademarks of Harlequin Enterprises ULC.

 Harlequin Enterprises ULC
22 Adelaide St. West, 41st Floor
Toronto, Ontario M5H 4E3, Canada
www.Harlequin.com

Printed in Lithuania

MIX
Paper | Supporting
responsible forestry
FSC® C021394

Karen Whiddon started weaving fanciful tales for her younger brothers at the age of eleven. Amid the gorgeous Catskill Mountains, then the majestic Rocky Mountains, she fueled her imagination with the natural beauty surrounding her. Karen now lives in north Texas, writes full-time and volunteers for a boxer dog rescue. She shares her life with her hero of a husband and four to five dogs, depending on if she is fostering. You can email Karen at kwhiddon1@aol.com. Fans can also check out her website, karenwhiddon.com.

Books by Karen Whiddon

Harlequin Romantic Suspense

Texas Sheriff's Deadly Mission
Texas Rancher's Hidden Danger
Finding the Rancher's Son
The Spy Switch
Protected by the Texas Rancher
Secret Alaskan Hideaway
Saved by the Texas Cowboy
Missing in Texas
Murder at the Alaskan Lodge
Vanished in Texas

The Coltons of Owl Creek

Colton Mountain Search

Visit the Author Profile page
at Harlequin.com for more titles.

Almost every book I write, I dedicate to my husband, Lonnie. We've been together for a long time and seen each other through many ups and downs. He reads every single book I write once it's published and that's a lot. He's the model for every romantic hero! Love you, Lonnie.

Chapter 1

The instant Willow Allen caught sight of her grandmother's white-frame ranch house, something inside her unclenched. West Texas might be flat, the earth dry and desert like, and the weather in July hotter than most people would consider hospitable, but no matter where Willow currently lived, she'd always consider it home.

For the past five years, Willow had lived in California, with its perfect weather, palm trees and beaches. She'd taken a job there right out of college, working as an actuary for a large insurance company. The work was not particularly glamorous, but she'd always loved numbers and considered it a good fit.

But then her grandmama had mentioned going to the hospital with chest pains and, after returning home, had refused to discuss her health further. She'd steadfastly said she was fine, claiming nothing was wrong. Alarmed, Willow had immediately put in for some of her accumulated PTO and made the long drive back to Getaway, Texas. She'd decided not to tell her grandmother, aware Isla would tell her not to come.

She hadn't been home since Christmas. Seven months ago, her grandmother had been just fine. At least, as far as Willow had been able to tell. But Isla lived alone, and despite expressing happiness with her new relationship with a local rancher, Willow worried. The woman she considered her mother had single-handedly raised her and loved her without reservation after Willow's birth mother, Isla's daughter, had died of a drug overdose. She was and would always be the most important person in Willow's life. Willow couldn't wait to surprise her. She planned to wrap her arms around her grandmother's tiny frame, breathe in her unique patchouli scent and spend the next three weeks catching up.

Parking her shiny, new red Ford Bronco in the driveway, Willow got her suitcase out of the back and pulled it up to the front door. She used her own key and entered, calling out to alert her grandmother to her presence.

Nothing but silence answered her. Just her luck. Grandma mustn't be home. She dug out her phone and called her. Immediately, a phone in the master bedroom started ringing.

That was odd, to say the least. Willow hurried over and, sure enough, spotted her grandmother's cell on the nightstand next to the neatly made bed.

Concerned, Willow began searching the house. What if Isla had experienced another chest pain episode and fallen? She might even now be lying unconscious. Heart racing, Willow went through every room, checking in the closet and shower, the kitchen pantry and laundry room and, finally, the garage.

Her grandmother's silver Toyota Corolla still sat parked inside.

What the…? Willow backtracked to the master bedroom and opened the closet. While she wasn't an expert on Isla's wardrobe, it didn't look like much, if anything, was missing.

Maybe her grandma's new beau had picked her up and taken her out somewhere, and she'd simply forgotten her phone. That had to be it. Willow would simply call him, make sure her grandmother was okay and wait for her return.

She grabbed Isla's phone and realized she didn't know the passcode. Despite trying several combinations, from her grandmother's birthday to her own, she couldn't get in. Frustrated, she went back to her own phone and scrolled through the texts between the two of them, trying to find the guy's name. Finally, she located it. Carl. No last name. And while Willow knew most of the families in town, without more information, she had no idea who Carl might be.

Still concerned, she called her friend Amanda. Unlike Willow, Amanda had never left Getaway. After graduating from cosmetology school, Amanda had opened her own beauty salon right on Main Street. No one had better access to the local gossip than the proprietor of Hair Affair. But the receptionist who answered said Amanda was with a client and offered to take a message.

Instead of leaving her name and number, Willow hung up. No way did she intend to sit around aimlessly and wait for Amanda to return her call. Patience had never been one of her virtues.

She grabbed her car keys and decided to head downtown. She might as well ask Amanda in person. That way, she could go directly to this Carl's house and see if her grandmother was there. If not, maybe Carl might know where Isla had gone.

While she hated to take such drastic measures, Willow didn't see how she had a choice. None of this was like her mom. Even if Isla hadn't been aware her daughter was coming to pay her a surprise visit, she had her self-imposed routine. Ever since becoming an empty nester, she'd filled her days with various activities, all scheduled. She attended yoga on Tuesdays, book club on Thursdays, and she volunteered at the local animal shelter on Friday afternoons. She'd taken up knitting and gardening and took great pride in her rose bushes. By her own unvarying schedule, Isla should be home right now, making something for the noon meal.

Pushing away her niggling worry, Willow went back outside to get in her SUV to make the short drive back to town. But before she could even start the engine, a large dually pickup pulled up in front of the house.

Maybe her grandmother had arrived home. Excited, Willow got out of her SUV and started toward the huge truck. As she approached, instead of Isla, a tall man wearing a black cowboy hat got out. He wore well-fitting Wranglers and boots. Ignoring her, he started for the front door.

"Excuse me," she said, causing him to break stride. "No one's home."

This finally caught his attention. He turned, muscles rippling under his tan Western shirt. His handsome, rugged face seemed vaguely familiar, as if she might have seen him on a television show or in a movie.

She froze, her first thought *rodeo cowboy*. But then again, maybe not. He had a strong profile and chiseled features. And he moved with a kind of easy grace that she found somehow sensual. A true West Texas specimen brimming over with masculinity. And absolutely everything that she'd once found unbearably sexy and now abhorred in a man.

Or thought she did, right up until this very moment.

"I'm looking for my father," he said, his husky voice tinged with the familiar West Texas drawl. "Carl Johnson. His, er, lady friend lives in this house."

Crossing her arms, she took a deep breath. "My grandmother lives here. And she's gone. I just arrived in from out of state. I was hoping she was with him."

Now she'd caught his attention. "Gone?" His narrow gaze swept over her. "Where is she?"

"I don't know. Her car is in the garage. And she left her cell phone in her bedroom. I have no idea where she might be. In fact, I was heading into town to see if I could find out where your father lives so I could check there."

"His truck is still at the ranch too," the man mused. "I wonder if they had friends pick them up."

"What about your dad's cell? Did you try calling it?"

Slowly, he nodded. "I did. He left it behind too." Moving a few steps closer, he held out his hand. "Rey Johnson."

"Willow Allen." She took his hand and shook it, hiding her amazement at how easily his large hand engulfed hers. "I need to find my grandmother. And since your father is missing too, maybe we can team up to make the search easier."

"I wouldn't say missing," he began, then shrugged and shook his head. "Though I guess you could call it that."

With that, he turned to go.

"Wait!" Stunned, she rushed after him. "What are we going to do about it? We have to find them."

"We?" He turned and stared.

Deciding to continue pushing, since she had no idea what else to do, she nodded. "Yes, *we*. Two heads are better than one, don't you think? And since our parents, are likely together, it only makes sense."

When her plea didn't appear to convince him, she continued. "I grew up here. And while I don't live here now, I know enough about Getaway to know all of us stick together and help each other."

"Did you go to school with my younger brother, Sam?" he asked.

It took her a moment to put the name together. "Sam Johnson?" Stunned, now it was her turn to stare. "I did. I had no idea my grandmother was dating his father."

"Our father," he corrected. "But, yes. The two of them have been seeing each other for several months."

She took a moment to fully digest this. When she and her grandmom had talked on the phone, Isla had been uncharacteristically giddy about her new relationship. Willow had been happy for her. After all, her grandmother had been alone for as long as Willow could re-member. She'd dated, certainly. But she'd also cultivated a wide circle of friends, and between social activities and her volunteer work, her life had seemed full.

Until the health scare. The mere fact that Isla refused to talk about it, when she and Willow kept no secrets from one another, had been really concerning. This, more than anything else, had made Willow drive home.

Right now though, she needed to find her grand-mother. "What about their other friends? Do you think they might be out somewhere with another couple?"

He shrugged. "I have no idea, but since neither of

them took their own vehicles, that has to be what happened. I just got back from Colorado, where I picked up livestock. Since my dad was really excited about them, and he knew when I'd be back, I was surprised when I couldn't find him. Sam has been busy repairing fence all day, so he didn't know anything."

The undercurrent of worry she thought she heard in his voice gave her pause. "Do you think something might have happened to them?"

When he met her gaze, his brown eyes seemed kind. "Let's not jump to conclusions. I'm sure there's a rational explanation."

She wanted to believe him. Yet she couldn't seem to shake the feeling that something was wrong. "I'm going to go into town and ask around. One lunch at the Tumbleweed Café should catch me up on all the local gossip."

This comment made him laugh. "Truer words have never been spoken."

"What about you? Would you like to join me?" she asked.

"Maybe another time," he replied, holding her gaze. The warmth in his expression made her mouth go dry. "I need to head back to the ranch. How about I give you my number and you can text me so I have yours. That way, if either of us gets any new information, we can let the other know."

She entered his number into her phone contacts and then sent him a text so he'd have hers. Then she watched as he strode to his truck, an unfamiliar ache warring with the worry inside of her.

Just as he reached for his door handle, he stopped and turned. "I changed my mind," he said. "If you still want to, let's go grab lunch. I haven't eaten since sunrise and could go for one of the Tumbleweed's burgers."

"Sounds great." She hurried to join him before he changed his mind.

To her surprise, he went around to the passenger side and opened the door for her. "Thanks," she said, realizing she'd almost forgotten what it was like to live in small-town West Texas.

Buckling up, she waited for him to get in and start the engine. Now she could only hope they'd run into both their parents, so she could put this sense of foreboding behind her.

Damn. Drumming his fingers on the steering wheel as he drove, Rey Johnson tried to reconcile his admittedly vague memories of the teenaged girl who'd hung around with his younger brother with the stunning woman in his passenger seat.

He'd known, of course, that his father's girlfriend had a daughter who lived in California. Sam had mentioned bitterly several times how much he envied Willow for having the courage to get out of West Texas and start a new life somewhere better. For all his talk, Sam seemed awfully content to stick around the family ranch and do the bare minimum to help keep the place running.

Both Rey and their father humored him. Carl because Sam was his youngest son, aka the baby, and Rey because he understood what made his brother tick. While Sam might be a dreamer, he hadn't yet made the connection between dreams and the hard work necessary to accomplish them.

Shaking off these thoughts, Rey glanced at Willow.

"I'm guessing it's been a while since you visited your grandmother?"

"Christmas," she answered, clearly distracted. "Just about seven months ago. I work in LA. I usually save up my vacation days so I can come home. Though my grandmom and I talk on the phone at least once a week. Sometimes more."

"LA?" He could understand why she'd gone to California. Whether her dream had been to model or to become an actor, someone who looked like her would be sure to get noticed. "Do you act?"

"Act?" Frowning, she eyed him as if he'd suggested she'd taken up cliff diving as a hobby. "No. I work in insurance. I'm an actuary. My job is to analyze the financial costs of risk and uncertainty." She took a deep breath and then smiled. "I absolutely love it."

Her smile lit up the inside of his truck and made his heart beat just a little bit faster.

"An actuary," he repeated, trying not to show his surprise. "I take it you must also love math."

"And spreadsheets," she countered, still smiling. "But yes. Math is my jam."

Not sure how to respond, he nodded.

"What about you?" she asked. "Since you're a rancher, I'm guessing you work around the place with your father."

"And brother," he added. "Sam works there too. We raise cattle, though recently we expanded to include bison. That's what I was doing in Colorado."

"Yet neither of you noticed when your dad left? Why wouldn't he have mentioned he was going somewhere?"

"That's just it," he replied, frustrated. "He's been really looking forward to seeing the bison we purchased.

He knew what time I'd be getting back. I actually expected him to be there to help me unload."

Turning onto Main Street, he noticed the way Willow sat up straight. "The Tumbleweed looks busy as always," she said, her lips curving. "I think out of all the places to eat in Getaway, I missed this one the most."

Since he'd never even once wanted to live anywhere else besides the town where he'd grown up, he simply shrugged. "Some things never change."

He found a parking spot close to the entrance. When he and Willow walked in together, several patrons sent interested glances their way. Which meant they'd be talking about him later.

The hostess, a quiet girl named Barbi who looked like a college student, led them to a booth close to a front window. Busy scanning the restaurant, Willow nearly ran her over when she stopped in front of their seats.

"I'm so sorry," Willow said. "I'm just looking for my mother or even some of her friends. Maybe you've seen her? Isla Allen?"

Barbi stared and then shook her head. "I'm new," she replied. "This is only my second day. I'm home from Tech for the summer. So if she's a regular here, I wouldn't know her. I can ask around though, if you want."

"I'd appreciate it." Willow slid into the booth and accepted the menu.

A moment later, Rey did the same. He'd barely glanced at the menu when an older man wearing a Western shirt, Wranglers and boots walked up. "Afternoon, Rey."

Rey pushed to his feet and held out his hand. "Good to see you, Walter. You haven't happened to have seen my father around town today, have you?"

"Nope. I haven't seen much of Carl ever since he went and got himself a lady friend." Walter eyed Willow curiously. "And who's this here pretty young thing?"

"My name is Willow Allen," Willow said, smiling. "I'm Isla Allen's daughter."

Walter's faded blue gaze sharpened. "Nice to see you back in town. I remember when you were just knee high."

"We're looking for them both," Willow continued. "As you seem to know, his father, Carl, and my grandma, Isla, are a couple. We're hoping someone around here might have seen them."

"You can't find them?" Walter asked. "Are you saying they're missing?"

"Not at all," Rey said, aware he needed to step in before Walter started a panic over the gossip grapevine. "Both of us just got back in town—separately—and we're thinking maybe the two of them are out doing something fun together. Willow here wants to surprise her grandmother. That's all."

"Oh." Clearly disappointed, Walter shrugged. "If I happen to see them, I'll let them know you're looking for them." Dipping his chin at Rey, the older man left.

The waitress appeared. "Can I get you something to drink?"

"Iced tea, please," Willow responded. Rey seconded that.

"Are you two ready to order or do you need another minute?"

"I'm ready," Willow said, sliding her menu across the table so the waitress could grab it. "I'll have the mushroom Swiss burger with fries."

"Bacon burger for me, please." Rey handed over his

menu as well. Once the waitress left, he leaned over and spoke quietly so he wouldn't be overheard. "I know you've been gone for a while, but I know you have to remember how quickly the gossip spreads around here."

"I do." She sighed. "And you're right. My grandmom wouldn't be happy if I started rumors about her. I just can't help but be worried. She's never done anything like this before."

"Like what?" he asked. "From what you've told me, she had no idea you were even coming to visit. I really think she and my dad are out somewhere enjoying themselves with friends. They'll show up eventually."

Expression enigmatic, she eyed him. "You sound awfully certain."

"I am." He sat back in his seat to make room for the waitress with their tea. He waited until she'd left before continuing. "Seriously, what are the alternatives?"

She sighed. "You're probably right, but I tend to have an overactive imagination. I worry."

"I get that. But give it until tonight. If she doesn't return home by then, we'll talk again."

Some of the tenseness seemed to leave her expression. Slowly, she nodded. "Sounds like a plan." For a moment, she studied him. "How is it that your dad is around the same age as my granny? You don't seem to be more than a couple of years older than me, and I know Sam and I are the same age."

"Carl is actually my uncle. He and my father ran the ranch together. When my mom died giving birth to Sam, he became like a second father to us." He took a deep breath, since he hated dredging up the painful past. "I was five when my father died during a bull-riding incident out in Cheyenne. He'd taken up rodeo when Sam and I were both toddlers and left us with Carl most of the time. He's Dad to us now and has been for a long time."

Her sweet smile contained a hint of sadness. "Same with my grandmother. She raised me up and is the only mom I ever knew. I don't know what I'd do if something happened to her."

Their food arrived then. Though his burger made his mouth water, he found himself watching as she picked hers up and took a bite. She ate with gusto, which he appreciated, and yet there was somehow something sensual about the way she enjoyed her meal. His body reacted immediately, and he busied himself with eating to get it back under control.

When he looked up again, he realized they'd finished at the same time. Each of them had a few fries remaining, but nothing more.

"You must have been hungry," she said, touching her napkin to the corners of her mouth. "I know I was."

"Starving," he agreed. "Maybe once our folks reappear, we can all go out to dinner together."

"Definitely." Her quick answer made him exhale. "And Sam should come along. He and I have a lot to catch up on."

Since there was no way to counter that suggestion without making himself look bad, he nodded. While he hadn't meant a date, not really, he was actually hoping to get to know her a little better. At least until she went back to California.

Just the thought was enough to put a damper on the moment of brief foolishness he'd allowed himself to entertain. Willow might be beautiful, she might be the most interesting woman he'd met in a long time. Sexy too, he definitely couldn't forget that.

But she wasn't going to stay. Which, in years past, might have made her a perfect woman with whom to indulge in a hot and heavy, no-emotional-baggage relationship. Not anymore. While he loved his life, he'd reached the stage where he thought he might be open to something more.

In addition, her mother and his father wouldn't appreciate their offspring indulging in a no-holds-barred erotic fling. That alone would be enough to counter any temptation.

"Are you okay?" she asked, interrupting his musing.

Blinking, he looked up, glad she couldn't read his mind. "I'm good," he replied, his voice a bit husky. "Lunch is on me."

Just as Willow started to protest, the waitress arrived with the check, as if on cue. They both reached for it at the same time, their fingers colliding. Somehow, Willow managed to come away with it.

"My treat," she insisted. "After all, you drove. And took pity on an exhausted, overly stressed stranger. I appreciate that more than I can say."

Her words touched him. Dipping his chin in a rancher's way of saying thanks, he abandoned any further effort to convince her to let him pay.

"The next one's on me," he said instead.

She considered him for a moment. "Deal."

On their way out, several old-timers stopped them to talk. Unfortunately, none of them had seen his father or her mother in the last couple of days.

He and Willow walked out to his truck without speaking.

After helping her in, he went around to the driver's side and got in. When she looked at him, he swore he could see the worry in her eyes.

"They'll show up soon," he said, feeling quite certain. "And we'll all have a good laugh over this later."

"I hope so." Finally, she sighed. "I'm exhausted. It's a long drive, and now that I've eaten, I can barely keep my eyes open. When I get back to the house, I'm going to take a nap. Hopefully, when I wake up, my mother will be back."

Chapter 2

After Rey drove away, Willow went back inside her mother's house. Despite her overwhelming urge to sleep, she found herself wandering from room to room, hoping she'd see an obvious clue as to her mom's whereabouts.

But the neat and tidy house yielded nothing unusual. Finally, Willow gave up and went into her childhood bedroom, now a guest room, pulled back the covers and climbed into bed.

She must have been more tired than she'd recognized because when she next opened her eyes, she realized she'd slept four hours. A quick glance at the nightstand clock showed it was nearly six, which meant her mother would soon be messing around in the kitchen, making supper.

Except the house remained eerily quiet. With a sense of dread settling in her stomach, she got up and made her way to the kitchen. As she'd guessed, it was empty. Once again, she went through the entire house, almost as if she hoped her mother might simply be hiding. Heck, as weird as that sounded, she'd take her grandmother jumping out to surprise her over this silent disappearance.

Despite knowing better, Willow checked her phone.

While her mom clearly couldn't reply to Willow's texts or phone calls since she didn't have her phone with her, if she'd gotten into some kind of trouble, she might attempt to reach out another way, like through social media. But all three of her mother's online accounts were stagnant, with no new posts at all within the last week. Not even the usual sharing of funny memes, something her mom had taken delight in doing.

Which made Willow wonder how long her mother might have been missing. The last time they'd talked was after Isla had the medical incident that she refused to discuss other than claiming to be fine. To Willow's astonishment, she realized this had been almost a week ago. She'd gotten so busy making sure her work was caught up before she left, she hadn't realized how much time had passed.

What if Isla had been gone all that time? Wouldn't someone have noticed? Her mother lived an active and full life and had many friends. Willow planned to check with them as well. Unfortunately, since she couldn't access her mom's phone, she had no way to contact them. And while Isla had remained friends with a few women whom Willow had known as a child, after Willow had moved away to California, her mom had broadened her interests and circle of friends. Willow didn't know much about them other than their first names.

However, since Getaway wasn't that big of a town, it shouldn't be too difficult to track these people down. Surely one of Isla's friends would know where she'd gone. She'd head into town first thing in the morning and get started. Unless, of course, her mom arrived home before then.

Having a plan of action helped somewhat. Realizing she needed to eat, Willow rummaged in the kitchen looking for something. She found a can of tomato soup and decided to make a comfort meal with that and a grilled cheese sandwich.

After she ate, she found herself roaming the house yet again. What she hated the most was the sense of powerlessness. She ought to be doing *something* to locate her mom instead of sitting around waiting for her to show up. At this point, she realized it was unlikely that Isla would.

For a few minutes, she debated whether it would make sense to go talk to the neighbors. She'd grown up here and knew them all well. While she didn't want to stir up the powerful neighborhood gossip group, who would know more about Isla's comings and goings than the neighbors closest to the house? Only the certainty that her mom would be absolutely horrified to have them involved in her "business" made Willow hesitate.

She decided she'd locate her mom's friends first. Hopefully, doing that would solve the riddle of her mother's whereabouts quietly and without fuss.

After several hours of mindless television, interspersed with pacing the house and checking out the front window for headlights that never pulled into the driveway, she knew she had to go to bed. Despite her exhaustion, she knew she wouldn't sleep well but wanted to try and get some rest so she'd be alert to start her search in the morning.

Though she tossed and turned some, she woke up shortly after sunrise feeling surprisingly refreshed. She checked the entire house again, in case her mom had come home during the night. Unsurprised to see that she hadn't, Willow took a shower, made herself some coffee and a couple of fried eggs with toast and then got ready to go into town.

Before she left, Willow checked her phone several times for a text from Rey but decided against contacting him just yet. She imagined he would be working on his own strategy to find his father and he'd contact her if he learned anything. She'd do the same for him.

Walking out of the house and locking the front door behind her, she got into her Bronco and sat for a moment behind the steering wheel. None of this felt real. Aware she was on the verge of having a panic attack, she concentrated on her breathing. It had taken years of therapy to learn how to train herself away from allowing these to take over. In fact, she hadn't had one in a long time.

And she refused to have one now. Where once she'd believed herself powerless, the focusing techniques she'd learned helped her regain control. Gradually, the tremors subsided, her heart rate slowed and she started the car.

Despite having gone to the Tumbleweed with Rey yesterday, she'd been too preoccupied worrying about her mother and battling her instant attraction to him to really look around.

Today, as she drove, everything came into focus with a sharp clarity. The familiar restored Western storefronts were reminders of how different Getaway was from Southern California.

She found a parking space a few doors down from the hair salon, killed her engine and got out. Her comfy shorts, soft T-shirt and flip-flops had been perfect for her casual life on the West Coast but might look out of place in downtown Getaway.

None of that mattered, she told herself. Growing up here, she'd always dressed how she wanted. Summers were hot, and trying to stay cool could be a challenge.

She just needed to find her mother, make sure she was safe and get in a big hug. After that, the two of them could catch up and have a nice, long visit. Taking a deep breath, she held on to that thought as she headed to the only hair salon in town.

Hair Affair looked busy as always, with every stylist's chair full. The receptionist, a young woman who had spiky purple hair and looked as if she'd recently graduated high school, smiled. "Can I help you?"

"I need to see Amanda," Willow said, smiling back. "Not for hair or anything. I just need a quick word."

Before the receptionist could speak, Amanda came rushing over. "Willow!" she squealed, wrapping Willow up in a tight hug. "I thought I recognized you! What brings you back to our neck of the woods?"

"I'm visiting my mom," Willow replied. "But she's not home." She shrugged, aware she needed to be careful not to add any new information for potential gossip. "She didn't know I was coming, and I want to surprise her. I know she's been seeing someone, and since you do her hair, I thought maybe she might have confided in you about her whereabouts."

Amanda cocked her head. "You mean Carl? Carl Johnson? We went to school with one of his sons. Sam. Remember him?"

"I do. Sam was a lot of fun."

"He still is." Amanda waved one perfectly manicured hand. "But it's his older brother, Rey, who's driving all the single gals crazy."

"Okay." Blinking, Willow debated whether or not to mention that she'd met him. Deciding it didn't matter, she touched Amanda's arm. "I'm assuming they still live out at that ranch near the county line."

"Yep. We were all there once, for Sam's sixteenth birthday."

"I remember." Willow took a deep breath. "Anyway, did Mom mention anything to you about any travel plans?"

Frowning, Amanda shook her head. "No. But she hasn't been in to get her hair done in at least a month. The last time I saw her, she seemed really happy. She couldn't stop talking about how much fun she and Carl were having. I bet she went somewhere with him."

"I'm thinking so too." Careful to keep her voice casual, Willow looked around the packed salon. "Are any of my mother's friends here today? Maybe I can ask them."

Amanda shook her head. "I don't think so. It's a bit early for that group of ladies. You should stop by the yoga studio. They all take a morning class there."

"My mom mentioned that. Where's it located?"

"That's right." With a sigh, Amanda signaled to her client she'd be right there. "It opened up after you moved away. It's on Main, right next to Serenity's. The owner is one of Serenity's sisters, I think. I'm sorry, but I've got to get back to work."

"Thank you." Willow hugged her friend again. "Once all this is settled, you and I will have to catch up over lunch. Right now, I'm going to drive over there and see if I can still surprise my mom. I'm hoping she's there." Even though she knew dang good and well that she wasn't.

"Good luck." Amanda hurried back to her client. "I'll hold you to that lunch," she said over her shoulder.

Back outside in the unrelenting West Texas sun, Willow glanced around before getting into her Bronco. Some things never changed, and downtown Getaway appeared to be one of them. Which she appreciated. Home was like a beacon of stability in an ever-changing world of chaos.

Since Serenity's little shop was only a few blocks away, Willow could have walked. She definitely could use the exercise. Except her time in the temperate climate of California had lowered her tolerance for the heat of Texas in the summer, and she knew she'd be a sweaty mess if she did. So instead, she climbed back into her vehicle and drove the short distance.

There were no parking spots anywhere even remotely close. Which meant the yoga class must have a great turn out. She found a place the next block over and took it. Looked like she'd be walking a little bit after all. At least it wasn't uphill.

In California, Willow had attended a few yoga classes before deciding to learn the moves via an app. She'd practiced it faithfully several mornings a week, since the flexibility she gained helped her surf. But riding the waves had become her true passion, and she'd thrown herself into learning and practicing until she was skilled enough to teach her own beginner class. Surfing had helped her get over her homesickness at first, and then the sport had made her feel connected to the sea.

Shaking off a sudden longing for the Pacific Ocean, Willow opened the door to the yoga studio and stepped inside. She stood in a small foyer with an empty reception desk. In a larger room off to the side, she could see about twenty-five women, all engaged in the same variation of the Bharadvaja's twist pose.

She moved closer, keeping a respectful silence as she scanned the room for any sign of her mom. While she didn't see Isla, she spotted several of her mother's friends. These women appeared to be not only skilled, but completely comfortable.

The instructor noticed Willow watching and acknowledged her with a quick dip of her head. She had her students finish up with several slow stretching moves. Then she announced in a quiet voice that the class had finished and made her way over to Willow.

"Can I help you?" she asked, her expression pleasant. She bore a striking resemblance to Serenity, though instead of flowy, colorful clothes and lots of jewelry, she wore black yoga pants and a pale yellow workout tank. Her shorty, spiky, silver hair wasn't anything like Serenity's long braids, but their facial features were almost identical.

"I'm Willow Allen. My mother, Isla, takes your class."

"She does." Beaming now, the older woman held out one graceful hand. "I'm Velma, by the way."

They shook. Then Velma gestured back at her students, who were now rolling up their mats and chatting. "Is Isla all right? She almost never misses a class, but I haven't seen her for the last three. All her friends have been worried about her too."

Right then and there, Willow's stomach sank. "Actually, that's why I stopped by. I just got in from out of town and was hoping someone might know where she went off to."

Velma's smile dimmed. "Oh. Have you checked with Carl Johnson? He and Isla have been an item for several months now. Maybe they took off together for a bit of a romantic getaway."

"He's missing too, so that's a definite possibility." It took a major effort, but Willow tried to sound upbeat as she thanked Velma and hurried out the door. She made it to her SUV before any of the other women left. Since she had no idea where else to look, she decided she might as well head out to Carl's ranch. Maybe Rey had learned something new.

The Johnson ranch was a good fifteen- to twenty-minute drive from downtown. Willow remembered the way, but only because she and Sam had been good friends back in the day. She'd actually been out to the place more times than she could count. And she figured it, like everything else around here, would look exactly the same.

Fifteen minutes later, she turned her blinker on, waiting to make the turn onto the gravel drive. She could only hope Rey would be home. While she knew she should have texted first, she hadn't taken the time to think. She just needed to talk to someone else who understood how it felt to have a missing parent.

The sound of tires pulling up the gravel drive had Rey's heart skipping a beat. Had his father finally arrived back home?

He hurried over to the window to look. A new Ford Bronco had just parked. The door opened, and Willow Allen got out. She wore flip-flops, a T-shirt and a pair of denim shorts that showed off her long legs. Her long, dark hair swirled around her tanned shoulders.

For a second, he couldn't breathe, couldn't think, could barely move. And then, he rushed to the door and opened it, ridiculously glad to see her. Because he was hopeful she might have some new information, of course. Nothing more.

"Any word?" she asked, by way of greeting. Just like that, she dashed his hopes.

"No. What about you?"

She shifted her weight from foot to foot, drawing attention to her pretty pink painted toenails. "Nothing. My mom didn't come home last night. This morning I stopped by the hair salon and then a place where she takes yoga classes, but no one has seen her. It's looking like she might have gone missing a week ago or more."

"A week ago?" He frowned. "My father was here when I left for Colorado to pick up the bison. That was six days ago."

"Surely someone else was here with him after you left," she said. "What about Sam?"

As if saying his name invoked some sort of magic, Sam appeared, the porch screen door swinging open. "I thought it was you!" he exclaimed. Rushing over, he enveloped Willow in a hug. "How have you been?"

"I'm good." Smiling, she extricated herself. "I'm guessing you were here when Rey left for Colorado?"

He looked to Rey and back to Willow. "I was. Why?"

"Do you have any idea when your father disappeared?" she asked.

Sam groaned. "Not you too. This morning, Rey called every single one of Dad's buddies looking for him."

"I did," Rey said, managing to keep his voice level. "And when the fifth guy acted surprised to hear I was looking for Carl, I gave up. No one has seen hide nor hair of him."

Willow groaned. "This is getting more and more worrisome. I'm thinking it's time to talk to the sheriff."

Crossing his arms, Sam finally appeared to pick up on their concern. "Willow, I know you and your grandmother are close. Don't tell me you haven't heard from her either."

"I haven't," Willow responded. "She's missing too. I came home from Cali to surprise her, but she isn't home. Even though her car is parked in the garage."

"Do you think they're together?" Sam asked Willow.

Rey shook his head, annoyed since he and Sam had already had a similar discussion. "Who else would they be with?" he asked.

Sam barely glanced at his brother, keeping all his attention focused on Willow. "I bet they went on a trip with another couple. Maybe someone from their church."

"I didn't think of that," Willow said. "For as long as I can remember, my grandmother has attended Sunday services at that small, nondenominational church on the south side of town. Straightline Church."

"Yes, that's the one. I remember you went there when we were in high school." Sam smiled. "You even dragged me to a couple of those youth activities back then."

Willow ignored Sam's attempt to reminisce. She turned to look at Rey, her expression hopeful. "That's a great suggestion, don't you think?" she asked. "It's entirely possible a group of them from church went on some kind of outing. I'll run over there and talk to Pastor Clayton."

"I have his number." Keeping his gaze locked on hers, Rey dug out his phone. "Let me just call and ask."

The elderly pastor answered on the second ring. After exchanging a few pleasantries, Rey asked his question.

"Church social events? We don't have anything scheduled until the ice-cream social after services this Sunday. Are you planning to attend?"

"I'm not sure," Rey answered. He took a moment to find the right words before asking his next question. Finally, he decided to just come right out with it. "My father and Isla Allen appear to be missing. You don't happen to have any idea where they might be, do you?"

"Missing? For how long?"

"We're not sure." Catching Willow's eye, Rey slowly shook his head. "I just got back from picking up some livestock in Denver, and he was gone. Sam was here, but he claims he doesn't know."

At this, Sam made a sound of protest. Rey ignored it.

"I had no idea," Pastor Clayton said. "I'll mention this in my sermon on Sunday. Maybe someone in the congregation will know something."

Rey thanked him and ended the call. When he repeated what the elderly man had said, Willow made a face. "Well, that will definitely get the gossip going."

"If it helps find them, it's worth it," Rey replied.

"Come on, you two." Sam rolled his eyes. "I still think you're making too much out of this. Honestly, what do you think happened to them? They're adults. They're fine."

Instead of responding, Willow looked down at her feet. Her worry and anguish seemed palpable, and it was all Rey could do not to reach out and pull her into his arms.

Clearly oblivious, Sam continued. "So, Willow. How long are you in town?"

Willow simply shook her head instead of answering.

"Sam, just stop," Rey warned. As Willow turned blindly to make her way to her vehicle, he took her arm. When she glanced at him as if to thank him, he was unsurprised to see tears in her eyes.

"It's going to be all right," he told her, helping her into her vehicle.

"Is it?" Expression as bleak as her voice, she pressed the button to start her engine. "Please let me know if you hear anything."

He promised he would. Jamming his hands into his pockets, he stood and watched as she drove away.

"What the hell was that?" Sam asked, his voice hard. "Are you seriously trying to make a move on Willow Allen?"

"Make a move?" Rey spun around so fast that Sam had to take a step back. "I don't know what's wrong with you, but you need to stop. She's worried about her mother. I'm concerned about our dad. And you should be too, if you had a lick of sense."

Sam grimaced. "She's not your type, you know."

Gaping at him, Rey took a deep breath. "Who, Sam?"

"Willow."

Sometimes, Rey wondered if he'd ever understand his younger brother. Refusing to dignify that statement with a response, Rey went back inside the house. He wasn't sure how Sam had picked up on Rey's attraction toward Willow, but with their father missing, that would be the last thing Sam needed to focus on.

Because work on a ranch waited for no man, chores

kept Rey busy for the rest of the day. He'd turned the small herd of bison out into one of the larger pastures, keeping them separate from their main herd of cattle. Saddling up Roscoe, he rode out to check on them. Every single time that he stopped, he pulled out his phone and checked it, hoping against hope that his dad would have turned up back home.

But there were no texts. Not from his brother or the pastor or Willow. Finally, after ensuring the bison were doing well and checking on the cattle, he decided the time had come to bring in the sheriff. This, he wanted to do in person. He'd ask Willow if she wanted to meet him there.

Decision made, he rode Roscoe back to the barn, unsaddled him and brushed him down. He noticed Sam's horse's stall was now empty, which meant Sam had finally gotten around to heading out to finish repairing one of the fences. Luckily, they didn't have any livestock in that pasture, but they were due to rotate some of the cattle there within the next few weeks.

Inside the house, he poured himself a glass of iced tea and got out his phone. Willow answered on the second ring.

"I'm about to leave and go into town," he said. "I think we need to bring the sheriff in. Rayna's very thorough, and if anyone can figure this out, she can."

"I agree." Willow hesitated. "Are we going to file missing person reports?"

"I think that would be best. Do you want to meet me there?"

"Yes," Willow replied. "I can leave here in about five minutes."

After ending the call, he called ahead, just to make sure Rayna would have time to talk to them. She agreed to meet with him and Willow. "I've been expecting the two of you to come by," she said. "I'll see you in about twenty minutes."

Hopping into his truck, he drove into town. When he reached the sheriff's office, he waited inside the air-conditioned cab of his truck until he saw Willow's red Bronco pull into the parking lot. Jumping down, he reached her just as she opened her door to get out.

Offering his hand to help her, he couldn't help but smile when she took it. The softness of her skin and the way she gave his hand a quick squeeze before letting go brought a rush of warmth inside him.

"I called ahead to let Rayna know we were coming," he told her, holding the glass door open so she could enter the building before him.

"Thank you." Expression serious, Willow took a deep breath.

Side by side, they made their way through the busy room toward Rayna's space in the back. Several uniformed officers glanced up at them. A few smiled and waved, but no one made any attempt to question or stop them. Which meant, Rey figured, that everyone had known they were coming.

"Come on back." Rayna appeared in her doorway, motioning at them. She went around her desk and pointed to a couple of chairs in front of her. "Have a seat. And go ahead and close the door behind you."

Once they were all situated, Rayna dropped into her own chair and leaned forward. "You're here because Carl Johnson and Isla Allen are missing."

Rey and Willow exchanged a quick glance before they nodded. "Exactly. Both of their vehicles were left at home, as well as their cell phones," Rey said. "This is not like my father at all."

"Or my mom," Willow chimed in. "Granted, she had no idea that I was coming to visit, but she hasn't been to yoga class, and none of her friends have any idea where she might be."

"They aren't the only seniors who have gone missing." Expression serious, Rayna slid a photocopy of a missing poster across her desk toward them. "Do either of you know Ernesto and Yolanda Alvarez?"

Rey stared at the poster. The grainy photo showed a couple of people about the same age as his father. Mid to late sixties or early seventies, the woman appeared to have streaks of silver in her hair. "I don't," Rey answered, glancing at Willow. "How about you?"

"I don't recognize them either." She slid the poster back toward the sheriff. "Do you think there's a chance they all went missing together?"

Chapter 3

Heart pounding, Willow waited to hear what Rayna had to say. The redheaded sheriff took the poster back and considered them both for a moment.

"I don't know yet," she finally said. "Right now, I'd prefer not to speculate. But the Alvarez family reported those two missing yesterday. They had a family reunion scheduled for Saturday, and when everyone arrived, Ernesto and Yolanda were nowhere to be found. Like your folks, both their cars were still at the house, and they left their cell phones. They also didn't leave a note."

Stumped, Willow sat back in her chair. Glancing at Rey, she could tell from his expression that he too had no idea what to make of all this.

"We have no clues as to their whereabouts," Rayna continued. "We've just begun the process of interviewing their friends. So far, they don't appear to have told a single soul where they were going."

Blindly, Willow reached for Rey. He met her halfway, enfolding her hand in his larger one. Though she barely knew him, she found this tremendously comforting.

"I stopped by my grandmother's regular yoga class earlier," Willow offered. "While I didn't speak directly with her friends, the instructor told me they were all wondering where Isla had gone off to. It isn't like her to miss a class."

Rayna nodded, her sharp gaze missing nothing. "I promise to look into this. Will you let me know if you hear anything?"

"Of course," Rey answered for both of them.

"Perfect." Pushing to her feet, Rayna gave them a friendly smile. "And, of course, I'll do the same. Try not to worry, you two. It's entirely possible they got a wild hare and took off on a spontaneous vacation."

"Which isn't likely," Willow pointed out. Rey seconded her comment.

"But you never know." Clearly determined to be positive, Rayna led the way to the door. "I'll be in touch."

Once back outside, Willow had to stop herself from reaching for Rey's hand. While she barely knew this man, his quiet strength gave her sorely needed comfort.

He walked her to her vehicle and waited silently while she unlocked her doors. "Try not to worry," he said. "Rayna's good at what she does."

"I heard she caught a serial killer a while back."

"Two actually." He shrugged. "Hard to believe our little town seemed to be a magnet for them for a little bit. At least it's been quiet since then."

Until now. Though neither of them said the words out loud, she knew they were thinking them.

"I wonder if we should ask Rayna to make sure they're both still locked up and out of commission," she said, getting into her Bronco.

He nodded. "I'm sure she will. But both of them had

specific types, and older couples don't fit those particular profiles."

"That's good." From somewhere, she summoned a smile.

"Stay in touch," he told her, stepping back so she could close her door.

Driving home, she tried to hang on to her composure. The last thing she needed was to break down. Isla would want her to be strong. After all, she'd raised Willow by example.

Back at the house, which felt achingly empty, Willow roamed around. Yet again, she tried to find some clue, some hint, of where her grandmother might have gone. For as long as Willow could remember, Isla had used an old, built-in desk in a corner of the kitchen to pay her bills and to store relevant documents. Willow dropped into the ancient office chair and opened one of the large side drawers. Rows of manila folders filled several hanging files. She went through them. Most of them appeared to be for various bills. Electricity, gas and water were packed full. After that, she found folders for receipts, also neatly labeled. She pulled out one marked Restaurants and began leafing through that. Nothing out of the ordinary jumped out. They were all local eateries here in town.

Putting the file back, she reached for the next one, marked Medical. There she found the discharge notes from her gram's recent hospital stay and a referral to a cardiologist in Midland. As far as Willow could tell, it didn't look like Isla had ever gone. And anything related to a diagnosis had been left out—either stored elsewhere or destroyed. Which made no sense, because Isla had always been a stickler about keeping everything in the right place.

She went through the rest of the medical records and found nothing else related to the ER visit and hospitalization. There'd been the usual routine doctor visits, for physicals and prescription refills. Isla had gotten her annual mammogram in March.

Closing the folder, Willow returned it to its place and sighed. She riffled through a few more, but there wasn't anything out of the ordinary.

A thorough search through the rest of the desk yielded nothing interesting. Which meant she was exactly where she'd started. With nothing.

The flashing light on her grandma's answering machine indicated a message had been left. Since she hadn't even heard the landline ring, this startled Willow. Maybe the call had come in when she'd been out. Heart pounding, she walked over to the outdated piece of equipment and pressed the button to play.

"This is Marlene, the city secretary. I'm calling to let you know that we'll be holding a meeting tonight at the Rattlesnake Pub to discuss recent developments in the disappearance of several of our residents. The meeting will begin at seven, and everyone is welcome. We hope to see you there."

Recent developments? Immediately, she wanted to call Rayna. The sheriff had promised to call her with any news regarding her grandmother. Which likely meant any developments were related to some of the other missing people.

Should she touch base with Rey? Right now, he was the only one she knew who could relate to what was going on. The fact that he was easy on the eyes didn't hurt either. Every time they got together, the physical attraction nearly overwhelmed her. Part of her felt guilty that she could even think of such things when her grandma was missing. But she also realized she was only human. Her body wanted what her body wanted. Since she had zero plans to act on them, she figured she might as well enjoy her little fantasies. Once her grandmother returned, the two of them would have a good chuckle over that.

Returned. For a moment, Willow's breath caught in her throat. Obviously, she couldn't go back to California until Isla had been found. And even then, Willow wasn't sure she'd be able to ever leave her again.

Which meant she had a lot of thinking to do. For now, she'd continue to try and stay anchored in the present. Take things one day at a time.

Until she could come up with something better to do, she decided she'd continue her search of the house. Previously, it had felt too intrusive to do a deep dive through her grandmother's things. Now, Willow didn't see how she had any choice.

She decided to start with the master bedroom, beginning with the main dresser. Once she started opening drawers, she realized that some of Isla's things had to be missing. Though the clothes were still neatly folded, there weren't enough of them for a person to make it through an entire week. Undergarments, pajamas, even socks. Either her grandmother had become seriously minimalistic, or she'd packed some of these things for her trip.

Her trip. The thought made Willow feel better. She

checked the closet out next and once again, she thought some of the clothing had been removed. There were actually empty hangers, which she considered proof.

The shoes, neatly lined up in the bottom of the closet, had a couple of empty spots too. While Willow had no idea where Isla stored her suitcases, she had a feeling one of them had been packed for a getaway.

The next time she talked to Rey, she'd ask him to check out his father's dresser and closet. She'd bet he'd find some indications of packing for a trip there too.

A trip, but to where? And why leave the cell phones behind? And keep the entire thing such a secret, especially from the ones who loved you?

Maybe this topic would be covered at the meeting that evening.

She wondered if she'd see Rey there. Just the thought had her heart skipping a beat. Resisting the urge to text him, she went into her old bedroom and finished unpacking instead.

When she got to the new yellow sundress she'd purchased to wear out to dinner with her grandmother, she found herself blinking back tears. Yellow was Isla's favorite color. The instant Willow had seen the dress in the window of her favorite shop, she'd known she had to have it for her time back home.

She'd wear it to the meeting tonight, she decided. The simple act of having yellow on would help her feel more connected to her missing grandmother.

After she finished unpacking, she rummaged through the refrigerator and made herself a sandwich for lunch. She figured she'd call Rey before the meeting and see if he maybe wanted to grab a drink or something after.

Right now, a nap fit the bill. She turned the TV on low, lay down on the couch and pulled a light blanket over her. Since Isla's disappearance, she hadn't slept well and figured she could use the nap to catch up on some much needed rest.

After a quick lunch, Rey managed to get all his chores done in record time. He planned to take a little of his newly freed up time to do a more thorough search of the house. Hopefully, he could find something that might offer a clue as to where Carl had gone.

When he reached the house, he was surprised to find Sam already there. Since they'd been expecting a hay delivery earlier that day, he'd figured Sam would still be out overseeing the hands as they unloaded and stored it.

"You finished up early," Rey commented, heading to the fridge to pour himself a glass of iced tea.

Sam grunted. "Oh, they're probably still unloading. I didn't see any reason for me to hang around in the heat and watch them. They seem to know what they're doing."

"You didn't help them unload?" Rey asked.

"Heck no. Why would I do that?" Sam scoffed. "We're paying them to unload."

Eyeing his younger brother, Rey couldn't help but think Carl had gone too easy on him. Sam always seemed to do the bare minimum, nothing more. Instead of calloused hands, his were soft. Though to be fair, Sam had never claimed to want the life of a rancher. Unfortunately, he'd never made an effort to do anything else.

Deciding not to say anything, Rey took a long drink from his tea. Sweaty and hot, he needed a shower, but he wanted to rehydrate first.

"There's going to be a town meeting tonight at seven," Sam said, his voice casual. "They left a message on the landline answering machine. I didn't erase it in case you want to replay it."

Rey paused. "Meeting for what? Did they say?"

When Sam turned around, he appeared slightly apprehensive. "Though they only said recent developments, I've heard that another older couple has disappeared. That's up to six people now, three couples. People are starting to freak out."

With his blood running cold, Rey took a second to answer.

"As they should. It scares the hell out of me."

"Did you know?" Sam asked, his voice hard. "Did you know that many people were missing?"

"No. I knew about Dad and Isla, and one other couple. Rayna told us about them when Willow and I went to see her."

"You and Willow?" Sam narrowed his gaze. "Are you still making a play for her? I can't believe you're taking advantage of this situation to hit on her."

Tamping down a flash of anger, Rey clenched his teeth and took a moment before responding. "I'm not sure how meeting her at the sheriff's office to file missing person reports qualifies as hitting on her. But you need to stop. Willow is rightfully concerned about her grandmother. I'm worried about Dad. Nothing more, nothing less."

Instead of appearing appeased, Sam shook his head, his jaw tight. "You know what? I'm going to call her and invite her out to dinner after the meeting. We have a lot to catch up on. I imagine she'll be glad to put aside all the doom and gloom for a minute or two."

"Maybe so," Rey conceded. He refused to even acknowledge the way the idea of her going out with his younger brother made him feel. In fact, now that Sam had announced his plan, Rey wished he'd thought of it. No matter who took her, she deserved to go somewhere nice, to give herself a couple of hours to let her worry and fears take a back seat. Sam was right about that.

"Are you going to the meeting?" Rey asked.

Muttering under his breath and ignoring the question, Sam got out his phone and began scrolling through his contacts. "I know I have her number here somewhere," he mumbled, wandering outside onto the back patio.

Glad he didn't have to offer to give it to him, Rey went over to the desk he and his father shared to begin his search. All the accounting for the ranch was stored there. He hadn't thought to check it before but wanted to go through everything just in case there might be a clue to Carl's whereabouts.

He sat down and pulled out several manila folders, all crammed full of papers. While wading through receipts, he heard Sam come back inside, slamming the door behind him. He glanced up to see Sam scowling.

"She didn't want to go," he said, glaring at Rey as if he thought his brother had something to do with Willow's decision. "Says we can catch up another time, but right now she's putting all of her energy into locating her grandmother."

"Maybe that's how you should have approached it," Rey suggested. "So far, you haven't been very sympathetic, never mind concerned."

Half expecting his brother to explode, Rey exhaled when Sam visibly deflated. "I am worried," he admitted. "Because you're right, none of this is like Dad. I just don't like to dwell on it the way you do. It makes me feel too powerless."

Surprised at Sam's candor, Rey nodded. "I get that. I feel pretty powerless too. When I stop to think about all the possibilities that might have occurred, I can't sleep at night. I'm sure Willow feels the same way."

"That makes sense." Sam grimaced. "I'll give it a few days, and then I'll try again. Maybe Willow will want to meet up if I want to commiserate."

"Maybe so." Rey took a deep breath, about to ask his brother yet again if he planned to attend the meeting. Just then, Rey's phone rang. Glancing at the screen, he saw it was Willow. Luckily, Sam had already lost interest in the conversation and had taken off to his room.

"Afternoon," Rey answered. "How are you holding up?"

"I'm a mess," she admitted. "But I wanted to tell you to go through your dad's dresser drawers and his closet. I just finished looking through my grandmother's, and I feel there's enough missing to prove she did pack for a trip."

"Interesting," he replied. "I've kind of hesitated to do that because I didn't want to be too intrusive, but I guess I'd better."

"I felt the same way, but now that I have, I feel a little better." She took a deep breath before continuing. "I'm sure you've heard about the town meeting tonight."

"I have. I heard another older couple has disappeared."

"What?" She sounded shocked. "My message didn't say anything about that. How many is that now?"

"Six. I definitely hope we're not about to learn there's even more."

"Me too. All of this is seriously freaking me out," she said. "Are you going to the meeting?"

Even though he'd just now heard about it, he said he was. "There's no way I'm missing out on getting more information."

"Same," she replied. "I really need to get out of the house, so I'm glad to have a reason to go into town. Anyway, I'm wondering if you wanted to meet for a drink after."

Deciding not to mention that he knew Sam had just called her and invited her out, he agreed. While he didn't feel hanging out with Willow was like hitting on her, he saw no reason to muddy the waters.

"Perfect," she said, then paused. "Do you want to grab something to eat too? We can go either before or after, though I guess it would depend on how long the meeting runs."

"Before," he answered quickly. "I've been so busy today that I haven't had time to eat lunch. We could eat around five thirty, if that's okay with you."

"Sounds good. I've been craving Tres Corazones. It's been forever since I've had it. California doesn't do good Tex-Mex."

Thinking of his brother, he felt a quick twinge of guilt. But then he wasn't about to turn her down simply because she didn't want to go out with Sam. Their parents were missing. Maybe Sam couldn't focus on that, but Rey could. "That sounds great."

"Perfect. I can meet you there." She waited for him to confirm.

"Sure," he said. "Just remember, the meal is my treat this time."

"As long as any drinks after the meeting are on me," she replied.

That made her go quiet. "We'll see."

After ending the call, he decided not to say anything to Sam. Since he and Willow were meeting up and taking separate vehicles, it wasn't even close to being a date. And if Sam attended the town meeting, maybe after he could join them for drinks to discuss any new information they'd learned.

Since he'd need to clean up early in order to meet Willow at Tres Corazones, he rushed through the remainder of his chores. When he arrived back at the house at four thirty with the intention of taking a shower, he found Sam parked in front of the television, munching on popcorn.

"Did you knock off early today?" Rey asked.

"Did you?" Sam barely looked away from the TV. "I'm assuming you're going to the town meeting?"

For the first time, Rey wondered what he'd do if Sam wanted to go with him. Bring him along to dinner, he supposed. Even if Willow hadn't wanted to go out with Sam by himself, surely she wouldn't object if it was the three of them. "I am. What about you?"

Mouth full of popcorn, Sam shrugged. "I might. And I might not. I figure you'll tell me whatever you hear."

Suppressing a small flare of anger, Rey bit back a retort. "I'm going to take a shower," he said and left the room.

When he emerged later, Sam had shut off the television and left. Since his bedroom door was closed, Rey figured Sam was in there.

A little after five, Rey went out to his truck to make the drive into town. He looked forward to seeing Willow again, even if just to have someone to commiserate with who actually was willing to do whatever it took to help find Carl and Isla.

Even though he arrived early, he spotted Willow's red Bronco already in the parking lot. The restaurant seemed busier than usual at this earlier hour, and he guessed numerous people had decided to grab dinner before the town meeting.

As he parked and got out, Willow emerged from her SUV. She wore a bright yellow sundress, her long hair in a neat braid down her back. The color flattered her skin, and her legs seemed to go on forever. Her beauty had him catching his breath.

"Are you okay?" she asked, making him realize he'd been staring. Without waiting for him to answer, she took his arm. "I wish it wasn't so hot. I love eating outside on the patio."

He recognized the nervousness that underscored her voice. Liking how it felt to have her arm linked in his, he patted her hand. "It's going to be okay."

Her grateful smile made his heart skip a beat.

"Thanks," she said. "I do tend to talk a lot when I'm stressed."

Inside, the hostess greeted them and led them to a small booth near the window. They sat, and she handed them menus and left. Almost instantly, someone else brought them a large basket of warm tortilla chips and two small bowls of salsa.

Rey watched Willow as she studied the menu. With her delicately carved features and lush mouth, she had a kind of sensual beauty of which she appeared completely unaware.

The soft curve of her shoulders captivated him. It might be the worst timing ever, but he ached with desire. As long as she didn't realize how she affected him, he figured he'd be okay.

The waitress arrived and took their drink orders. Willow asked for a small margarita on the rocks, and Rey ordered a Mexican beer with a lime.

While they waited for their food, she told him more about her life in California. Since he'd never been there, he listened closely as she described the beaches and the ocean, enjoying the way her eyes sparkled as she talked.

"You love it there," he observed.

"Not really." She shrugged. "The weather is nicer, but everything is so expensive. I miss Texas sometimes. The ocean is the only thing that makes me feel connected to the earth."

This was something he understood. Something about the wide-open spaces of his home, the way the sky colored orange and yellow and pink at sunrise, tethered him to the ground. "Do you go to the beach often so you can watch the waves?"

Her grin lit up her entire face. "No. I go almost every day so I can surf."

Their food arrived just then, saving him from having to come up with a reasonably intelligent response. What he knew of surfing was next to nothing.

Once the waitress left, he eyed Willow over his fajitas. "Are you any good at it?"

"Surfing?" Her grin widened as she picked up her fork. "I think so. I actually teach beginner surf classes every Saturday."

With that, she dug into her food with gusto, leaving him no choice but to do the same.

"I'm even listed on the surfing school's website," she said, in between bites. "If you do an internet search for my name along with surfing lessons, I'll come up."

He had to fight himself not to reach for his phone to do exactly that. Because now he couldn't get the image of Willow, her sun-kissed skin glistening, riding a surfboard in a bikini.

Pushing the thoughts away, he focused on his meal. By the time he'd finished eating, his arousal had mostly subsided, and he felt normal.

Heaven help him if she ever found out how she affected him.

He paid the check, and she let him, though she apparently couldn't resist telling him the next meal would be on her. She smiled and nodded, giving him hope that there would be a next time.

They walked out to their vehicles.

"I'll follow you," Willow said.

Since the town meeting was being held at the Rattlesnake Pub, which was just down the street from Tres Corazones, Willow and Rey were slightly early. Despite that, the parking lot had begun to fill up, which meant the overflow would spill out onto Main Street.

After getting out of their vehicles, they walked into the pub side by side. The tables had been pushed to one side, and rows of folding chairs had been set up facing a lectern that had been placed on the stage where bands usually played.

Several people greeted him and waved. Rey waved back but didn't stop to talk.

Most of the seats in the first four rows were already occupied. Rey and Willow took chairs near the aisle in row five.

"I recognize so many people," Willow said. "But I'm guessing they forgot what I look like because not one single person has greeted me."

"You can go around and reintroduce yourself after," he said, trying to comfort her.

"Maybe." She shrugged. "I'm not sure I want to, actually."

He guessed that was because she wouldn't be around long enough after her mother was found for it to matter.

By the time seven o'clock arrived, every seat was full and still more people continued to fill the back of the room. Willow kept turning and eyeing the growing crowd. "I had no idea so many people were worried about this," she murmured. "It's now standing room only."

Rey didn't tell her that most of them were there out of a combination of curiosity and boredom.

The sheriff walked in, flanked by several of her deputies. All of them were in full uniform. They took their seats up on the stage, behind the lectern. The meeting was about to begin.

Chapter 4

Bracing herself, Willow reached for Rey's hand without thinking. To her relief, he enveloped her fingers with his larger ones, offering comfort.

Tony Hutchins, the owner of the Rattlesnake Pub and, from what her mom had told her, Getaway's newly elected mayor as of a couple of months ago, made his way through the room. This took him a while as he constantly stopped to talk with people. He finally walked to the center of the stage and eyed the assembled group before tapping on the microphone.

"I need your attention, please." Once the room had gone silent, he continued. "We are all here because we're concerned for one of the most vulnerable groups in our society—our senior citizens. We've recently learned that several of our beloved townsfolk have gone missing."

Murmuring broke out, and for a moment Tony let the sound swell. Then he cleared his throat, tapped the microphone again and, once he had everyone's attention, announced he would be turning things over to Sheriff Coombs.

At this, Willow sat up even straighter. While Rayna had definitely promised to keep her posted, she supposed that meant only regarding information related to Isla and Carl. The other missing couples, while a new development, might not directly impact the case. Either that, or, Willow figured, the sheriff had just been too busy.

"Right now, we've been made aware of six people, all over the age of sixty-five, who have virtually disappeared," Rayna began. "At this time, foul play is not suspected. This means that we have to assume that wherever they went, they went willingly."

Again, people started talking, the swell of voices rising. Standing motionless, Rayna waited this out until eventually everyone quieted and focused again on her.

"We wanted to call this meeting," she continued, "because we need each and every one of you to help. If you have security cameras at your businesses, check your footage. None of these missing individuals took their personal vehicles, which is in itself unusual. We've checked with bus rental and passenger van companies and haven't found anything helpful. But someone in this room might have video of a large van or bus driving by. If you find something like that, I need you to contact me."

"Have you checked with Myrna?" someone shouted. Myrna ran the small travel agency part-time, when she wasn't weaving elaborate shawls and table runners to sell.

"Yes, we did," Rayna answered, her tone level. "None of the missing people booked any kind of trip with her."

Serenity, the self-proclaimed town psychic, who'd attended with her sister, Velma, the yoga instructor, stood. "I have a feeling they are all safe and well."

Since most times her *feelings* turned out to be accurate, no one contradicted her. Not even the sheriff, who, like the rest of the town, knew better.

Even Willow, who wasn't exactly sure how she felt about Serenity's psychic abilities, took comfort from hearing those words.

And then Serenity took a deep breath and continued. "However, just because they don't believe themselves to be in danger at this moment, doesn't mean the threat isn't there. It's just hidden."

She pinned her steady gaze on the sheriff. "This means you have to find them, before trouble manifests itself."

As soon as Serenity sat back down, everyone started talking at once. Again, Rayna stood motionless at the podium, waiting. When the noise finally died down, Rayna asked if anyone had any specific questions. "Bear in mind, we don't know much about this case at the moment. Which means we're extremely limited on answers."

Despite her disclaimer, people began shouting out questions. Most of them, Rayna couldn't answer, and she finally told everyone she would not get into speculation about where the missing people might be. With that, she reminded them to check their video camera footage and then declared the meeting to be over.

Instead of leaving, almost everyone pitched in to help move the tables that had been pushed up against the wall back where they belonged. Tony put country music on over the speakers and announced that the kitchen and bar were now open.

"Do you want to stay and have a drink?" Rey asked. "It looks like that's what most people are doing."

Suddenly, Willow wanted out of there. "I'd rather go somewhere else," she said. "Have you ever been to that place on the other side of town called The Bar?"

"That new place?"

Even though The Bar had opened up a few years ago, everyone still called it new. "Yes," she answered. "I know it's different. Not as down-home and familiar as here, but I'm willing to bet it will be a lot less crowded."

"Sounds good." He held out his arm, and she took it. Together, they wound their way through the crowd toward the door.

Once outside, Willow exhaled in relief. "I'm sorry, but I just don't feel up to any questions. Once everything settled down, I just knew people were going to start figuring out whose family members are among the missing. I don't think we would have gotten a moment of peace."

Gaze steady, he studied her for a moment. "You're probably right. I'll follow you over to The Bar."

"Willow Allen!" a voice called. "I thought that was you."

Slowly turning, Willow tried to summon up a smile and failed. She vaguely recognized the woman hurrying toward them as someone she'd gone to high school with, but couldn't remember her name.

"I'm sorry." Rey took Willow's arm. "We're late for another appointment and have to go. Hopefully you two can catch up another time. Come on, Willow."

More relieved than she could express, Willow allowed him to hustle her over to their vehicles. "Thank you," she muttered, climbing in hers. "I owe you one."

He laughed. "See you in a few."

As she'd expected, only a few cars and pickups were parked in the lot outside. Rey took a spot next to her, and they walked into the place together.

"I haven't ever been here," Rey said, glancing around curiously.

"I've been a few times," she told him. "Though I get why most people go to the Rattlesnake Pub." Gesturing around the smaller, dimly lit space, she made her way to a booth. "This place reminds me of California."

"I take it that's a good thing," he commented, sliding into the booth opposite her.

Before she could answer, a waiter appeared and handed them drink menus. "It's really slow in here tonight," he said. "I'm hoping some of the people who went to the town meeting decide the Rattlesnake is too crowded and come here."

Willow smiled. "I hope so too. That's what we did."

They ordered drinks. Beer for him and a small margarita for her.

Once the waiter left, Willow leaned forward. "I'm not sure what to make of all this. I couldn't help but notice Rayna didn't offer up a hypothesis on where all the missing couples might be."

"Because law enforcement doesn't work with guesses," he replied. "She's just stating the facts. Nothing more, nothing less. I'm sure she's working every angle she can."

She nodded and took a deep breath. "Are you as worried as I am? This is completely out of character for my grandmother."

"Same with my dad," he said. "And if you're like me, you have to stop yourself from coming up with multiple bad scenarios."

"Exactly. I've watched way too many true-crime shows."

Their drinks arrived. The bartender had taken the time to make Willow's margarita look festive. Instead of the usual lime color, hers was gold, shot through with ribbons of pink. "He made you our house specialty," the waiter explained, setting it down in front of her with a flourish. "It's a prickly pear infused with agave. I hope you enjoy it."

Willow took a sip, aware both the waiter and the bartender were watching her from the bar. "Delicious," she said, loud enough for them to hear.

After drinking from his beer, Rey sighed. "While Carl and Isla certainly appear to be enjoying dating each other, neither of them have ever given any indication that they'd do something like this. Which is one of the reasons I'm so worried."

"Same. But tell me something. Why isn't Sam concerned? Every time I talk to him, he acts as if nothing out of the ordinary is going on."

Rey's gaze sharpened. "I don't understand that either. Is that why you turned down his offer to meet you for dinner?"

"He told you about that?" she asked. When Rey nodded, she took another sip of her drink. "I don't want to talk badly about your younger brother, but his determination to pretend everything is normal wears me out. When we were teenagers, Sam and I were good friends."

"And if anyone should understand what it feels like to be worried about a parent, he should," Rey finished for her. "I have a feeling this is his way of coping. If he pretends nothing is wrong, it's easier on him."

The door opened and another couple came in. Willow recognized them as two more who were missing family members. She lifted her hand in a wave.

"Your grandmother is missing, right?" the woman asked. When Willow nodded, the woman held out her hand. "I'm Sofia Alvarez, and this is my brother, Tomas. Our parents, Ernesto and Yolanda, have disappeared too."

"Why don't you join us?" Willow invited. "I'd love to swap details, if you don't mind. There are bound to be some similarities."

Sofia's sad smile touched Willow's heart. "I'd like that," she said, dropping into the seat next to Willow. A moment later, her brother did the same next to Rey.

As it turned out, Sofia's mother and Isla knew each other. They belonged to the same book club. "My mom always talked about her meeting with the book ladies," Sofia said, her gaze sad. "She mentioned Isla Allen more than once."

While Willow and Sofia talked, Tomas sat silent. He barely responded to Rey's attempts to bring him into the conversation. Finally, Tomas pushed to his feet and glared at them. "We shouldn't be talking about this," he said. "That just makes it worse. Come on, Sofia. We need to go by Mom and Dad's house again."

Slugging back the rest of his beer, he slammed his bottle on the table and strode to the door.

Expression apologetic, Sofia stood. "He's having a hard time dealing with all this," she said. "He still lives here in town, just a few blocks away from our parents' place. I think he feels like he should have been able to prevent this from happening."

"I get it." Impulsively, Willow stood too and touched the older woman's hand. "How about we exchange numbers so we can keep in touch if anything changes?"

Sofia got out her phone, and once Willow recited her number, sent her a text. "I'd better go," she said. "Since heart problems apparently run in the family, I don't want anything to happen to Tomas."

With that, she hurried out the door.

Shocked, Willow stared after her. She dropped back into her seat. "Did you hear that?" she asked Rey. "She said heart problems run in the family."

"Okay," Rey replied. "Clearly, I'm missing something."

"My mom had a heart incident. She went to the ER. She kept saying it was nothing, but I don't know for sure. That's the main reason I scheduled PTO and came home."

He eyed her, his expression calm. "And you think there's a connection?"

Just like that, her excitement deflated. "I'm grasping at straws, aren't I?"

"Maybe." He reached across the table and touched her arm. "How about this? Mention it to Rayna. Let her investigate. It might be something, or it might not."

Slowly, she nodded. Taking another drink of her delicious margarita, she realized she wanted to go home. When she told Rey, he nodded. After signaling for the check, he paid the bill and walked her to her Bronco.

Opening Willow's door for her, he nearly leaned in to kiss her. The urge to do so had been strong. If he'd done that, he figured she'd think he was as bad as Sam. Even if she didn't, he knew he would.

Instead, he'd stepped back, plastering what he hoped was a pleasant expression on his face. "Stay in touch," he said.

She nodded, buckled her seat belt and closed her door. He didn't get into his truck until she'd driven away.

Pulling out onto Main Street, he almost stopped back in at the Rattlesnake but decided against it. No one knew anything more than what Rayna had told them, so he'd be wasting his time. He'd done about as much socializing for one day as he could stand.

When he arrived back at the ranch, Sam's pickup was still in the usual spot. Which meant he hadn't gone anywhere, not even a quick stop at the Rattlesnake to hear Rayna speak. Rey supposed he hadn't really expected him to. Still, it would have been nice if he'd shown just a small bit of concern.

Pushing back his irritation, Rey walked inside to find Sam once again lounging in front of the TV. He barely looked up when Rey approached. After standing beside the couch for a minute, Rey finally reached over and grabbed the remote to turn off the television.

"Hey," Sam protested, finally glancing at his brother. "I was watching that."

Rey dropped down onto the cushion next to him. "I thought you might want to hear about the meeting. I take it you didn't go."

"Nope. I figured if anything new happened, you could just tell me. Did you happen to see Willow there?"

At this point, Rey felt like he had nothing to hide. "I did. Willow and I actually grabbed some food before the meeting and went for a drink after. If you'd have come with me, maybe you could have done some of that catching up you claim you want to do."

Sam's expression darkened. "I can't believe you. You're doing what you told me was wrong."

"No, I'm not." Rey kept his voice level. "Willow is worried about her mom, the same way I am about Dad.

That's what we talked about. We sat with each other at the meeting, and then talked to two other people—a brother and a sister—who were worried about their parents."

Narrow-eyed, Sam glared at him, as if trying to ascertain whether or not Rey was telling the truth. "Did Willow ask about me?"

With difficulty, Rey suppressed a groan. "This is not about you, Sam. It's about Isla and Carl. They're missing, remember?"

"How could I forget." Sam pushed to his feet. "You'd never let me." And he stormed into his bedroom, slamming the door behind him.

Some things never changed. Sometimes, Rey thought Sam remained a perennial angry teenager.

Rey picked up the remote and turned the TV back on. If Sam cooled off and wanted to talk, Rey would be there. Otherwise, he didn't have the energy to worry about it.

The next morning, Rey got up before the sun rose and showered and dressed. He made his way into the kitchen for coffee and food. At first light, he intended to head out to check on the cattle, with a stop by the hay barn to make sure all the new bales had been put up.

To his surprise, he'd barely sat down at the table to drink his coffee when a sleepy-eyed Sam stumbled in.

"Mornin'," Sam mumbled. He made himself a cup of coffee and then sat in the chair across from Rey. "Listen, just because I'm not all worried about Dad doesn't mean I don't care. I'm just more optimistic than you. There's nothing wrong with that."

Since Rey didn't want to start something this early in the day, he simply nodded. He could only hope Sam would lose interest if he realized Rey couldn't be provoked.

"I'm sure they're fine," Sam continued. "A group of them probably went away together for a spontaneous trip and didn't want to be disturbed." Sam raised his mug and took a long swig. "You're just being pessimistic for thinking they might be in trouble."

Again, Rey didn't respond. He continued drinking his coffee, hoping Sam would leave him in peace.

Instead, Sam leaned forward. "You never answered my question last night. Did Willow ask about me?"

Rey took a deep breath, barely able to hide his exasperation. "Actually, we didn't discuss you. Last night was all about the missing people."

Eyes narrowed, Sam continued to stare. "I know you're worried, but it seems to me that you're just trying to bond with Willow."

"Come on, Sam." Rey lost the battle to keep his voice level. "How can you not be concerned? There are six people from town who just up and disappeared, leaving their cell phones and vehicles behind. Not a single one left a note. Even if your theory about them all going on vacation were to pan out, you have to admit this is not like Dad. He couldn't wait to see the bison. He must have texted me like twelve times, in between several phone calls. He knew when I'd be back, and he planned to be here to help me unload our new breeding stock. You honestly don't see anything worrisome about the fact that he wasn't? He never goes anywhere without checking in with one of us."

"Okay, okay." Sam shook his head, wincing. "No need to yell. One thing you have to remember is that Dad and Isla are both grown adults. They don't need our permission to go away together. None of those missing people do."

That statement alone meant his younger brother was going to willfully continue to miss the point.

Jaw clenched, Rey knew he had to get out of the house and away from Sam before he said or did something he'd regret later. Even though he hadn't had his breakfast yet, he strode for the back door, yanked it open and left.

"What about breakfast?" Sam called after him.

Rey didn't bother to answer. Sam knew how to cook. He made his way to the barn, headed to Roscoe, the gray gelding he preferred to ride, and saddled him up. Then he rode out, heading down the gravel road for the far pasture. This was one of the places he'd gone as a kid when he needed to think. He still went there every now and then, though less frequently.

Despite Rayna's assurances that she was handling this, with every hour that passed, Rey's worry increased.

What had happened to his dad? Even though he himself had kept reassuring Willow that the two parents would show up, he'd begun to have serious doubts. Carl had never been an impulsive man, and he did everything with a well-thought-out purpose. Running away from not only his responsibilities but also his family without a single word of explanation was the last thing he would do.

All his life, Rey had been what his father called a fixer. He'd always been good at identifying a problem and then finding a solution. But this, he couldn't fix. Not when he had no idea what the problem might be.

He rode for an hour, trying to let the quiet seep inside him. Instead, he found himself imagining various scenarios as to why his father had vanished, none of them good. Even his horse sensed his unsettled mood and acted skittish, shying sideways at shadows.

Since he had work to do, he and Roscoe headed out to check on the herd. Bison weren't like cattle, he realized. They wandered more, and even though some of the terrain where he'd put them to pasture seemed steep, they didn't seem averse to climbing. He'd been advised to keep them separate from the cattle, at least until he could have a vet make sure none were carriers of brucellosis, a deadly livestock disease.

He'd also been told they could be aggressive. While he personally hadn't witnessed that, he made sure to keep his distance so he didn't accidentally provoke them.

After he'd located the herd and done a head count to make sure they were all there, he rode Roscoe down the road a bit to check on cattle in three other pastures. Sam had done recent fence repairs to the second one, which made it even more shocking to see the fence down and two of the groups of cattle in one large herd.

Had Sam forgotten to fix this section of fence? Or had the damage come after that?

Without enlisting the help of his ranch hands, Rey didn't have a prayer of separating out the herd, so he dismounted and made some temporary repairs to the broken section. Without the proper tools and materials, he knew anything he fixed wouldn't last for long. Once again, it seemed he'd be having another talk with Sam. To bolster his case, he snapped some photos with his phone.

About to leave, he spotted another section that appeared to be on the verge of collapse and rode over there. He propped it up as best he could, took a few more pictures and then rode down the rest of the fence line, checking for any more problem spots.

Finally, he'd checked all the fencing in the immediate area. Wondering now if he'd have to check the fencing on the entire ranch, his frustration with his brother threatened to turn to anger. Sam had been given this task for a reason. Once he'd identified problem areas, he had the ability to assemble a crew and materials and get the repairs done as soon as possible. He knew as well as anyone how vital maintaining good fencing was to the safety of the herd.

If he couldn't even handle this simple task, maybe Sam needed to go ahead and get a job in town.

Seething, Rey returned to the barn. After removing the saddle, he brushed Roscoe down. The repetitive motion of currying the horse usually did a lot to soothe him, but not this time.

When he'd gotten Roscoe all brushed, he put his horse back in the stall. Aware he needed to calm down, he slowly made his way back to the main house. On the walk there, he rehearsed what he needed to say several times, hoping he could chastise his younger brother without too much anger. He wanted to be rational and collected. Otherwise, he knew Sam would try to turn the narrative to be about their missing father, rather than his complete and utter dereliction of duty.

But as he got closer, he realized Sam's pickup wasn't there. Sam had left. Which might be a good thing, as that meant Rey would have to wait to talk to him until he returned.

Chapter 5

The morning after the town meeting, Willow woke to the still too silent and empty house with a sinking feeling in the pit of her stomach. She felt like she'd missed something, though she couldn't put her finger on exactly what.

Getting up, she headed straight for the kitchen to grab a cup of coffee and try to think. Hopefully, once she cleared the sleep cobwebs out of her mind, she'd be able to focus and pinpoint what she might have missed.

Sipping her drink, she replayed what Rayna had said at the meeting yesterday, but she kept coming back to Sofia Alvarez's comment about heart issues running in the family. Had one or both of her missing parents struggled with issues similar to what Isla had? If so, what about the other missing people? Had they possibly gone off together for treatment?

Grabbing her phone, she called Rayna. When she got the sheriff on the line, she outlined what she thought.

"Interesting," Rayna commented. "I wasn't aware of that. I'll contact the families of the other missing people and see if they had any heart issues. What I need from you is contact information for your grandmother's doctors. While I know they won't release any personal information, at least I can find out if they recommend any particular heart specialists or facilities."

"Thank you," Willow said. "I'm thinking maybe they went to some sort of inpatient place, like a healing resort."

"This is West Texas, not California," Rayna reminded her. "I can't see someone like Carl Johnson going for something like that."

"Maybe not for himself, but he might for the woman he loved."

"Good point." Rayna sighed. "But even if your theory is valid, how on earth would they get six people to sign up? Places like that are expensive. Not all of the missing individuals would have the funds for a medical retreat or resort."

"I don't know." Deflated, Willow took another sip of coffee. "I was looking for the common denominator. What do these people have in common? Did they disappear together or separately?"

"The timing would seem to suggest together," Rayna said, her tone thoughtful. "And I've got my people looking into any possible connections between the group. By the way, did Isla still attend church?"

"As far as I know, she still went to Straightline Church."

"Well, that eliminates one more possibility," Rayna said. "The Alvarez family went to St. Francis. And the other couple were Baptist. Let me check into the doctor angle, and I'll get back with you."

After ending the call, Willow drank the last of her coffee and made another round of the house. For whatever reason, searching for clues as to Isla's disappearance helped settle her mind.

Her thoughts kept returning to last night. For one,

heart-stopping moment, she'd thought Rey had been about to kiss her. Even worse, she'd longed for the press of his lips on hers.

Was she that desperate for a distraction? Her cheeks warm, she began searching the cabinet under the sink in her grandmother's bathroom. Even though she'd checked it once before, she pulled everything out one at a time, setting them aside until she'd emptied it. Nothing but the usual toiletries.

After she'd put every item back, she did the same to the medicine cabinet above the sink. Here, she hoped to find prescriptions that might give her a clue about her granny's health. But Isla had evidently taken all of that with her, as most people did when traveling.

Instead of starting on the bedroom, which she'd already searched more than once, she decided to jump in the shower and get ready to go into town. She didn't think she could stay alone in the house any longer. Even though she guessed Rayna had already done so, she wanted to stop by her grandmother's church and talk to the pastor and the church secretary in person. Even though Rey had called them, she felt like a visit just to chat might help jog their memories. And she also planned to swing by the bookstore where Isla liked to get her reading material. Then last but not least, Serenity's on Main Street.

Most people in town, even those who considered themselves too hard-nosed realistic to be true psychic believers, respected Serenity and her "visions." After all, she'd been right far more than she'd been wrong. And everyone liked her. Unfailingly kind and supportive, people tended to go to her when they found themselves in need of comfort or wisdom.

Willow could use both right now. Though she hadn't been to her shop since her last time home during the holidays, she knew Serenity would welcome her as if no time had elapsed at all.

In her teens, she had spent quite a few pleasant hours browsing through Serenity's shop. Specifically, the part of the store dedicated to rocks and crystals. Willow had bought her first rock, an inexpensive piece of polished tourmaline, at sixteen. Since then, she'd slowly and steadily added to her collection. She kept them on display in the living room of her apartment.

The heat could be brutal this time of the year, and though she'd normally wear jean shorts, a tank top and flip-flops, this time Willow dressed in a nice pair of khaki shorts, a cap-sleeve blouse and strappy wedge-heeled sandals. She put her long hair up in a high ponytail and grabbed her purse and keys.

Driving into town, she headed for her mom's church first. Willow had grown up attending services there. She'd known Pastor Clayton her entire life. On every visit home, her mother had made sure she got to church on Sunday. Personally, Willow thought it was long past time for the elderly pastor to retire, but he joked that as long as he could stand upright, he planned to preach.

Bertha, the gray-haired church secretary who seemed nearly as old as her boss, looked up from her desk when Willow knocked. Squinting through her glasses, she clearly didn't recognize her guest at first.

"Bertha, it's me. Willow Allen. Isla's daughter," she added for good measure.

The older woman's face creased in a smile. "I thought that was you. Come in, come in. Pastor Clayton will be so happy to see you."

Willow stepped into the small office and went around the desk to give Bertha a quick hug.

"It's a shame about your grandmother," Bertha mused. "We've all been praying for that entire group to be found."

Just then, Pastor Clayton came around the corner. His stooped shoulders and shuffling gait revealed his age. He stopped short when he caught sight of Willow. "My stars!" he exclaimed, clapping his hands together once in excitement. "Willow Allen! To what do I owe the honor of this visit?"

Before she could answer, he took her arm and shepherded her into his office. "Have a seat," he invited. He offered her water, iced tea or coffee, but she declined. She waited until he got settled behind his desk before asking her questions.

"I came to see you about my grandmother," she began. "As her pastor and spiritual advisor, did she come to you with any problems or issues?"

"You should know Ms. Rayna has already been here asking me the same thing," he said, clasping his hands in a steeple on his desk. "And I'll tell you what I told her. If Isla had asked for my counsel on any personal issues, I would not be able to reveal them. However, since she did not, in that respect, there is nothing for you to worry about. In fact, I'm more concerned with the fact that she hasn't attended services in two months."

"What?" Shocked, Willow leaned forward. "She stopped coming to church? That isn't like her."

"I know, I know." He sighed. "I was so worried that I tried calling her and left several messages. When she didn't return my calls, I stopped by her house unannounced."

"When was this?"

"A few weeks ago," he replied, his grave expression matching his tone.

Bracing herself, Willow waited.

"She actually answered the door. Apologized for not inviting me in, but said she had a doctor's appointment. Naturally, I asked after her health, but she waved me away. I never did get a chance to ask her why she'd stopped coming to services."

"How did she look?" Willow asked. "Did she appear to be ill?"

"Not really." He frowned. "Has she been having health issues?"

"I'm not sure," Willow admitted. "She had some sort of heart episode but refused to elaborate. She just said it wasn't anything serious."

"I'm sorry I can't be of more assistance," the pastor said. "I told Rayna the same thing."

Getting up, Willow thanked him for his time. She waved to Bertha on her way out.

When she got into her vehicle, she let the engine run and sat a moment, hoping the AC would cool down the interior. Isla prided herself on being a creature of habit. She liked her routines and seldom, if ever, varied from them. For her to have stopped attending services at Straightline Church and not have mentioned it to Willow set off all kinds of alarms.

Next, she drove to the bookstore. When she parked

and went inside, she didn't recognize the teenager working behind the counter. "Is Mr. Smith in?" she asked, hoping to see the owner.

The kid, a tall, gangly boy with a mullet and wire-rim glasses, looked up at her and blinked. "No," he answered. "He hasn't been here in a few weeks. My older sister Kathy is the manager, and she opens and closes the store. I work here in between my shifts at Pizza Perfect."

Alarmed, Willow swallowed. "Is Mr. Smith all right? He never missed a day coming into his bookstore."

"He never *used* to," the kid corrected. "But he stopped coming in a couple weeks ago. Kathy says she talked to him, and he asked her to keep the place running until he could get back."

She froze. "Got back from where?"

"I have no idea." Clearly losing interest, he looked down at the tablet on the counter in front of him. "If there's something I can help you find, please let me know."

Willow thanked him and left. Had Mr. Smith also disappeared, along with the six others? He was about the same age as her grandmother, late sixties, early seventies. And while she couldn't remember if he was married, she figured she might as well mention him to Rayna, just in case.

The thought that even more older people might have gone missing sent a chill down her spine. Pushing the thought away, she drove the couple blocks north to Serenity's. She parked, took a deep breath and walked inside.

The bells on the door set off a cheerful sound to announce her arrival. Willow took a quick look around. Except for the expansion of the flower shop Serenity ran in conjunction with her metaphysical store, not much had changed since her last visit.

"Willow!" Serenity came from the back, her multitude of bracelets jingling, her colorful skirt making her appear to float. "It's so nice to see you."

She enveloped Willow in a quick hug. When she stepped back, her earlier smile had vanished from her face. "You're worried about your grandmother, aren't you?"

Slowly, Willow nodded. "Very. But I appreciated you letting us know that she and all the others are okay."

Expression distracted, Serenity made a dismissing motion with her hand, which sent the bracelets jingling again. "Come, sit and have a cup of tea. I'll read the leaves after we finish."

Willow followed her through a multicolor beaded curtain to the back. She took a chair at the small, round table and eyed the large crystal ball Serenity kept in a glass case on the counter.

Serenity used an old-fashioned tea kettle on her small, electric stove. When it whistled, she poured the water into two cups that each held a small metal tea diffuser. While the tea steeped, she went to the refrigerator and removed a foil-wrapped pound cake. She didn't bother asking Willow if she wanted a piece. Instead, she sliced off two pieces, put them on saucers and set them on the table.

"My favorite," Willow said, unexpected tears springing to her eyes. Serenity had often served her this dessert when Willow was a teen. She didn't question how the older woman had known to have it on hand.

Bringing over both cups, Serenity smiled. "It's so good to see you again. Yes, the circumstances are terrible, but it hurts nothing to take a few minutes and enjoy each other's company."

She'd just started to relax when Serenity stiffened. "Oh no," the older woman said. "I think someone near Isla might be in trouble."

Though he'd already gone through most of his dad's desk, this time Rey decided to search the entire house. He couldn't shake the feeling that he was missing something. And while he didn't really think it had to do with heart issues or Isla's health like Willow had suggested, at this point, he wasn't willing to rule anything out.

He started in the kitchen. Opening and closing all the cabinets, he saw nothing out of the ordinary. Dishes and glasses, pots and pans. When he reached the junk drawer by the landline, he took the entire drawer out and carried it to the table.

First, he took out every pen and pencil and set them aside. Then he sifted through the rest of the contents, finding nothing of interest. Disappointed, he put everything back and replaced the drawer in its proper spot.

Now what? What should he search next?

The sound of tires on gravel had him looking up. Had Sam finally returned? Pushing to his feet, Rey went to the window to look.

Instead of Sam, he saw Willow's red Ford pulling up.

Just like that, his pulse went into overdrive. He watched as she parked and got out, transfixed by her beauty. Though he knew she'd been born and raised here in Getaway the same as him, she looked like an exotic flower.

Heart in his throat, he hurried for the door. She knocked

just as he reached it. Opening the door, he stepped aside and motioned for her to enter. "Willow! What brings you here?"

As she brushed past him, bringing with her the scent of peaches, he inhaled sharply. She whirled around to face him, her ponytail swinging. Her stormy eyes and troubled expression had him once again yearning to pull her into his arms. Somehow, he managed to resist.

"I just left Serenity's," she said, her voice uneven. "While we were sitting there talking, she suddenly said she thought someone near my grandmother might be in trouble."

Not sure how to react to that, he motioned for her to follow him into the kitchen. While most everyone in town had a healthy respect for Serenity and her prophesies, Rey himself wasn't too sure. Sometimes it seemed she put things in the vaguest terms possible, playing it safe.

Once she'd taken a seat at the farm table, he poured them each a glass of sweet tea and brought them over. "What exactly did she say?"

She sighed. "As usual, she didn't go into any specifics. But we were having cake and tea and chatting when all of a sudden she sat up straight and said she thinks someone near Isla is in trouble."

Near Isla? Like Carl?

"And?" he asked. "Using the word *someone* is pretty darn generic, don't you think?"

"Yes, I agree. If she hadn't followed that up with saying *near Isla*, I wouldn't have paid any attention. But I know Isla and your dad are together, so it worried me." She sighed. "Probably more than it should have."

"Did she say anything else?"

"No. After making that pronouncement, she got very rattled and said I needed to go. I tried to question her, but she refused to say anything else. When I left, I drove right over here."

"I wouldn't put too much stock in that," he said. "Even the words she used—*in trouble*—can mean numerous things."

"True." Visibly trying to relax, Willow blinked rapidly. "I took it to mean in danger, but you're right. It doesn't have to be that."

He tried to think of something else he could say to help her feel better, but short of saying he didn't put any stock in Serenity's so-called prophecies, he hit a wall. "Well, I hope if Serenity *sees* something else, she contacts you."

"Me too." She took a long drink of her tea. "Thank you for this. I didn't realize I was so thirsty."

The back door opened, and Sam breezed inside. He stopped short when he caught sight of Willow. "What are you doing here?" he asked, his gaze going from her to Rey and back again.

"Well, hello to you too," Willow said, raising her brows. Rey half-expected her to jump to her feet and hug his brother, but instead she remained seated, regarding Sam without smiling.

To his credit, her response made Sam grimace. "I'm sorry," he said, his voice sheepish. "It's just you're the last person I expected to find in my kitchen."

"Really? Why is that?" she asked.

Since it seemed Willow might be spoiling for a fight with Sam, Rey figured now might be a good time to excuse himself. He started to get to his feet, planning to claim he needed to go check on something in the barn. But Willow reached out and touched his arm.

"Please wait," she asked, the entreaty in her gaze making him realize he'd do anything for her. "We aren't finished talking, and since Sam here clearly has no interest in the topic we're discussing, we can continue once he's gone."

Ouch. Rey braced himself for his younger brother's response.

"Wow. That's not fair." Expression wounded, Sam went to the fridge to get his own glass of iced tea. Once he'd poured it, he plunked it down on the table and took the seat next to Willow. "We used to be good friends," he said, studying her. "What happened?"

"My grandmother and your father went missing," she said, her voice quiet. "And any time I've tried to talk to you about it, you change the subject. You seem to want to act like everything is normal, that nothing has changed."

Sam took a long drink of his tea, his gaze never leaving her. "I'm well aware of what's going on. I just thought you might want a distraction, that's all."

More than anything, Rey wished he could silently leave the room. But Willow had asked him to stay, so he would. His presence didn't seem to bother Sam, who appeared to be doing his best to pretend he wasn't there.

"You just don't get it." The sadness in Willow's eyes made Rey's chest ache. "I just want to find Isla, to make sure she's safe."

"And Carl," Rey added, earning a sideways glare from Sam. "Actually, all of the missing townspeople," he continued for good measure.

Sam returned his full attention to Willow and nodded. "I'll do better," he said. "What do you need from me?"

She sighed. "Nothing, Sam. Though I do appreciate you offering. Right now, I have zero energy to devote to anything other than searching for our loved ones."

"I can help with that." Sam placed his hand on her arm, which made Rey fight a fierce urge to knock it away. A second later, Willow did it herself.

"Thanks. I've spent several hours talking to people in town to see if they know anything. I need to call Rayna and give her some information that may or may not be relevant." She stood. "Please excuse me."

And she stepped outside to make her call.

Rey and Sam watched her go. Once she'd disappeared from view, Sam turned to eye Rey.

"What is going on here?" Sam asked, his gaze hard. "Willow and I have been friends for years. Why are you trying to ruin that?"

Rey pushed to his feet. "Sam, I'm not sure what you think I've done or what exactly you're trying to say. But not everything is about you."

"Fine." Sam continued to stare. "But I see what you're doing. You're using Dad's disappearance to get close to a hot woman. I get it, because that was my plan, but you beat me to it."

Though he wanted to throttle his brother, Rey took a deep breath and tried to keep his voice level. "That's not what I'm doing, and I'm pretty sure you know that. Willow and I are both trying to find Carl and Isla. I don't think anyone rational could turn a desperate search for loved ones into something else."

Sam put his head down on his arms on the table,

just like he'd done when he'd been a teenager trying to get his way. From experience, Rey knew he could either wait it out or simply walk away. But he didn't want to intrude on Willow's phone call, nor did he want to leave and let her come back and have to be alone in the kitchen with Sam.

Which meant waiting it out would be his choice. He sat back down and took a drink of his tea.

The back door opened, and Willow came inside. Her gaze slid over Sam, still with his head down, and met Rey's. "When I was in town, I stopped at the bookstore. My grandmother is a regular customer there. I learned that Mr. Smith, the owner, hasn't been seen or heard from in a couple of weeks."

Sam raised his head. "What about Mrs. Smith? Did anyone think to ask her?"

Rey and Willow looked at each other, then back to him. "Sam, Mrs. Smith died last year," Rey said. "Mr. Smith has been living alone."

"I didn't know that." Sam shrugged. "Guess I should have gone into the bookstore more often."

"Rayna is going to check on him," Willow continued, ignoring Sam's comment. "He's about the same age as all the others. He might be with them." She sat back down and picked up her drink. "I wonder how many more missing people there might be."

"Just out of curiosity, what do you think happened to them?" Sam looked from one to the other. "Alien abduction? I mean, seriously. What are the actual possibilities?"

"That's just it," Rey answered. "We don't know."

"They might have gone on a trip," Sam said. "Like,

taken a bus somewhere. Maybe Vegas. Old people love to gamble. Or to a spa resort. Who knows? But for this many people to disappear all at the same time, it has to be a coordinated effort."

"That's what worries me." Willow sighed. "Because whatever happened, it was really out of character. Even if you go on vacation, you bring your phone. You tell your family."

"Then what happened?" Clearly frustrated, Sam dragged his fingers through his hair. For once, he appeared to actually be focused on the situation rather than how it affected him.

"That's what we're trying to figure out," Rey said. "Rayna is working on it. She's good. If anyone can get answers, she can."

"I'll start asking around too," Sam promised. "And I'll let you two know if I hear anything."

"Thank you," Willow said, looking at him. "I stopped in at the church my grandmother attends. The pastor said she hasn't been in several weeks. That's not like her."

"Weird," Sam replied. "She even had Carl going to services with her."

Rey noticed she didn't mention her conversation with Serenity. He supposed he couldn't blame her.

"Well, thanks for the tea." Willow stood. "I guess I'd better run. I just wanted to give you an update."

"Do you want to stay for dinner?" Rey asked, giving in to impulse. Sam snapped his head around to stare.

"I might," Willow admitted, her soft gaze locked on his. "Honestly, I dread going back to grandma's empty house. But only if I can help cook."

Rey smiled. "That can be arranged. Most of our meals

are simple, especially in the summer. I usually throw something on the grill. Maybe you can make a side dish."

"I can do that."

In the background, Sam snorted. "We usually just open a can of beans or microwave some frozen vegetables."

Which was only because Sam was in charge of making the sides, though Rey kept that truth to himself.

"Well, I think I can figure out something," Willow said, still smiling. "What are you grilling tonight?"

"Chicken breast," Rey answered.

"Perfect." She glanced at the pantry and fridge. "Do you mind if I take a look and see what you have?"

"Go ahead." Sam smiled. "I can be your assistant while Rey mans the grill."

They ended up having grilled chicken and a delicious corn salad. Even Sam's earlier bad mood appeared to have lifted. He complimented Rey on the chicken, something he never did. Willow's spirits seemed better too. She seemed more relaxed and happy. Rey loved seeing the light in her eyes.

She insisted on helping clean up. Sam, for once, pitched in. Rey went outside to clean his grill. When he'd finished and went back in, Willow thanked him for the meal and headed out.

About to walk her to the door, Rey stopped when Sam stepped in and did it instead. The second he'd closed the door behind her, he turned to Rey and grinned. "I think I'm in love with Willow," he said. "And I'm confident she feels the same way. I think the time has come for me to settle down and start a family."

Chapter 6

A puppy, Willow thought, driving away from the ranch. Sam reminded her of an overeager puppy. Instead of helping as she'd prepared the corn salad, Sam had tripped all over himself and gotten in the way. Even worse, he'd clearly decided she hadn't meant it when she'd told him she wasn't interested. He'd been flirty and had kept touching her. Only when she'd told him sharply to stop had he kept his hands to himself. Which was a good thing, since she'd seriously begun to consider walloping him.

Somehow, even with his interference, she'd managed to whip together her special corn salad. Back in California, she'd prepared this to bring to every beach party and cook out she'd attended, so she knew the ingredients by heart. She could tell it wasn't something Rey and Sam usually ate, so she'd enjoyed watching their reactions when they'd taken their first bite. Especially Rey's.

Despite everything going on, she couldn't seem to stop looking at Rey's handsome face. Oddly enough, he hadn't had this effect on her at all when she'd hung around with Sam as a teenager. But now...

Her breath caught every time their eyes met. She found herself wanting to be closer to him, to touch him.

With Sam's watchful gaze on her every time she looked up, she struggled to act unaffected.

Multiple times during the meal, she found herself about to say something to Rey, but bit back the words due to Sam's presence. Despite his attempt to be empathetic, she knew he still believed Isla, Carl and the rest of the missing people would show up any day. Whether he was overly optimistic or deluded, she wished she could share his belief. With every day that passed with her grandmother gone, her worry grew.

She arrived home and let herself into the house, hoping against hope that Isla would pop out of the kitchen and envelop her in a hug.

But the empty house remained still and quiet. Closing the blinds, she changed into an old T-shirt and soft shorts, poured herself a glass of wine and settled down to watch TV.

Her phone rang. Amanda Epps, her friend who owned the hair salon.

"Hey, girl," Amanda said. "Any luck finding your grandmother?"

Willow told her no.

"Oh. I'm sorry. But listen, I just got off the phone with Sam. It sounds like you and I have something to celebrate, right? I know the timing seems a bit off, but we need to take good news when we can. So congratulations!"

Confused, Willow took a deep breath. "Congratulations on what?"

Amanda went silent. "Oh, dang. I didn't realize…"

"Didn't realize what?"

"That it was supposed to be a secret. You know how

Sam is. He can run on at the mouth. He asked me to organize a get-together for the two of you."

Though she'd begun to feel like a broken record, Willow asked why.

"I don't know," Amanda replied. "All he said was to
celebrate your good news."

Finally, Willow let her exasperation show. "There is
no good news. Please don't plan any sort of gathering or
party, because I won't be attending. Right now, all my
focus is centered on finding my grandmother."

"But Sam said—"

"I don't care what he said. He and I are only friends.
As a matter of fact, I'm going to call him right now and
get this straightened out."

"Oh, wow. I'm so sorry. I thought for sure you two
had gotten engaged," Amanda said.

Engaged? Willow nearly spit out her wine.

"I hope I didn't spoil any surprises," Amanda continued.

After taking a couple of deep breaths, Willow was able
to speak normally. "Don't worry, you didn't. It's all good,
I promise. But I am going to have to let you go now."

As soon as she ended the call, Willow dialed Sam,
simmering. When he didn't pick up, instead of leaving
a message, she phoned Rey. He answered on the second ring.

"What the heck is going on with Sam right now?" she
demanded. "I just got a phone call from Amanda, one
of my high school friends, offering her congratulations
at my and Sam's good news."

"Good news?" Rey sounded carefully noncommittal.
"Are some sort of congratulations in order?"

"Don't you start too!" Frustrated, she took a deep gulp of wine. "Did he say something to you?"

Rey went silent. When he spoke again, the pitch of his low voice sounded intense. "Willow, are you sure you want me involved in whatever you two have got going on?"

Though she rarely, if ever, cursed, Willow did now. "Damn it, Rey. I was just there. You know as well as I do that Sam and I have nothing going on. Now please, tell me what he said. If he's calling people in town and spreading some kind of rumor about me, I need to stop it now."

"I think you should call him."

"I tried to, but he didn't pick up." She could no longer hide her frustration. "Come on, Rey. What's going on?"

"Sam has convinced himself that you are in love," he finally said, reluctance coloring his tone.

"With *him*?" she squeaked. "Are you serious?"

Before he could respond, she heard the sound of Sam's voice in the background. "Is that Sam? Put him on."

"But—"

"Put him on *now*!" she demanded.

"Hold on. Sam, Willow wants to talk to you."

"Tell her I'm not here," Sam said.

"She can hear you," Rey replied. "Here."

He must have handed Sam the phone because a second later Sam greeted her. "Hey, Willow. What's up?"

"What did you say to Amanda?" she asked, not bothering to try and contain her anger. "What celebration are you planning?"

"Oh, geez," Sam said, sounding sheepish. "I was trying to get something set up in advance, that's all. She shouldn't have called you."

"Set up in advance for what?"

"Um, I'd rather not say," he replied.

"Since it involves me, I think you have to. Now, spill."

"Just a sec." Sam sounded weird, like he might choke on his words. "Let me go outside so we can talk in private."

In the background, she heard the sound of a door opening and closing.

"Okay," Sam finally said. "We're alone now."

Silent, she waited. She could hear the nervousness in his voice.

"Willow, I was going to ask you to marry me. That's what the celebration was going to be for. So everyone could share in our happiness."

Dumbfounded, she struggled to find words and failed.

"Willow, are you there?" Sam asked anxiously. "What do you say? Obviously, I haven't got a ring yet or anything, but we could pick out one together."

Though she wanted to ask what planet he lived on, she'd known Sam for years, and if he was serious, she didn't want to break his heart. She thought about playing this off as a joke, giving him an easy way out, but he clearly seemed to think this was an actual possibility. Why, she had no idea.

"Sam, we're not even dating," she said, as gently as she could. "I've made it abundantly clear to you that we are friends, and I'm not interested in anything more."

"But the connection," he said, his tone serious and desperate. "Earlier, when we made that corn salad. Don't tell me you didn't feel it too."

"There was no connection, Sam. We are just two old friends, helping out in the kitchen." Then, just in case she hadn't made it clear enough, she continued. "There will be no celebration, no engagement, heck, no dating. I need you to understand this. Please tell me you do."

Sam was silent for so long, she thought he might have ended the call. "Are you there?" she finally asked.

"I am." He sounded distant now. "I apologize for misunderstanding. Let me take the phone back inside, so you can talk to my brother. Obviously, you've chosen him over me."

"This isn't a competition," she said, but Sam didn't reply.

A moment later, Rey came on. "Willow?" he asked, his voice hesitant. "Are you all right?"

"I'm not sure," she answered honestly. "I have no idea what's going on with Sam. He helped me make the salad tonight for dinner, and somehow he got it into his head that we are a couple."

"He said as much to me," Rey admitted. "I was kind of shocked, but I figured I'd just stay out of it."

"There's nothing to stay out of." She wasn't sure whether to laugh or cry. "This feels almost like a prank. I just wanted to fill you in because your brother is not okay. I'm worried about him."

"I'll talk to him later, once he's calmed down. Maybe Dad being missing has finally hit home with him, and this is his way of dealing with it."

She swallowed. "I think he needs help, Rey. Maybe he should talk to a therapist or a doctor."

"Maybe," Rey agreed. "I promise I'll bring that up too, when the time seems right. To be honest, he's always been a bit immature, but this is next-level stuff. I'm worried about him also."

She wished she were there with him, ached to be able

to take comfort in his strong embrace. Shaking her head at her own untoward thoughts, she took a deep breath.

"I promise I'll talk to him," Rey continued. "Try not to worry. I'll fill you in as soon as I have more answers."

"Thanks." She needed to get off the phone before she said something she'd regret, like how much she needed him. "I'll talk to you later."

"Definitely." Rey hesitated. "And Willow, don't let yourself feel bad about this. None of it's your fault."

The empathy in his voice nearly undid her. Somehow, she managed to hold it together long enough to tell him goodbye.

Putting her phone down on the end table, she knew he was right. She'd done nothing wrong. But now, in addition to battling her overwhelming attraction to Rey, she was honestly concerned about Sam. She might not be romantically interested in him, but he was one of her oldest friends. If he needed help, she would do her best to make sure he got it.

After talking to Willow, Rey went looking for Sam. Sam had been acting erratically, even for him. While Rey wasn't exactly sure what might be going on with his younger brother, he couldn't help but hope Sam might open up to him.

Before he could reach his brother's room, the doorbell rang. That in itself was unusual. Out here at the ranch, visitors were few and far between, and most people let him know in advance they were coming. Frowning, Rey pivoted and headed toward the front door.

He opened it to find a sheriff's deputy in full uniform standing on his porch. Immediately, Rey's heart sank.

"Are you here about my father?" he asked, his voice breaking despite his best efforts.

The man, a deputy Rey didn't recognize, removed his cowboy hat. "I'm sorry, sir. Are you Rey Johnson?"

"I am."

"I'll need you to come with me. Rayna asked me to bring you down to the hospital," the man said.

"The hospital?" Hearing that gave Rey hope. "Can you at least tell me if he's all right?"

"Sir, I've only been instructed to fetch you. I don't know any details."

Which seemed fair. "Just one second," Rey said, calling for Sam. "My brother needs to come too."

When Sam didn't answer, Rey hurried inside to knock on Sam's door. But again, Sam didn't respond. Rey turned the knob and peeked inside. No Sam. Which meant he was somewhere out on the ranch.

Deciding he didn't have time to look for him but would call him on the way to the hospital, Rey hurried out front to rejoin the deputy. He got into the passenger seat at the man's direction.

"I need to make a few calls," Rey said.

"Go ahead, it's a long drive," the deputy said.

"Thanks." Rey punched the contact to make the call. But Sam didn't pick up. Leaving a voice mail, he outlined what he knew and where he was headed. Since he didn't have too much information to go on, he said that too. "Anyway, if you want to head to Midland, that's good. If not, give me a call when you get this. I'll update you when I know more."

Next, he tried Willow. She answered almost immediately. "What's going on?" she asked. "Did you get a chance to talk to Sam?"

"Not yet." He filled her in on what was going on.

She gasped. "Serenity's warning. She said someone with Isla was in trouble."

"She just didn't say who or what kind of trouble," he said, deciding he'd concede this one to Serenity. "I guess we're about to find out."

"Have you called Rayna?" she asked, the tremor in her voice echoing the way he felt inside. "I'm guessing since she only sent for you that my grandmother wasn't found."

"I don't know." His gut twisted. "Let me try her now. If I hear anything new, I'll call you back. If not, I'll update you once I get to the hospital."

But Rayna didn't pick up. Since he really hadn't expected her to, he put his phone away and settled in for the drive to Midland, the location of their closest hospital.

The deputy, whose name Rey still hadn't gotten, wasn't much of a talker. In fact, he barely even glanced at Rey, preferring to keep his focus on the road.

Which suited Rey just fine. He had a million questions, and since this guy clearly had zero answers, he'd make the ride in silence.

Finally, they arrived at the hospital. The deputy parked his cruiser and looked at Rey. "I'll need you to stay with me," he said.

"Fine." Impatience churning inside him, Rey followed the man into the emergency department waiting room, where they were met by another uniformed officer.

"This way, please."

The triage nurse buzzed them back. Down a long hallway past several rooms. Finally, Rey spotted Rayna, sitting in a chair outside a room marked ICU. She jumped up as they approached.

"Is he okay?" Rey asked. "Please tell me he's all right."

"It's not Carl," Rayna said. "When I got the call, the description made it sound like it might be, but when I got here about fifteen minutes ago, they allowed me back to see him. Once I did, I realized it's Floyd Smith. Willow might have told you, but he's been missing too."

Just like that, all the jumbled emotions of hope and fear and relief vanished. "Not Carl," he repeated. Then, realizing they'd recovered at least one of the missing people, he took a deep breath. "Has he been able to tell you where he's been?"

Slowly, the sheriff shook her head. "He's not conscious. In fact, he's in pretty bad shape. Someone found him half naked, wandering a county road out near the edge of Getaway limits. The doctor says he's severely malnourished and dehydrated. I'm hoping they can fix him up quickly so he can give us some information."

Since Rey sensed his legs might give out, he dropped into the chair Rayna had just vacated. "It's not Carl," he repeated, his throat aching as he shook his head. "I honestly thought you'd found my father. I'm not sure whether to be relieved or disappointed."

"I get that, and I'm sorry." Rayna squeezed his shoulder. "I thought, from the description I was given, they'd found your father. Now that we know it's not, we can go from there. Honestly, this is the first real lead we've had in this case. Until now, there's been nothing."

"Nothing?" Rey repeated. "Nothing at all?"

"Yes. No matter how hard we look for evidence, it's like an entire group of people vanished without a trace.

The only thing they have in common is their age. All of them are senior citizens."

Rey took a deep breath, trying to slow his racing pulse.

"So I'm really hopeful once Mr. Smith can tell us where he's been, we'll know where to find the others," Rayna continued. "Assuming they are all together, which seems likely."

Rey nodded. "I need to call Sam and Willow," he said.

"Go right ahead." Rayna moved away to give him some privacy. "I'm going to grab a soft drink from the vending machine. Do you want anything?"

"No thanks." Waiting until Rayna rounded the corner, Rey pulled out his phone. He called Sam first, just in case his brother had jumped into his truck and might be on the way to the hospital. The call went straight to voice mail. Rey went ahead and left a message with all the details he'd just learned from Rayna. "Call me back when you get this," he said.

Next, he phoned Willow. She answered on the first ring, clearly waiting. "The guy isn't Carl," he told her. "Rayna said it's Mr. Smith, the bookstore owner. He's in pretty bad shape and unconscious, so no one has been able to question him to see if he was with the others."

"Oh, that poor man." Willow took a deep breath. "I hope he's going to be all right."

"Me too." He debated whether or not to tell her what Rayna had said about there being no other leads in the case. In the end, he went ahead and passed that on. He didn't want to start hiding things from her.

"No other leads?" She sounded stunned. "She doesn't have anything at all?"

"Unfortunately not."

His answer made her groan. "Great. I really hope Mr. Smith knows something."

"Me too." He found himself wanting to linger on the call. Hearing her voice brought him both comfort and an aching sort of need.

"Please let me know if you learn anything," Willow continued.

He promised he would before saying goodbye. After, he sat and stared at his phone for a moment, wishing he could see her.

Then, shaking his head at his own foolishness, he went to find Rayna.

Walking down the adjacent hall, he located her standing near the vending machine, drinking a cola and talking to one of her deputies. They went silent when he walked up.

"I couldn't reach Sam," he said. "Though, I was able to fill Willow in."

"You might as well go home," Rayna said, her tired smile matching the hint of exhaustion in her eyes. "I'm going to stay here in the hopes that Mr. Smith wakes up. I'll call you once he does."

"Are you sure?" Rey asked, torn between trying to help out and getting the heck out of the hospital. "I'll need to catch a ride back with one of your guys."

"Yes, I'm sure and that's fine. I've got more deputies here too. There's no reason for you to stay."

More relieved than he should have been, Rey thanked her and headed out to the lobby to wait for his ride. Before the deputy got there, he checked his phone just in case Sam had called or texted, but there wasn't anything. Had his brother even gotten his messages?

He tried again, though this time he hung up without

leaving a message. Unsure whether to be angry or just annoyed, he shoved all of that into the back of his mind and greeted the deputy. He wished he could ask to drive. Driving had always been therapeutic for him, so by the time he made it home, he figured he'd have been in a much better frame of mind. Instead, he had no choice but to ride shotgun.

Leaving Midland to head east toward Getaway, the deputy cranked up the radio when an old Brooks & Dunn song came on. By the time the Welcome to Getaway sign came into view, the sunset had turned the sky to purple overlaid with swirls of orange, pink and yellow. In other words, a typical West Texas summer sky.

Once the deputy had dropped him off at the ranch, instead of going inside, he found himself getting in his truck and heading in the opposite direction toward Willow's house. He couldn't articulate why, not even to himself, but he needed to see her. After the emotional upheaval he'd just been through, being with Willow felt like the only thing that could even begin to calm the rawness.

He didn't take the time to think or call her or text her. Instead, he drove with a single-minded intent, focusing only on her.

Finally, after what felt like forever, he turned onto her street and pulled in front of her house. Now that darkness had fallen, the yellow lights she'd turned on inside lit up the front bay window from behind the closed curtains. He sat in his truck for a moment, marveling at the suburban cheeriness of the place, before he turned off the motor. Jumping out, he headed up the sidewalk with a brisk stride. Hoping she'd be as eager to see him as he was her, he took a deep breath and pressed the doorbell.

Chapter 7

When Willow opened her door to find Rey standing there, her pulse went into immediate overdrive. Taking a shaky breath, she stepped aside and motioned him in. He'd barely moved past, brushing lightly against her, when she closed the door and turned to face him. Something intense flared in that instant. The smoldering heat in his gaze made her entire body tingle.

Neither of them spoke. No words were necessary. Instead, they locked gazes and moved toward each other, as if pulled by unseen forces. She couldn't speak, or think. Dizzy with desire, she couldn't look away. Rey took up all her focus.

Claiming her lips with his, the raw hunger in his kiss sent a ripple of excitement through her. She raised herself to meet him, shuddering at the delicious sensation of his kiss. His touch, almost unbearably tender, ignited in her a frenzy of need.

She deepened the kiss, demanding more, craving more. His breath hitched as his tongue met hers. *This*, she thought, her knees trembling. She'd been waiting all her life for *this* man.

On fire, she fumbled with his shirt, needing to feel

the heat of his skin under her fingers. His fingers seared a path across her abdomen as he helped her shed her clothes. Finally, both naked, they came together again, skin to skin. His hardness matched her softness.

Still locked together, they made it to her couch, still kissing as they fell against the cushions.

"Are you sure?" he rasped, lifting his mouth long enough from hers to ask.

This made her chuckle, even as desire thrummed through her blood. "A little late for that, aren't you?" she asked, unable to keep her quivering body from rubbing like a cat against his oh-so-perfect arousal. "And yes, I'm sure. Are you?"

Instead of an answer, he made a low growl deep in his throat. The primal sound sent her already sensitive nerves ablaze.

He lowered his body over hers. She gasped as he entered her, then arched up to meet him, welcoming him into her body.

Moving slowly, he filled her completely before he withdrew and then did it all over again. He intoxicated her, captivated her and drove her utterly mad.

"More," she ordered.

To her surprise and delight, he took her at her word, releasing whatever leash he'd put on his self-control. He took her, fast and deep and hard, driving himself into her with a fury that matched her own frenzied need.

Again and again, each time she met him halfway, nails raking down his skin. Their mutual passion, raw and primal, felt like nothing she'd ever experienced before.

As her climax built, shuddering with tremors that

warned of an impending tsunami, she finally surrendered and gave herself over to an explosion of pure pleasure, sweet and raw. Drowning, she moaned as waves of ecstasy crashed over her, while she rode the crest of the tide.

After, she curled into him, the solid thrum of his heartbeat under her ear. They held on tightly to each other, each reluctant to move away.

For the first time in her life, she allowed a man to sleep beside her in her childhood bed in her mother's house. More than right, or convenient, having Rey there felt necessary.

The next morning, Willow woke before sunrise. Even so, Rey had risen before her. She went into the bathroom and washed her face and brushed her teeth. After dragging a brush through her hair, she followed the smell of coffee to the kitchen, where Rey sat at the table drinking a cup. At the sight of him, her body stirred again.

"I hope you don't mind," he said, gesturing toward her grandmother's old coffeepot. "I need my caffeine, or I'm worthless."

"Of course I don't mind," she replied, aching to kiss him again. "You're up early."

He shrugged. "I always get up at five. Old habits are hard to break."

"I get it. I'm an early riser too." After making her own cup of coffee, she carried it over to the table. "One of my true joys in life is being on the beach when the sun comes up."

"Do you miss it?" he asked. "The ocean, I mean."

"I do," she answered honestly. "But I missed Getaway too. West Texas has a way of getting into your soul and leaving a mark. If I could bring the ocean closer to here, I'd have paradise."

Which would mean she'd stay. She didn't give voice to that thought, which was something that had been rattling around in her head for some time now. Even before her grandmother had disappeared, Willow had missed her. Plus, as Isla grew older, Willow wanted to be around to help her, enjoy her company and learn from her seemingly endless well of wisdom. Now, she had to wonder if she'd ever get the chance again.

Throat aching, she turned her head away to hide the sudden tears in her eyes. But Rey must have noticed. He covered her hand with his. "We're going to find them," he said. "Alive and well."

Slowly, she nodded, grateful for his touch. "I'm going to ask for more time off from my job. I still have vacation days remaining, though I'd planned to use those during the holidays. But there's no way I can leave, not with my grandmother still missing."

Instead of replying, he leaned over and kissed her. Which was much better anyway. When they broke apart, they breathed heavily.

"Do you want to go back to bed?" he asked, the heat in his eyes matching his husky voice.

The thought made her shiver. "I have a better idea," she said. "We both could use a shower. How about you join me?"

Grinning, he got to his feet and pulled her up with him. "You don't need to ask me twice. Let me see if I have one last condom, and I'll meet you there."

The hot shower wasn't as steamy as their lovemaking. Slick, soapy skin, water running down his muscular, hard body. Allowing herself to explore, she loved the way he held perfectly still so she could. Only the immensity of his arousal and the banked heat in his eyes testified how her touch affected him.

Meanwhile, she thought she might melt into a molten puddle. Every nerve ending tingling, her touch became bold, demanding. When he finally gave in, he entered her fiercely, filling her and almost sending her over the edge.

Though they'd spent the night in each other's arms, and their lovemaking had varied from the initial frenzy to a more leisurely pace, this was different. Quick and rough, both standing, when the pleasure overtook her, she let it. Head back, she cried out with wild abandon. A moment later, Rey joined her.

They took turns cleaning each other off. She marveled at his tenderness, giving the same back to him.

She wondered if she'd ever get enough of this man. When around him, her senses heightened. The world looked brighter, sounded softer, and she felt more alive than ever before, except for when riding the crest of a huge wave on the Pacific.

If only Isla, Carl and the others could be found, she thought life would be pretty darn good. Maybe even complete.

Stunned at the turn her thoughts had taken, she grabbed a towel and handed it to him. Then she dried herself off and escaped to her room to compose herself while she got dressed.

When she emerged, dressed but with her hair still damp, she found him fully clothed and waiting. His smile made her catch her breath. "I just talked to Rayna," he said. "There hasn't been any change on Mr. Smith, so he still hasn't regained consciousness. He's still in the ICU."

"I wonder if I should drive out there and see him," she mused. "He was always so kind to me when I stopped in the bookstore."

"Rayna said he isn't allowed any visitors other than immediate family."

"Which means he won't have any." She couldn't keep the sadness from her voice. "Other than his staff and friends, he's completely alone."

He hugged her. "Since he's not conscious yet, I think it'll be all right. If I hear anything else, I'll let you know."

"Thank you."

"I'd better go," he said. "I've got a crew working on fence repair today, and I need to join them."

Since she wasn't sure what to do with herself today, she briefly considered asking if she could join him. But she knew absolutely nothing about fixing fences, and her presence would be more of a hindrance than a help, so she didn't.

Instead, she followed him to the door. Absolutely stunned when he turned to kiss her, she kissed him back and then stood on her front porch to watch him leave.

Rey kissed Willow goodbye and got into his truck to drive home. The familiarity of the simple gesture made his chest ache. Unable to help himself, he glanced back as he pulled away, catching sight of her standing on her doorstep watching him go. Though he didn't want to leave her, work called.

All the way home, he sang along to the radio, his

mood buoyant despite the knowledge that Rayna still hadn't been able to speak to Mr. Smith to get information. If he didn't hear from her by this afternoon, he'd give her another call just to check in. He really hoped Mr. Smith survived and made a full recovery, and not only because everyone wanted to know where he'd been and what had happened to him.

It was still early when he pulled into the ranch drive. His stomach growled, reminding him that he hadn't eaten. He figured he had time enough to make a bowl of oatmeal or something.

"Where were you last night?" Sam demanded, meeting him at the door. "You didn't come home at all. I was worried."

Rey stared, shouldering past his brother. "Do you ever check your text messages or voice mail?" he asked, his voice harsh. "It would have been nice to get some sort of response."

"I checked them." Crossing his arms defensively, Sam continued to give him the stink eye. "You said the guy in the hospital wasn't Dad. I didn't know you wanted me to reply to that. I figured we'd talk about it once you got home. But you didn't come here. I waited up for you too."

Since it clearly hadn't occurred to Sam to pick up the phone and call, Rey wasn't sure he wanted to waste his breath.

Instead, he shrugged and headed to his bedroom to change his clothes before going out to meet his hired hands. "We're repairing more fence today," he called over his shoulder. "Just in case you want to join us and help. There's quite a large section down."

"You still haven't told me where you were. Did you spend the night in town or stay at the hospital?"

Rey turned, eyeing his brother. "I stayed in town. Why didn't you at least call me? I was worried when I didn't hear from you."

"I fell asleep in front of the TV," Sam replied. "By the time I woke up, it was after two a.m., and it was way too late to call."

Exhaling, Rey decided to let it go. Venting frustration had never had any effect on Sam. "It's all good," he said. "Do you want to help with the fence? We can use an extra pair of hands."

"We'll see. You know, you seem awfully happy," Sam mused, following right behind him. "After all the traumatic stuff with the misidentification at the hospital, I'd think you'd be exhausted and crabby."

If Rey felt any exhaustion, it would be due to him and Willow making love several times over the course of the evening. But since he had no intention of mentioning that to his brother, he simply shrugged, went into the bedroom and closed the door behind him. Since he'd indulged in a shower with Willow earlier, he simply needed to change and head out.

By the time he emerged a few minutes later, Sam had disappeared. A quick glance out the window showed he'd taken his truck, which meant he had no intention of working on the ranch.

Figured. Refusing to let his younger brother's antics ruin his mood, Rey went out to the barn to saddle up Roscoe and meet his crew.

He rode over to the same pasture where he'd made temporary fixes the day before. The crew had already arrived, having driven in and parked on the gravel road that abutted the pasture. Rey greeted them and dismounted, tying Roscoe to a low tree branch so he could be in the shade while he worked.

Physical labor turned out to be exactly what he needed. He found himself wishing Sam had shown up because Sam might have benefited from an outlet for whatever was bothering him. Though Rey planned to try to have a sit-down talk with his brother, he knew from past experience that Sam had to be in the mood for a discussion. Otherwise, trying to get him to share anything would only enrage him or cause him to completely shut down.

Finally, the fence repair had been completed. The crew left, and Rey rode Roscoe back to the barn.

When he arrived back at the house, tired and sweaty, he headed straight for the shower. Though Sam's truck once again sat parked in the drive, Rey didn't encounter him on his way to clean up.

His phone rang just as he finished toweling himself off. Though he didn't recognize the number, he answered anyway.

"Rey?" His father's voice, very faint. "Can you hear me?"

"Dad?" Heart racing, Rey gripped the phone. "Where are you? Are you all right?"

Whatever else Carl tried to say broke up, making it unintelligible.

"I can't understand you," Rey said urgently. "Please, just tell me where you are, and I'll come get you."

But only silence greeted his request, indicating the call had dropped.

Immediately, Rey called the number back. It rang

once and then nothing. Not even voice mail or any way to leave a message. He tried again and again, each time with the same result. Then he dialed Rayna.

"Still no change," she said when she answered. "I'm driving home now. I've got men posted to his room around the clock, and someone will call me if and when he's awake and alert."

"That's not why I'm calling." He told her about Carl phoning him and how he hadn't been able to make out what he'd said. "I didn't recognize the number, and I've called it back several times with no luck."

"Text it to me," Rayna ordered. "I'll check it out when I'm back in town."

After ending the call, he did as she asked. Then, just in case he might get lucky, he called the number again. Same result.

"Damn," he said, resisting the urge to hurl his phone at the wall. Next, he dialed Willow. But she didn't answer, so when her voice mail came on, he left her a message to call him when she got a chance.

Once he'd gotten dressed, he went looking for Sam. He found him in the kitchen, eating a sandwich with potato chips.

"I made you one too," Sam said, pointing toward the fridge. "I wasn't sure what time you'd be back, but I figured you'd be hungry."

Not sure what to make of his brother's jovial mood, Rey thanked him before telling him about the phone call.

"He *called* you?" Eyes huge, Sam put his half-eaten sandwich down on the plate. "Can I see your phone? I want to call him back."

"I've already tried that, several times." Rey retrieved

his sandwich from the refrigerator and took the chair opposite Sam. "I've also called Rayna and given her the number. She's going to see what she can find out. I'm hopeful they can ping the location, so we know where to go look for Dad."

Picking up his sandwich again, Sam took a huge bite and chewed before responding. "See? I told you Dad went somewhere on vacation. He's fine. He probably just had bad cell service or something. Since he accidentally left his own phone at home, he probably had to buy one of those cheap, disposable phones."

Not sure what planet his brother might be living on, Rey decided not to reply to that comment. Instead, he concentrated on wolfing down his sandwich, along with a handful of chips. He washed everything down with a diet cola.

"Oh, when I was in town earlier, Gia Barrera asked about you," Sam said, grinning.

Rey didn't recognize the name. "Who?"

"Buddy Barrera's younger sister," Sam said. "The one who used to have a crush on you back in the day?"

Since Rey only vaguely remembered and hadn't seen Buddy in years, he shrugged.

"Don't you want to know what she was asking?"

Eyeing his brother, Rey polished off his sandwich. "Not really. I'm more concerned with figuring out where Dad is and if he's in trouble."

"You should see her now," Sam continued, as if he hadn't spoken. "She's super hot."

"Are you trying to tell me you're going to start dating her?" Rey asked. Maybe a new girlfriend would help get Sam out of whatever rut he'd found himself in.

"Dating her?" Sam laughed. "She's interested in you. I'm just passing on the good news. I told her I'd give you her number." And he slid a piece of paper across the table. "Here you go. Good luck."

Rey didn't even look at the paper. "Thanks, but no thanks. I'm not interested. If you think she's all that great, go ahead and ask her out."

Just then, his phone rang. Willow. His heart skipped a beat. "Hey," he answered, pushing up from the table. "You're not going to believe what just happened."

Though he walked into the living room to continue the conversation, Sam followed. Deciding to ignore Sam's stares, Rey filled Willow in.

"Oh, wow. Did he sound…okay?" Willowed asked, her voice breaking.

"It was hard to tell," he replied, softening his voice. "He kept breaking up. I couldn't even make out any of his words. I tried to call him back several times, but he never picked up. I couldn't leave a message because there was no voice mail."

"But at least you know he's alive," she said, her sniffling letting him know she was on the verge of tears. "I'd give anything to hear my grandmother's voice."

"I know." Lowering his voice again, he glanced up to find Sam not even bothering to pretend to not be eavesdropping. "I've given the information to Rayna, and hopefully she'll be able to get something for us."

"Thank you." She sighed. "I wish you were here. This all gets so discouraging sometimes."

Glancing at his brother again, he decided what the hell. "I can be there in an hour. Would that work for you?"

"Definitely." Her relief seemed palpable. "And bring a change of clothes in case you end up spending the night."

This made him grin. "I'll keep that under consideration. See you soon."

After ending the call, still smiling, Rey turned to go to his room and pack a small bag. Just in case, as she'd said.

"Who was that?" Sam followed him to his room.

Rey turned. Briefly, he considered telling his brother it wasn't any of his business. Then, deciding he had nothing to hide, he shrugged. "Willow. I'm heading over to her place now."

Arms crossed, Sam eyed him. "What for?"

Right then, Rey realized the time had come for them to talk. "Sam, what's going on with you? I know you and Willow were—are—friends, but I'm also aware there's nothing else happening between the two of you."

"There could be," Sam answered sullenly. "If she'd at least give it a chance. But now I know why she won't. Because you're making a play for her."

"Sit down." Rey gestured at his bed. "Please."

Expression hostile, Sam sat. A second later, Rey sat down next to him. "This isn't a competition," he said. "And I think you know that."

"But you're my brother. You're not supposed to go after a girl that I have feelings for."

Rey knew he needed to tread gently. "Sam, talk to me. Willow is a person, not an object you can decide to stake a claim to. You know this. I know you do."

Scowling, Sam considered. "True. But I still don't like the way you're acting, making her be with you."

"We're all adults here. I can't make Willow do anything." Rey took a deep breath. "Now, why don't you tell me what's really going on? You aren't acting like yourself, and it's got me a bit worried."

Sam started to shake his head but then stopped. When he met Rey's gaze, the look of naked vulnerability on his face made him appear much younger. "I don't like change," he finally admitted. "I want things to stay the way they are. First, Dad started dating Isla. That was weird, but kind of nice. I always liked her back when I was in school. But now..."

Sam took a deep breath before continuing. "It's too much, Rey. Like one thing stacked on top of a bunch of others. First, you left to go get bison, leaving me here to try to run things. I'd never tried to manage this place on my own before. Then Dad disappears, and I know you blame me, even if you don't say it. And my old friend Willow comes back. Instead of wanting to hang out with me, the two of you are doing your own thing. Once again, I'm left hanging out here on my own."

Clapping his hand on his brother's shoulder, Rey met and held his gaze. "No one blames you for Dad going missing. How could we? Whatever happened, he made his own choice. I know you were busy because I'm well aware of what it takes to keep this place running."

"Thanks for that," Sam said. "Because I've been feeling pretty guilty. I've been pretty worried about Dad."

"Have you? You sure haven't acted like it."

"It's easier to pretend everything is fine," Sam said, shrugging. "That's what I've been doing. Otherwise, it's way too stressful."

"I know," Rey replied, dropping his hand. "The worry

eats me up sometimes. Willow too. She's quietly trying not to freak out."

They sat in silence for a moment. Then, Sam gestured to Rey's packed bag. "Do you really like her?"

"I do," Rey answered immediately.

Still staring, Sam finally nodded. "You know she lives in California. She'll go back there once Isla is found."

"I know that too." Even if he sometimes had trouble remembering that. "But that doesn't mean we can't spend time together and even enjoy each other's company while she's here." Rey took a deep breath. "Are you going to be okay with that?"

Finally, Sam looked away. When he raised his head again to meet Rey's gaze, a slight smile curved his lips. "Do I have a choice?" he asked. "I mean, it's not like you'd be willing to stop seeing her if I asked, would you?"

"No." Hearing a trace of humor in his brother's voice, Rey chanced a smile back "I like her too much to do that. And I think the feeling might be mutual."

Groaning, Sam rolled his eyes. But when he looked at Rey again, he grinned. "You deserve it, you know. You work harder than anyone I know, and you're always there for me and Dad."

"Thanks." The unexpected praise made Rey's throat ache. "I appreciate you saying that."

Sam stood. "Now all you need to do is find Dad and Isla, and maybe we can all live happily ever after."

Chapter 8

Seeing Rey's truck pull up in front of her house, Willow stood at the window and watched as he strode up her sidewalk. She wondered if she'd ever get used to the way her heartbeat accelerated and her mouth went dry at the first sight of him.

She opened the front door and managed to wait until he'd made it all the way inside before wrapping her arms around him. Despite the fact that they'd spent most of the previous evening making love, she already wanted him again. And judging from his instant bulge of arousal, he felt the same way about her.

Mouths locked together, they stumbled backward toward her couch. But the sound of a ringing phone penetrated her daze of arousal.

"Is that you?" She wrenched her mouth away long enough to ask.

"I…" Fumbling in his pocket, he pulled out his still ringing phone. "It's Rayna," he said, shaking his head as if to clear it. "I think I'd better take this."

Though he was still breathing heavily, he managed to answer. He listened for a second, clearly working at getting himself under control.

"Rayna, I'm going to put the call on speaker," he said, punching the icon to do exactly that. "Willow is here with me, and I know she'd like to hear whatever you have to say." He then placed the phone on the coffee table.

"Sounds good." Rayna's voice sounded clear, though a bit grim. "Theodore Smith is awake. The medical team says he had such severe heatstroke that some of his organs started shutting down. The doctor isn't sure if it caused brain damage or not. But judging from some of the unbelievable things he's saying, I'm afraid it might have."

Willow's heart sank. "I'm sorry to hear that. Were you able to learn anything useful, like if he'd seen Isla, Carl or any of the others?"

"Unfortunately, he's not coherent. He kept saying the same two words, over and over and over. *Prophecy* and *servitude*. And the more we tried to get him to elaborate or explain, the more agitated he became. The nurse finally had to put something in his IV to get him to calm down."

Swallowing back her bitter disappointment, Willow met Rey's gaze. When he moved behind her to put his arms around her, she leaned into the comfort of his embrace.

"Maybe he'll be able to talk more once he's had some rest," Rey said.

"It's possible." Rayna sighed. "I don't know anymore."

"Are you okay?" Willow asked.

"I'm exhausted. I rushed to Midland once my deputy called to tell me Mr. Smith was awake. I'd only just gotten to sleep. Now, I'm going to drive all the way back to Getaway and go home and try to get a few more hours of rest." She took a deep breath. "Rey, I've got people working on trying to figure out where your father called from. So far, they haven't had much success. It's difficult, since he used a burner phone."

Though Rey's expression reflected his disappointment, he didn't comment. Instead, both he and Willow thanked her. Rayna promised to touch base if anything changed and ended the call.

"That was weird," Rey mused, his arms still around her. "Is Mr. Smith super religious?"

She turned to face him. "I don't know. Maybe he became that way once he lost his wife. I guess we could ask some of his employees. They'd know better than anyone."

"True." Brushing his mouth across hers, he kissed her, making her shiver. "I'm sure Rayna will look into that."

Though she welcomed the distraction, something about the information Rayna had relayed about Mr. Smith bothered her. Obviously, Rey could tell that her heart wasn't into it, as he broke away. "What's wrong?" he asked.

"I don't know." Needing to move, she began pacing. "I grew up hanging out in that bookstore. I was around Mr. Smith a lot. He recommended books for me all the time, saying he wanted me to broaden my horizons. Him talking about prophecy and especially about servitude doesn't sound like him."

"Sometimes people turn to religion at times of great need. He'd lost his wife and, from all accounts, was completely alone."

"Maybe so," she allowed, still not entirely convinced. "I've only talked to Pastor Clayton about my grandmother. Tomorrow, I need to stop in at all the other churches in town and see if Mr. Smith attended."

"That's a good plan," he agreed, dropping down onto her sofa and dragging his hand through his hair.

Judging by his pensive expression, he had something to say.

"What's up?" she asked softly, sitting down next to him, close enough that they were hip to hip.

"I talked to Sam before I came over," he said, looking up and meeting her gaze.

She studied him, looking for hints of tension in his eyes or the set of his jaw. She didn't see any. "How'd that go?"

His slight smile caused the corners of his eyes to crinkle. Sexy, sexy man. "Actually, pretty well. He and I sat down like two adults and talked. He and I haven't had that kind of discussion in years."

While she knew she had to choose her words with care, she was also worried about Sam. "Did you mention that he might benefit from talking to a therapist?"

"Not yet." His response came too quickly.

Something must have shown in her face because he reached out and took her hand. "You have to understand. Sam and I haven't always had the greatest relationship. Plus, we come from a long line of stoic ranchers, whose motto has long been to suck it up and bear it. If Sam has something deeper bothering him other than basic immaturity, I can't insist he needs to go to counseling. If I did, even if it had been something he'd previously considered, he'd do the opposite."

He had a point. She'd known Sam for years. "You're probably right," she admitted. "It's just that I'm worried about him. He's always been so happy-go-lucky. But the way he acted the other day has me pretty concerned. Especially when he called my old high school friend to get her to plan a celebration for something that existed only inside his mind."

"I agree." He squeezed her hand. "But I don't think this is the kind of thing that can be rushed. Right now, he seems okay. I'm hoping he and I can keep the lines of communication open and maybe he'll feel comfortable confiding in me if something is wrong."

"Wisdom and good looks, what a combination," she teased, even though she was serious. "You're probably right. Sometimes, I tend to laser focus on what I think is a solution and run roughshod over anything that gets in my way. Sometimes, I have to force myself to stop and take a deep breath." She smiled. "It took more than a few therapy sessions for me to figure that out."

He kissed her then, driving all thoughts of Sam out of her head.

Later, as she got up to make them some microwave popcorn to munch on while they watched a movie, she noticed the light on her grandmother's ancient answering machine flashing. She never remembered to check the thing because most people these days didn't leave messages.

Curious, she pressed the play button, hoping against hope to hear Isla's voice. Instead, a woman said she was calling from a doctor's office. She wanted to remind Isla that she had a follow-up appointment scheduled for this Friday at two o'clock.

Sadder than she should have been, Willow jotted down the office number. She'd call them tomorrow and let them know that her grandmother wouldn't be able to make her appointment. Due to the privacy laws, she figured no one there would be willing to discuss any specifics about Isla's condition, but she might as well try.

Once she'd made the popcorn, she emptied the bag into a large bowl and carried it back to the living room. Rey had the remote and was scrolling through the movie offerings on Netflix.

"Hey." Looking up, he smiled when she approached. "What are you in the mood for?"

"Not rom-com," she said immediately, plopping down next to him. "Action-adventure or horror."

"Horror?" His brows rose. "Like what?"

"I've watched the entire *Halloween* series four or five times," she said proudly. "Same for *Friday the 13th*."

"What about *Texas Chainsaw Massacre*?" he asked.

"Not scary enough," she promptly answered. "But *Nightmare on Elm Street* is good. There are several of those."

"Hard pass." Shaking his head, he looked back at the screen. "I'm not a fan of horror."

She hid her disappointment. "Not many people are. How about action-adventure? Or I can do a Viking movie. I'm not picky. I just don't want to watch anything sappy."

"Sappy?" He turned again to look at her. "Give me some examples of what you consider sappy, please."

Embarrassed now, she grimaced. "I've just never been able to buy into the whole meet-cute movie setup. I'll take things that never happen in real life for ten dollars, please."

"Have you ever even watched one?"

She had to think about that for a moment. "Not for years. And by years, I think I was in middle school." She actually remembered exactly how old she'd been. She and her eighth-grade boyfriend, Tanner, had settled in to watch a movie, and she'd chosen an older romantic comedy. Tanner had spent the entire ninety minutes mocking everything that happened in the movie. When she'd protested, he'd begun ridiculing her too.

Things had gotten heated, and in the end, Tanner had gone home. The next day at school, any time she'd passed one of his buddies, they'd made snide comments. Some of the other girls had joined in. She'd had great difficulty watching another rom-com after that.

"That's terrible," Rey said, after she explained, pulling her close. "I'm sorry that happened to you."

"Thanks." She leaned into him. "It was a long time ago. I was just a teenager, so I probably need to get over it."

"Does that mean you want to try watching a rom-com?" he asked, a teasing note in his voice. "I'll let you choose."

Smiling, she glanced up at him. "I take it you're a huge fan of them?"

"Maybe." He shrugged. "I've been known to watch one or two. Though mostly when on a date." And then he laughed.

She swatted his arm. "Funny. Action-adventure, please. I just need something to get my mind off worrying about my grandmother."

Sometime in the middle of the movie, she must have dozed off. She woke to Rey covering her with a throw blanket. Smiling up at him, she managed to wake up enough to get to her feet and make her way to her bedroom.

Once there, she crawled in beneath her covers, invited him to join her, and promptly fell back asleep.

The next time she opened her eyes, the nightstand clock said 3:15.

She could get used to this, she thought, gazing at the

handsome hunk of man sleeping beside her. The instant that thought occurred to her, panic rose in her throat. She thought of California and her apartment a few blocks from the beach. She could see her surfboard, leaning up against the wall just inside her front door. She'd made a life there, with friends and a job and a sport she'd become really good at. Plus with the surfing classes she taught, she got to spread that love around to others.

Getaway represented her past. While she'd never forgotten where she'd come from, nor would she, the differences between the two places—not just in the landscape, but cultural—sometimes made her feel like they were alternate realities. Still, she'd often found herself yearning for the people and the landscape of home. Not to mention the food. She hadn't been able to find a decent chicken-fried steak or biscuits and gravy anywhere in California.

And to be honest, she'd missed her grandmother. Though she knew Isla had lots of friends and interests and lived a rich and satisfying life, Willow hated living so far away. She'd always felt she should be closer in order to help out when needed.

Now, with her grandmother missing, Willow knew she'd be staying until Isla was found. And even after that, Willow wasn't sure she could return permanently to California ever again. That was even without adding her growing feelings for Rey into the equation.

After waking up late, which felt decadent as hell, Rey shared a leisurely breakfast and coffee with Willow. He liked being with her, probably more than he should. But he'd decided not to worry about a murky future and enjoy the time they had together while he could.

On the way back to the ranch, Rey decided he'd stop off at the bookstore and talk to Mr. Smith's employees. Even though Willow had already gone by, he figured he might as well get their take on their boss's hospitalization. And Willow had made a great point about finding out if Mr. Smith had attended church, and if so, where.

The young kid behind the counter barely glanced up from his phone as Rey approached. Once Rey stopped in front of him at the counter, he reluctantly put his cell away. "Can I help you?"

Rey introduced himself. "I wanted to talk to you about the owner, Theodore Smith."

"He's in the hospital." The young boy swallowed hard. "The sheriff came by and let us know. We had no idea. Several of us are going to carpool to Midland and visit him after closing tonight."

"That's great, but I'd suggest you call first. Last I heard, they were only allowing immediate family in since he's in the ICU," Rey said.

"Oh. Thanks."

Taking a deep breath, Rey continued. "If you don't mind, I wanted to ask you if he's particularly religious?"

"Mr. Smith?" Confusion made the kid frown. "No. Why?"

Keeping his voice casual, Rey shrugged. "I don't know. He was talking about prophecy and stuff like that. I thought I'd see if you knew which church he attends. I wanted to let his pastor know what's happened and see if he might want to visit him."

"Mr. Smith didn't go to church. At least, not as far as I know. He didn't talk much about what he did in his private life. But he sure as heck didn't seem religious.

I know he'd been having some medical issues recently, but he never said what they were. He just went to the doctor a lot."

Now they were getting somewhere. "Do you know what doctor?"

"No." Picking his phone back up, the kid had clearly lost interest. "Let me know if I can help you find anything. A book, that is."

Since he'd been dismissed, Rey turned to go. As he passed a display, a photo book on surfing caught his eye. He picked it up, studying the cover, which showed someone riding the crest of a huge wave. Trying to imagine petite Willow bravely doing something like that, he carried the book over to the counter. "I'll take this," he said, surprising himself and the young clerk.

After making his purchase, he took the bag and his receipt and left. Though he told himself the book had been an impulse purchase, which it had, he also realized he wanted to know more about the things Willow loved.

Once he'd placed the bag on the passenger seat of his truck, he decided he might as well go and see Serenity. She'd told Willow that she'd *seen* someone around Isla was in trouble. He wanted to ask her about Mr. Smith.

Walking into the shop, the nearly overwhelming scent of the incense hit him first. Much stronger than the last time he'd visited. As he moved farther inside, he saw why. In addition to incense, Serenity also had a scented candle burning.

"I've been expecting you for days," Serenity announced, breezing in from the back. Today, instead of her normally vibrant colors, she wore a black-and-gray long, flowing dress. As usual, she had dozens of bracelets on one arm, and large earrings shaped like feathers hung from her ears.

"You look nice," Rey said, deciding not to react to her prediction.

"Do I?" Her smile told him she understood his deflection. "This outfit was a birthday gift from my sister, so I thought I'd better wear it. The dress is lovely, though I would have preferred brighter colors."

"It's a nice change," he said, meaning it. "I came to talk to you about what you told Willow. You said that someone near Isla was in trouble."

Serenity nodded. "Yes. But it wasn't your father. The man who cried out is getting medical help now."

Startled, Rey narrowed his eyes. "Did Rayna tell you?"

"I haven't talked to Rayna in a good while," Serenity replied. "She knows I'll reach out if I get anything concrete."

Rey sighed. He liked Serenity and sure as heck didn't want to offend her, but he couldn't help but speculate that if she had true psychic powers, she should put them to good use and find all the missing people.

"It doesn't work like that," Serenity told him. "And no, I didn't read your mind. You actually said your thoughts out loud."

"Did I?" He wasn't too sure. "Okay then, I'll bite. If it doesn't work like that, can you explain to me how it does?"

"Sure." She smiled. "Do you want to come into the back and have some tea? We can talk there."

Genuinely curious, he followed her through the colorful beaded curtain into the combination stock room, break room and kitchen.

"Sit." Gesturing toward her small table with two

chairs, she continued over to the counter. "I keep this coffeepot full of hot water plugged in so I can make tea anytime I want to."

He took a seat, watching as she made them both cups of hot tea. "Earl Grey," she announced, setting the steaming cup down in front of him. She then took a seat in the other chair, blowing lightly on her tea before taking a tiny sip.

"You're not the first rancher to be sitting in that chair," she said, smiling. "Nor will you be the last. To be honest, sometimes I don't understand how all this works myself. Things come to me. Sometimes in dreams, sometimes in visions. Once in a while, I hear voices."

"Do you see dead people?" he asked, purposely quoting from a movie. "And if so, are there any here right now?"

His question made her chuckle. "Not in the way you mean. Every so often, an entity who has passed has something important to say, and I listen and relay the message. Mostly, I take care not to keep myself open to that kind of thing. If I did, I would be bombarded."

"Okay." He nodded as if he understood, though he really had no idea what she meant. "When you mentioned to Willow that someone with Isla was in danger, how'd you get that message?"

"I didn't say in danger, I said in *trouble*," Serenity clarified. "And I believe the phrase I was told was *near* Isla. Someone near Isla was in trouble."

"Told? By who?"

Taking her time answering, Serenity took another sip of her tea. "Are you going to drink yours?" she asked, inclining her head toward his untouched cup. "It's really good."

Though he preferred his tea over ice, he didn't want to be rude, so he drank some. It tasted different. Trying to identify the taste, he took another sip.

"Oil of bergamot," Serenity said, correctly interpreting his expression. "That's what gives the black tea its unique taste."

"I see," he replied. "But you didn't answer my question. Who told you someone was in trouble?"

"I just *saw* it," she said. "A man, near Isla at first. She tried to help him. He appeared ill. Stumbling, asking for water. I clearly saw Isla get him some. But I got an overwhelmingly strong sense that he was in serious trouble."

"You got that part right." He told her about Mr. Smith and how he'd been found on a back road out in the blazing July sun. "He's still in the ICU. They think he had heatstroke."

She blinked. "Theodore Smith? The owner of the bookstore? That's terrible. I know he's had some health issues recently. And since his wife passed away, he's been completely alone."

Drinking a few more swallows of his tea, he nodded. "I just left the bookstore. His employees are planning to visit him in the hospital after they close for the day."

"That's nice," Serenity said.

"It is, but unless they've moved him out of the ICU, only family is allowed. Plus, I'm not sure if he'll even know they're there. He's not yet fully conscious."

Serenity watched him closely. "Has he said anything yet? Or is he unable to communicate?"

"He's said a couple of words. *Prophecy* and *servitude*."

Frown deepening, she made a clucking sound. "Oh, dear. That doesn't sound like him."

Now it was Rey's turn to watch her closely. "Do you know him well?"

"Not really. I visited him a few times to bring him meals after his wife passed. But he'd stop in occasionally. And we'd talk."

Rey nodded. "Since you said him saying those two words didn't sound like him, I'm guessing he wasn't religious?"

"Correct. He was not religious at all." Serenity sighed. "In fact, he believed there was nothing after death, nothing at all. Until his wife contacted me and asked me to talk to him. That shook him up."

Genuinely curious, Rey eyed her. "How did you prove it was really her?"

"That was easy. She mentioned something that only she could know. At first, he appeared startled. But then the poor man broke down in tears." Misty-eyed herself, she tossed back her drink as if it were whiskey. "I felt so bad for that poor man."

"I take all that to mean you don't think he was attending a church around here?"

Serenity straightened. "I'd be very surprised to learn that he was. Even if hearing from his departed wife shook him, he didn't seem inclined to seek out organized religion. But who knows? All I can tell you is if Theodore Smith did join a church, he didn't share that information with me."

Hiding his disappointment, Rey thanked her. "I'd better go," he said. "Please let me know if you get any other information from any source."

Slowly, the older woman nodded. "Will do."

As he left the shop and walked to his truck, his phone

rang. Seeing the sheriff's number on his caller ID, he answered.

"They've decided to call another town meeting," Rayna said, her tone a mixture of determination and exhaustion. "Not only do we need to provide an update on Theodore Smith, even though there isn't much to report on, but another older couple has gone missing."

Stunned, Rey swallowed. "Who? Do I know them?"

"Maybe," Rayna responded. But he didn't recognize either of the names she mentioned.

"Willow wasn't familiar with them either," Rayna continued. "I talked to her right before I called you."

"I see. And that's what we're going to discuss at this meeting?" He used his key fob to unlock the doors and climbed in behind the wheel.

"I wish that was all. With all of this going on, now we've got a small group of people spouting conspiracy theories. The meeting is mostly because we need to nip this kind of nonsense in the bud."

"What kind of conspiracy theories?" he asked. "I haven't heard any."

Her sigh reverberated over the phone. "Aliens."

It took a moment for her response to register. "Aliens? Are you serious?"

"Unfortunately, I am. This group is telling everyone who will listen that aliens are periodically abducting our elders. They've been lurking on the fringe for years, I'm told. But now, they think they finally have proof that their beliefs are valid. They've actually printed up pamphlets and are going around passing them out."

Rey laughed. "But no one actually gives this theory any credence, right?" he asked.

"There will always be gullible people," she responded. "My office has fielded more than one panicked phone call in the last twenty-four hours."

Dumbfounded, Rey thanked her for calling. When he got off the phone, he drove home. When he got there, he walked into the kitchen to be met by Sam.

"There's another town meeting tonight," Sam told him.

"I heard. I just got off the phone with Rayna. Apparently, there's a small group who believe all the missing people were abducted by aliens." Rey couldn't keep the stunned disbelief from his voice.

"That explains this," Sam said, grabbing a purple pamphlet off the counter and handing it over. "They were walking up and down Main Street and handing them out. Everyone in Rancher's Supply was making fun of them."

"Whoever made these didn't put a lot of time or thought into the design," Rey mused. "One simple fold, and text that appears to be a basic computer font. Not to mention some of the ideas they're presenting as facts are…"

"Out of this world," Sam quipped, then cracked himself up.

About to crumple up the flyer and toss it, Rey set it down on the counter instead. "Rayna also said another senior couple has gone missing."

"Really? Are you going to the meeting?"

"Most definitely. As a matter of fact, I need to call Willow and make sure she knows."

Sam made a face but then, catching Rey watching, shrugged. "Whatever. Do what you have to do. I just want Dad to be found."

Chapter 9

When Rayna had called her to let her know that another older couple had gone missing, Willow asked if they'd been able to learn anything from Mr. Smith. Unfortunately, the bookstore owner had lapsed into a coma. His doctors weren't even sure he was going to make it.

This news made Willow feel incredibly sad. Hearing about more missing senior citizens scared the heck out of her. When she said as much to the sheriff, Rayna agreed.

"I just don't understand what's going on," Rayna said. "I've worked other missing person cases in this town, though they were all young women. Each time, the abductor messed up and left clues. Or people escaped and were able to tell us what was going on."

Willow latched on to that one word—*abductor*. "Is that what you think?" she asked, unable to keep the panic from her voice. "That my grandmother and Rey's father were *abducted*?"

"Not really. I can't really see why anyone would abduct a bunch of older couples. Though I can't discount any possibility. Well, except maybe for one," Rayna replied. "But they've called another town meeting for tonight. Same place."

Trying not to hyperventilate, Willow took a deep breath before speaking. "I'm glad people are wanting to work toward a solution."

"Some of our townspeople are definitely trying to help with that, but there are others…" Rayna snorted. "Well, you wouldn't believe it if you heard it elsewhere. So I'm going to tell you. You know how I said I couldn't discount any possible scenario except for one? Well, there's a small but very vocal group claiming that the missing people were abducted by aliens."

"Aliens?" Willow repeated, shocked but somehow not. "Did they happen to say what evidence they're basing this theory on?"

"Nope. Because they're irrational. And people like that don't require proof."

Willow thought for a moment. "If that's all this meeting is going to be about, then I don't see any reason to attend."

"Oh, that's not all," Rayna hastened to reassure her. "I'll let them say their piece, after the main part of the meeting is over. That way, anyone who's feeling uncomfortable or disinterested can simply leave."

"Good thinking," Willow said. "I'll definitely be there."

Rey had called shortly after that, asking if she'd go with him. Of course, she'd agreed.

Now she stood on her front porch, wearing jeans and a T-shirt, impatiently waiting for Rey to pick her up. She didn't know how much more of this uncertainty she could take. All she wanted was to wrap her arms around her grandmother, once she knew Isla was safe. And watch all the other family members reunite with their own loved ones, especially Carl and his sons.

She could only hope that day would come soon. It had to, because she didn't know what she'd do if anything happened to her grandmother.

Rey's truck came around the corner. As always, her stomach did a little flip-flop at the prospect of seeing him. He pulled up in her driveway, and as she started down the sidewalk toward him, he jumped out and opened the passenger door for her. Something guys rarely, if ever, did anymore.

"Thanks," she told him, hopping on up inside. "I appreciate this."

As he got back in on the driver's side, he glanced at her, a half-smile on his handsome face. "No need for gratitude. Naturally, we go together?" he asked. "We're a team, remember?"

Her heart turned over at the warmth in his gaze. For a moment, she thought he might lean over and kiss her, but instead he shifted into Drive and pulled away.

Even though they arrived fifteen minutes early, the Rattlesnake was already packed. Luckily, they found two seats together in the third row. Glancing around, Willow spotted several people she knew. A few waved, a couple of others dipped their chins in acknowledgement, but no one came over and spoke. Which was fine because Willow wasn't in the mood for random chitchat.

At five minutes before seven, a tall, balding man with wire-rimmed glasses jumped up on the makeshift stage and stood behind the lectern. He leaned into the microphone, so close that when he spoke he caused a bunch of feedback. The high-pitched squeal had several people covering their ears. The man shrugged, clearly not embarrassed, and tried again.

"Let's talk about aliens," he said, the enthusiasm in his voice making Willow inwardly wince. "A group of us has been looking into these disappearances, and it seems clear that they've been abducted by extraterrestrial beings. We think they're targeting older individuals as they want to learn from their collective wisdom."

Several people in the audience groaned. Others tossed out disparaging comments. And one man yelled out, "Get off the stage, Ronald. None of us came to hear that kind of nonsense."

"It's not nonsense," Ronald said, his tone offended. The noise level in the room rose immediately. Everyone appeared to be trying to out talk the others.

Rayna chose that moment to stride up to the stage. She thanked Ronald for coming, mentioning that he hadn't been scheduled to speak until after the main part of the meeting. That said, she then asked him to please take a seat so they could start the meeting. She waited until he'd left the stage before turning once again to face the room.

"Moving on," she said, her tone hard. "As you may know, two more senior citizens have turned up missing. We still don't have any leads on where these people might have gone. Instead of discussing aliens, I've been approached by several individuals who would like to organize a search."

Again, everyone started talking at once. Rayna shook her head and held up her hand for silence. "Now, because we have no idea where to even begin, I've got a team of volunteers who are drawing up maps of search areas. We thought we'd begin in the various unfenced fields and pastures on the outskirts of town."

She pointed to three card tables that had been set up in the back of the room, near the bar. "We have sign-up sheets set up back there. Once we have enough people sign up, we'll start. I'm hoping for tomorrow."

Again, the noise level rose. Rayna stood patiently waiting until it died down. "Now these searches aren't going to be looking for the missing individuals, per se. Though it would be awesome to find them. What we will be looking for are clues. Anything, any hints that might explain where these people disappeared to. And even if you can't help with the search, you can help in other ways. Talk to your neighbors."

She scanned the room, which had once again gone quiet. "I know not everyone in town is in attendance. There might even be some people in more remote places nearby, the smaller ranches and such, who aren't even aware that people are missing. Talk to them. Ask questions. Maybe someone, somewhere noticed something out of the ordinary. Whatever it is, no matter how small, please call me. Now, does anyone have any questions?"

Several people raised their hands.

"As long as it's not about aliens," Rayna added. "You first."

After Rayna answered everything, she announced the meeting had ended. People got up and started milling around, some heading for the bar and others for the door. A few people stopped by the table Ronald had set up, accepting his brochures and talking to him.

Though Willow and Rey stood, they stayed near their seats, mutually agreeing to let the crowd thin out before moving.

"I'm not signing up to pair with anyone in the official

search," Willow said. "Mainly because I don't know who I'd end up with. But I do like the idea of going door to door at some of the more remote properties. It's a long shot, but who knows what might turn up."

"I agree," Rey replied. "If you don't mind, I'd like to join you. We can sign up to go as a team." He grinned. "That's becoming one of my favorite words."

"I'd like that." Willow smiled back. She almost told him she thought they made a dang good team in everything, especially the bedroom, but worried someone might overhear. Still, something of her thoughts must have shown in her face because Rey's eyes blazed with a sudden heat. She swayed toward him, entranced despite the fact that they were surrounded by people.

Just then, Sam walked up, accompanied by an attractive woman in a short white dress who looked vaguely familiar. "Hey, you two. I'd like you to meet Gia Barrera. Gia, I think you know my brother, Rey. And this is our friend Willow Allen."

"Pleased to meet you," Gia said, barely glancing at Willow. Instead, she gazed hungrily at Rey.

"I remember you," Willow said, drawing the other woman's attention. "You're Buddy's younger sister."

Gia dipped her chin in acknowledgment. "I am. That's how Rey and I first met." She continued eating Rey up with her eyes. "Do you remember, Rey?"

"I'm not sure." Rey took Willow's arm. "If you'll excuse us. We're making plans to help out with the search."

"I'd like to do that too," Gia exclaimed, batting her false eyelashes. "Rey, maybe you and I could team up."

This comment had Rey frowning. "Willow and I are

already a team. Why don't you and Sam work together?" He glared at his brother.

Then, without waiting for an answer, Rey turned away, taking Willow with him.

She managed to hide her laughter until they were outside. Once they'd stepped into the parking lot, she let it out. Half smiling, Rey watched her. He waited until she'd finally wound down, wiping at her eyes. "What?" he asked.

"As if you don't know." She shook her head. "Little Gia Barrera has the hots for you."

"Sam already told me," he admitted. "And I suggested that he date her."

"Instead, he brought her to the town meeting and came over to you." She shook her head. "I guess he was hoping once you saw her that you'd change your mind."

"Came over to *us*," Rey clarified, grinning. "I'm thinking she probably pressured him into it since I already told Sam that I wasn't interested."

Privately, she figured Sam had likely been all for it too. Despite Rey saying he and Sam had talked heart to heart, she doubted Sam had paid much attention to anything his older brother might have said. Though, she had to admit there might be a chance she was wrong. She'd been gone from Getaway a good while. Sam might have changed.

Rayna exited, waving as she and her deputies got into their sheriff's department vehicle and left.

Just as they turned the corner, Willow's cell phone pinged, announcing a text. She pulled it out and looked, not recognizing the number. Probably spam. But just in case, she clicked on it to open the message.

Help, it read. It's me, Isla. We need…

"Look." Willow tugged on Rey's arm, showing him the text.

His breath caught. "She didn't finish. Needs what?"

"I don't know. She's still typing." Instead of waiting for her grandmother, a notoriously slow typist, to finish, Willow fired off a message.

Where are you? Are you all right? Give me your location so I can come and get you.

The dots that indicated the other person was still typing disappeared. Both Willow and Rey continued to stare at the screen, waiting.

Where are you? Willow tried again. Please tell me.

Nothing. Tears stinging the back of her eyes, Willow fought the urge to throw her phone on the ground.

"Give her another minute," Rey advised. "If she's anything like Carl, it'll take her forever to type something out."

Slowly, Willow nodded. Clutching her phone in a death grip, she stared at the screen, willing more words to appear.

Instead, it remained blank. Willow bit back a cry and swallowed hard.

"Take a screenshot of that number and the messages and send them to Rayna," Rey said, squeezing her shoulder. "Maybe she can trace that number or figure out who it belongs to."

Instantly, she did as he'd suggested. "Hopefully, Rayna will have better luck with this one than she did with the phone call that you got from Carl."

He nodded. "It concerns me that both of them are trying to reach out and ask for help, but something or someone appears to be stopping them."

His words threatened to make her sick. "Do you think they're being held hostage?"

"Let's not jump to conclusions," he said, still squeezing her shoulder. "While it's normal to jump to worst-case scenario, without more information, we have to try and find a more positive possibility."

"Like what?" she snapped. "Because right now, I'm just about out of positivity."

Rey shared Willow's frustration. While he knew Rayna excelled at her job, it rankled that neither she nor any of her deputies had been able to find a single clue as to where those missing might have gone. As far as he could tell, they had these meetings for the sole purpose of appeasing distraught family members. For him, they had the opposite effect.

"Do you want to get out of here?" he asked, not bothering to modify his brusque tone. Then he noticed Willow's bowed head, and the way she seemed deep in thought.

For a moment, she didn't respond. When she raised her head, she simply stared at him, her eyes glistening. "I can't go home right now," she said. "I'd like to get a drink, but I'm not up for the crowd inside the Rattlesnake. Maybe we can go back to The Bar? I can follow you there."

His stomach growled, reminding him that he hadn't eaten. "I have an idea. How about Bob's Burgers? I need food, and they sell beer by the pitcher. A perfect combination, at least as far as I'm concerned."

Looking up from her phone, which still remained blank, she considered. "It's been years since I've had one of their burgers. Sure, I'd like that, though I'm not sure I can eat."

Slowly, he nodded. "Would you rather go home?"

"No," she answered immediately. "I can't handle being alone right now. I just need to talk to my grandmother."

He took her arm and steered her toward his truck. "Maybe you should try to eat something. How long has it been since you had food?"

"I don't know." Shrugging, she stopped. "But what about my SUV? I drove here."

"I can bring you back to it after we eat." He opened his truck door for her.

She thought for a moment and then nodded before she climbed into the passenger seat, still clutching her phone.

It made his chest hurt to watch the sorrow in her expression. He got into the driver's seat and started the engine.

While they drove, she kept sneaking peeks at her phone. Finally, she heaved a big sigh. "Why hasn't she responded? I'm going to try texting her again."

But, still no reply. In the course of the three-minute drive to Bob's, Willow must have checked her phone half a dozen times. She sent a couple more texts, made one phone call that wasn't answered and appeared to be on the verge of a total breakdown.

When they arrived at Bob's, he parked and killed the motor. Turning to her, he cupped her face in his hands.

"It's going to be okay," he said. "I don't know how I know, and I don't have proof, but deep inside I know Carl and Isla will be found."

Gaze locked on his, she swallowed. "But—"

He kissed her then, meaning only a quick press of his mouth to silence her doubts. But the instant their lips met, the usual passion blazed through him. With difficulty, he forced himself to lift his head. "How about we go inside and eat? You can try, and if you still can't, get a to-go box for later."

Slowly, she nodded. "Okay. That way you won't have to sit across from me and devour your burger while I stare at you."

"Exactly!" Smiling, he jumped out and hurried over to open her door. She took his hand and allowed him to help her down. Then, with her hand still clutching his, they walked into the restaurant.

The smell of delicious, all-beef burgers cooking made Rey's stomach growl again, louder this time. Eyes wide, Willow glanced at him. "You really *are* hungry, aren't you?"

He shrugged. "I am."

They were shown to a booth near the back wall with a good view of the front window and each handed laminated menus. "Your server will be with you shortly," the teenaged hostess chirped before flouncing away.

Rey had been here enough times that he didn't need to study the menu. For Willow, it had been a while, so she picked it up and began to peruse the offerings.

When she noticed him watching her, she gave him a small, sad smile. "I have to say, I might be able to eat something. I used to love their mushroom and Swiss burger."

The server came. They ordered their food, and Rey asked for a pitcher of beer. The waitress brought that out first, and Rey poured a glass for Willow and himself. She'd placed her phone faceup on the table and still kept checking it, clearly hoping Isla would try again.

He couldn't blame her. After his father had called, he'd been frantic to hear that beloved voice again. In that moment, he'd have done anything to locate Carl, moved mountains and rivers.

But he hadn't been able to. And somehow, he'd had to make himself accept that. Willow would too, in her own time.

"I wish she would call," Willow said. "Or text. Anything to let me know how to find her."

"I get it, believe me," he told her. "And I hope she does. But I know Isla. She wouldn't want you starving yourself while you wait."

This statement made the corners of her mouth lift. Just a little, but the look in her eyes didn't seem as sad. "Truth. I can hear her now, ordering me to get some food in my belly right this instant."

Since he knew Isla, he had to laugh. "You bet she would."

With that, Willow's mood appeared to lighten. She sipped her beer, and while she kept her phone out on the table, she didn't seem as fixated on it.

They talked about other things. He mentioned he'd picked up a book on surfing, and her face lit up. For the next several minutes, she told him about her adventures learning how to ride the waves and her excitement when she finally mastered it. While he enjoyed seeing the way her eyes glowed as she talked, he realized in that instant he had nothing to offer her that could even remotely compete with that.

When their food arrived, looking as good as it smelled, she eyed her plate and shook her head. "I forgot how huge they are. Good thing they cut it in half."

He grinned and picked his up. Gaze still locked on hers, he took a huge bite. "Mmmmm." The perfection of it made him roll his eyes.

A moment later, she did the same. "Oh, my!" she exclaimed, after chewing and swallowing. She took another bite and then another. Before long, they were both just devouring their meals. She finished her half burger and barely paused before picking up the rest. In between, she dipped her seasoned fries in ketchup and popped them in her mouth.

Initially, he'd slowed down to watch her eat. He found her single-minded intensity sensual. But realizing she didn't intend to stop until she'd completely demolished her meal, he focused on finishing his as well.

When all he had left were a few fries, he glanced up to find her lazily twirling one of her remaining fries in ketchup. "Thank you for getting me to eat," she said. "I feel much better now. Apparently, I needed that more than I realized."

He took a sip of his beer. "Me too."

Though he didn't think he could eat another bite, when Willow asked for the chocolate lava cake and two forks, he didn't say a word. The desert arrived a few minutes later, and she dug in with so much enthusiasm, he could have just sat and watched her.

Except she paused after her third bite, fork halfway to her mouth, and frowned at him. "Are you not going to have some? I can't eat this entire thing all by myself."

Then what could he do but help her finish. He'd never had the lava cake, but it tasted delicious.

Her phone pinged, indicating a text. She jumped, snatched it up off the table and entered her passcode. He knew the moment her face fell that the text wasn't from Isla.

"It's Rayna," she said, the dejection in her voice making his heart squeeze. "Acknowledging she got my screenshots and promising to look into it."

"That's good," he replied. "And she will."

Slowly, she nodded.

The check came, and they both reached for it. She lightly slapped his hand away. "My treat," she insisted. "I wouldn't have eaten at all if you hadn't gotten me to come here."

"Fine," he said. "I'll get the next one."

On the drive back to the Rattlesnake, Willow went quiet. Though she turned her phone over and over in her hands, she no longer seemed to think Isla would be texting again.

"At least we know they're alive," he blurted out, wincing the moment he spoke. "That's what kept going through my head when my dad called. Sure, I'm worried about him. But knowing he was able to reach out gives me hope."

"True. There's that." She sat up straight. "I refuse to allow myself to get worked up worrying about things that may not be true." Glancing at him, her expression determined, she exhaled. "I'm going to try to focus on the positive, like what you just said."

"Good." He turned into the parking lot, which had emptied quite a bit. Pulling up next to her Bronco, he left the engine idling.

Instead of getting out, she turned in the seat to face him. "Do you want to follow me to my place?"

"Any other time, I would. But tonight, I'm going to go on home," he said, as gently as he could. Part of him hoped that she'd ask him to go with her, that she didn't want to be alone. But he knew he couldn't spend every night at her place, and he wanted to have a talk with Sam after that stunt his brother had pulled at the town meeting earlier.

"Okay," she said, leaning over and kissing him. "I'll talk to you tomorrow? I'm planning to start talking to some of the older people who still remain in town. If someone is targeting that age group, surely someone else will have been contacted."

Though he figured Rayna had no doubt already done that, he wasn't sure. "That's a great idea. But I've got a lot to do around the ranch. I've got a couple of buyers coming to look at cattle, and I need to be there. One appointment is in the morning, but the other is early afternoon. I can text you if I get done early, but I'm thinking it's likely to be an all-day thing."

"I understand." Kissing him again, she opened her door and hopped out. "Good luck on the cattle sale. And I promise to keep you posted if I learn anything."

"I'd like that."

She closed her door and walked to her vehicle. He sat and waited until she got in the Bronco, ostensibly to make sure she was safe, but in reality, he didn't want to tear his gaze away.

But finally, he had to drive home. Pulling away, he felt he'd been separated from a part of himself. Too soon, he told himself, gripping the steering wheel. Not just that, but neither of them had ever made the slightest attempt to pretend their relationship was anything permanent. They were enjoying each other's company for as long as they could. But still, he had enough self-awareness to realize he might be in for all kinds of heartache. Hell, if he felt like this now, he couldn't even imagine what it would be like when Willow went back to California and left Getaway and him far behind.

Since the thought didn't bear thinking of, not right now with their parents still missing, he turned up the radio and concentrated on the road.

Chapter 10

Driving away from Rey felt more difficult than it should have. Weird how attached she had gotten to him in such a short amount of time. Somehow, she suspected Isla would approve.

This time, instead of letting thoughts of her grandmother make her sad, she refused to allow her mind to go down that path. Instead, she pulled up into the driveway, parked and went inside.

Isla would be found unharmed and safe. There could be no other alternative.

Going from room to room, turning on all the lights, she realized Rey had been right to go stay at his own home. She missed him, for sure, but they each needed to also have their own alone time. After all, it wasn't as if they were in some kind of long-term, committed relationship.

She washed her face and changed into some comfies. Then she went and got a glass of water, turned on the television and settled onto the couch to catch up on some of the shows she'd been streaming back in California.

Full and oddly content, she dozed off. When she woke, she realized it was nearly three in the morning. She went to her bed, crawled in between the sheets and drifted right back to dreamland again.

In the morning, she felt rejuvenated. She hummed under her breath while she showered and then carried her coffee out to her grandmother's back patio to drink. If things were normal, Isla would be bustling around the kitchen right now, insisting Willow eat a large breakfast in order to start her day right. In days past, Willow would have insisted her grandmother come out and enjoy a few minutes of the quiet morning with her. Most times, Isla would grumble a bit but would finally plop down into the chair next to Willow, mug in hand. Taking a long sip of her coffee, Willow sighed. She would give anything to have her grandmother here right now.

Soon, she reminded herself. Isla was fine and would be found soon, alive and unharmed. Then the two of them would have a heart-to-heart conversation about whatever health issue her grandmother was facing.

She spent the day cleaning the small house from top to bottom. She also did laundry, made a casserole for dinner, and made sure she didn't have a spare moment to think or worry.

When she finally went to bed, she fell into a deep and dreamless sleep.

The sound of someone pounding at her front door startled her awake. Heart racing, she sat up straight in bed and glanced at her nightstand clock. Two a.m.

She grabbed her phone and saw she had several missed calls, all of them from Rey. Since she kept her phone on Do Not Disturb at night, she'd had no idea.

Did that mean Rey was at her front door? If so, that meant something awful must have happened, as in her experience no one ever brought good news at this hour of the morning.

Peering through the peephole before unlocking the door, when she saw Rey standing on her front porch, she unlocked it and yanked the door open. "What's going on?" she asked, stepping back and gesturing for him to come in.

Pushing the door closed, he turned and gripped her arms. Expression intense, he met her gaze and held it. "I want you to stay calm, okay?"

Those words caused her heart to drop all the way to the bottom of her stomach. "Oh no." She swallowed hard. "What's happened? Please, tell me."

"A body has been found," he said. "Rayna is retrieving it and bringing it to the hospital morgue in Midland, until the medical examiner can be here from Abilene or Midland in the morning."

"Male or female?" she managed to ask. Inside, a litany kept running through her head—*Don't let it be Isla. Don't let it be Isla.*

"I don't know," Rey answered. "Rayna just called me and filled me in."

"Did she ask you to go to the hospital?"

"No. All she said was she'd fill me in as soon as she knew anything." He took a deep breath and dropped his hands from her arms. "I decided on my own to come get you."

"Thank you." Spinning around, she grabbed her purse and keys. "Let's go."

Once in his truck, she couldn't stop herself from jiggling her leg. *Please don't let it be Isla. Or Carl*, she amended.

"It's going to be all right," Rey told her. "I can't explain it, but I have a feeling. It's not going to be Carl or Isla."

"I hope you're right," she replied, her voice shaky. "But even if it's not, someone is going to have lost their loved one. It's awful enough that it's looking like Mr. Smith isn't going to make it."

"That's true, but we don't even know if this body is one of the people missing."

Throat tight, she nodded and turned to look out the front window. The flat road stretched out ahead of them, illuminated only by their headlights since there were no streetlights out here in the country. At this time of the morning, full dark with only a sliver of moon, the landscape took on a dystopian feel, which made her shiver.

"There." Rey pointed. "Looks like maybe an ambulance along with the sheriff's department vehicles."

They could see the red-and-blue flashing lights in the distance. Suddenly, Willow's tension returned. Stomach churning, she sat up straight, clenching her hands tightly in her lap.

Rey pulled his truck over to the shoulder behind the sheriff's car. Another one had parked right in front of her. He turned on his flashers and got out, crossing around the back of the vehicle to open the passenger door for Willow. Taking his hand, she jumped down. Then, still holding on to each other, they walked toward the small cluster of people standing a short distance beyond the sheriff's vehicles.

Arms crossed, Rayna watched them as they approached. "Why am I not surprised to see you? I take it you two were together when I called."

Though Willow's cheeks heated, she shook her head. "No, we weren't. Rey came pounding on my door and woke me up."

Meanwhile, Rey appeared to be trying to see past the sheriff.

"I can't let you go any closer," Rayna said, giving him a hard look. "I understand your concern, but I can promise you this isn't Carl or Isla."

"I'd like to see for myself," Rey replied.

"And I understand that, I really do. But I have to respect the family's privacy. Think about how you would feel if that was your loved one lying there. Would you want strangers gawking at their body?"

Willow squeezed Rey's hand. "We would not," she said. "But can you at least tell us who it is?"

"The identity of the victim will be withheld pending notification of their family," Rayna replied in her best law-enforcement-official voice. "And right now, I'm afraid I'm going to have to ask you to leave. This is an official crime scene investigation. I promise to update you both when I can."

That phrasing sent a shudder of dread through Willow. Rey evidently noticed it too because his grip on her hand tightened.

"We'll go," he said, his jaw tense. "But I do expect a full update as soon as possible."

"Definitely," Rayna agreed. "And you know how fast gossip spreads in this town. Pay no attention to anything you hear because all of it will be pure speculation. I'll release an official statement as soon as possible, hopefully by end of day today. Now go. Please. We still have work to do here."

"Thank you," Willow said. Rey echoed her statement. Together, they turned and made their way back to his truck.

They waited until they were inside the cab with the doors closed before turning to each other.

"Crime scene investigation?" Willow asked. "What exactly did she mean by that?"

"I'm guessing it was a clear case of murder." Rey's dark tone echoed Willow's thoughts. "Gunshot wound, run over by a car, a stabbing. Who knows? But apparently, it mustn't have been pretty, otherwise Rayna wouldn't have been working so hard to keep things hidden."

Willow groaned. "I can only imagine what kind of stories will be going around town tomorrow."

"Today," Rey corrected. "Even though the sun won't come up for several hours, it's already tomorrow."

"Thanks for pointing that out." Yawning, she covered her mouth with her hand. "I don't know about you, but I plan on going back to bed as soon as I get home."

"Me too." If he caught her subtle invitation to rest at her house, he didn't let on. "With those cattle buyers coming, I need to at least try and appear well rested."

"I forgot about that," she said, meaning it. "Have you always been the one who sells off your cattle?"

"No. My dad always took care of that. He took a lot of pride in our livestock. He loved to brag and could talk most buyers into almost any price. Since he'd been doing it for years, he knew them well and they knew him. People who buy from us know they're getting quality beef. We have a great reputation. But even so, Dad really enjoyed the whole song and dance."

"And you don't?"

He sighed. "No, not so much. I'm more of a work the land type guy. Not so much a salesman."

"I get that," she said. She thought about asking him if he'd considered having Sam handle it, but decided she already knew the answer. "I'm guessing you don't have much of a choice."

"I don't." His brusque tone told her that he really didn't want to discuss it any further. He started the engine and pulled a U-turn in the middle of the deserted road, and they headed back toward town.

With the mood somber, Willow wondered if she'd have trouble going back to sleep. Despite her exhaustion, her mind wouldn't stop spinning various scenarios as to how the body had gotten there. All of them were gruesome. She'd always had a vivid imagination, and sometimes she wished that she didn't.

Glancing at Rey, who'd turned up the radio in a clear indication he didn't want to talk, she wondered if he might be having similar thoughts. It was a terrible thing to have a loved one missing, with no idea where on earth they might be or if they were safe.

Finally, they turned onto her grandmother's street. When she saw a window lit up yellow in the house, her heart skipped a beat. For one amazing second, she thought Isla might have finally come home. But then she realized she must have left the light on in her hurry to leave earlier.

This made her eyes sting and her throat ache.

Rey pulled up into the driveway and left the engine idling. "I'll walk you to the door," he said.

True to his word, he went with her up the sidewalk, waiting while she fumbled with her key in the lock. Once she had the door open, he pulled her close and gave her a long, lingering kiss.

Returning the kiss, she'd just begun hoping he might change his mind and stay with her when he pulled away.

"I really have to go," he said. "Please try and get some rest. I'll talk to you tomorrow."

"You get some rest too." Hiding her disappointment, she took a step back.

He nodded and turned to make his way back to his truck. Instead of closing the door, she stood and watched him drive away, only going inside once his taillights turned the corner.

Though she'd lived alone in Cali for years, she couldn't get used to the emptiness of staying at her grandmother's house without her.

After dropping Willow off at her house, Rey headed for the ranch. Eyes scratchy, he wondered if he could manage to get a few more hours of sleep before he had to meet the first group of buyers. Since they were due to arrive at nine, he thought that might be doable, especially if he could get Sam to take care of the usual morning ranch chores like feeding and watering the horses. Though those were supposed to be Sam's responsibility, Rey often found himself doing them when Sam randomly disappeared or slept in.

Today though, Rey was really going to need his younger brother's help.

Once inside the dark house, he flipped on the kitchen light. Instead of going directly to his bedroom, he grabbed a pen and pad of paper off the desk and wrote a quick note. In it, he asked Sam to make sure to take care of the horses and the usual household chores since he'd need to sleep in and had cattle buyers coming at nine. He propped that up against the coffee machine. Since Sam always made coffee before doing anything else, that would ensure he would see it.

That done, Rey turned out the light and made his way to his own bed. He undressed in record time, set an alarm for eight on his phone and crawled beneath the sheets. Though he thought he might toss and turn, worrying about today's frightening developments, he didn't.

When his phone alarm woke him, he sat up and stretched before heading directly to the bathroom for a hot shower. The buyers would be here in an hour, which gave him enough time to have coffee and breakfast. Knowing that Sam would have taken care of everything else really helped.

Clean, dressed, and feeling surprisingly well rested, he went to the kitchen. There were breakfast dishes piled up in the sink, still dirty. Moving past, he found himself clenching his jaw and keeping his mouth shut. His note was gone at least, which meant that Sam had seen it.

After making instant oatmeal and a cup of coffee, he ate. From the other room, he heard the sound of the television. Odd, because he doubted Sam would have had enough time to get all the chores done. Unless he'd actually gotten up early for once.

Coffee cup in hand, he wandered into the living room. There, he found Sam kicked back on the couch, watching TV. Squelching a jolt of irritation, he wondered if Sam had been out to the barn to feed the horses. Or if he'd done any of the minor ranching chores essential to the survival of their livestock. He reminded himself not to jump to conclusions. Sam might have gotten everything done earlier and come back to take a break.

"Hey," Rey said, standing near the end of the sofa.

Sam barely glanced away from the TV. "Hey, yourself. I hope you get a good price for those cattle today."

"Thanks." Trying to figure out how to best bring up the subject, Rey decided he might as well be direct. "I appreciate you taking care of the horses this morning."

Now Sam did look up, his expression blank. "What are you talking about?"

"I left you a note," Rey replied, careful to keep his tone level. "I know you saw it."

"Oh, that. I did see it. But then I got busy and forgot about it." Sam turned his attention back to the TV.

Rey checked his fitness watch. "I'm going to need you to turn off the television and get that taken care of. The horses should have been fed and watered long before now. My buyers will be here in twenty minutes, which means I don't have time."

"It shouldn't take more than fifteen minutes," Sam said. "You've got time."

"No. I. Don't." Marching over to his brother, Rey snatched the remote off the coffee table and turned the TV off. "I really needed your help this morning. Actually, I still do," he amended. "Please get the horses taken care of and clean up the kitchen. I've got to meet the buyers and take them down in my truck."

Scowling, Sam pushed to his feet. "I'll do it, but you're wasting a great resource. Me."

Unsure what his brother meant, Rey waited. When Sam simply glowered at him and didn't elaborate, Rey finally asked him to explain.

"I should be the one selling the cattle, not you. Dad always took me with him, and he taught me everything he knows. I could do a great job, and I'd enjoy it. Unlike you, who clearly hates doing it."

"I don't hate…" Starting to explain, Rey let his sentence trail off as he realized his brother was right. Dealing with buyers ranked right up there with mucking out stalls.

"You know if Dad were able to contact us, he'd want me to handle this," Sam continued. "He trained me, after all. He always told me he wanted me to take over for him when he couldn't do it any longer."

"Why didn't you say something sooner?" Rey asked, trying to reconcile the idea of his father trusting Sam with something so important. "And why didn't Dad tell me?"

"Because you made it clear you weren't interested. Even at the dinner table, any time the subject came up, you said you preferred to handle the day-to-day operations and let someone else handle the salesmanship. You know you did."

Rey stared. In that regard, his brother was absolutely correct. "True," Rey admitted.

"Then let me handle this today," Sam pressed. "I know you're doing your best, but you have no idea how to do any of this. The buyers know me. They met me last year when I worked with Dad."

"I don't know." Rey considered. On the one hand, he'd never seen this kind of enthusiasm from his brother. On the other, this was far too important of a transaction to let slide. Sam was the absolute master of flaking out on things.

"You keep saying you want me to help out more." Sam continued. "Well, here's your chance. Give me a shot."

Right then and there, Rey decided to take a leap of faith and trust his younger brother. He could see no reason for Sam to lie about this, and to have him actually volunteer to handle a necessary task that Rey truthfully found burdensome spoke volumes.

"Take my truck," he said, tossing the keys at Sam. "I've got it all clean and ready to meet the buyers."

Though Sam caught the keys, the look on his face told Rey that he'd apparently done something wrong. "Thanks, but I don't need your truck." He tossed them back. "My truck will do just fine. The buyers like to know they're dealing with a real rancher, so the dirtier the truck that meets them, the better. Dad taught me that."

Not sure how to respond, Rey simply nodded.

Grinning, Sam grabbed his cowboy hat, dipped his chin in response and swaggered out the door.

Rey watched him go, hoping his trust was well placed. Either he'd made a huge mistake that he'd pay for later, or he'd done both the ranch and Sam a favor. He really hoped it would turn out to be the latter.

Then, since the horses needed to be fed and numerous other chores waited that Sam had left unattended, Rey got to work. Without the two important meetings hanging over his head, he found his mood lighter. Though the occasional doubt and worry over Sam's ability to sell their livestock at a good price surfaced, he managed to put them from his mind. More than anything else, he hoped that Sam had finally found his niche, an area where he excelled.

Rayna still hadn't called by the time Sam returned from the first meeting, his mood jubilant. "They doubled the usual order," he said. "Even with the increase in price."

"Seriously?" Rey gave his brother a high five. "How'd you know the amount to ask for? I was just going to use what Dad charged last year."

Expression horrified, Sam stopped moving and stared. "If you'd have gone with that strategy, you'd have cost us some serious cash. Dad and I had already discussed our pricing strategy for this year. So that meant I had a great general plan from which to operate."

"Oh." Rey swallowed. "Well, good work. I'm glad you talked me into having you represent our ranch."

"Yeah, you are." Sam practically danced around the room, throwing punches at an invisible foe. "And now that I've clinched this deal, signed paperwork and all, the second group has no choice but to match it."

"Is that how that works?" Rey asked, partly amused but mostly proud. Because once again, he'd have had no idea.

"It is." Sam beamed at him, once again still. "I can't wait to tell Dad!" Then, apparently realizing he wouldn't be able to do that anytime soon, he winced. "I mean, as soon as he gets back home."

Not wanting to kill his brother's mood, Rey decided to wait to tell him about the body that had been found until he'd heard more from Rayna.

"Sit." Rey gestured toward the kitchen. "Let me make us a couple of sandwiches for lunch. You need to eat something before you head out to the second meeting."

"Thanks." Instead of immediately grabbing a chair,

Sam went to the refrigerator and grabbed a couple of cans of Dr. Pepper. "We're celebrating," he said, lifting one can in a salute.

Now Rey grinned. "Sounds good to me. I better up my sandwich-making game."

"Nah." Dropping into a chair, Sam popped open his can and took a drink. "Just ham and cheese with mustard for me."

"Then I'll have the same."

After making the sandwiches, Rey got out some chips, and he and his brother ate lunch together in companionable silence.

When they'd finished, Sam drained the last of his soft drink and pushed to his feet. "I want to get washed up, and then I'm heading out," he said. "I have no doubt that this meeting will go about the same as the first one."

"I'm positive of that." Rey stood too, liking the way Sam carried himself with the new self-confidence.

After Sam left, Rey straightened up the kitchen and then headed out to the barn to clean up a couple of stalls. He usually hired teenagers to help with this, but since it was July, most of them had found summer jobs. If he hadn't heard from Rayna by the time he finished, he figured he'd call Willow and see if she wanted to grab dinner in town. Or maybe he could pick up something and take it to her house.

For the first time since Carl had disappeared, Rey had hope about Sam's role at the ranch. Evidently, Carl had seen something in his youngest son and had been quietly nurturing it.

Damn. Missing his father something fierce, Rey found enough busy work close to the house to clear his mind. When he finished up, tired and sweaty, he headed back with the intention of jumping in the shower.

Sam had already returned, and once again, his mood was jubilant. "I think another celebration is in order," he said the instant Rey walked through the door. "This one went even better than the first sale. I know Dad keeps logs, and this one has to break all records. I'm pumped!"

"Nice job!" Rey wasn't too exhausted to appreciate his brother's excitement. "Seems to me you found your calling."

"You know it. Dad would be so proud." Sam's face fell. "I wish he'd turn up. I really miss him."

"Me too," Rey said. "But I'm really glad you made the ranch a nice profit. That'll help us pay the bills."

"Yeah." Sam shrugged and then grabbed his hat. "You might want to get on that. I'm heading into town to celebrate. Want to go with?"

Looking down at his filthy, sweat-stained clothing, Rey shook his head. "I need to shower. How about if I meet you at the Rattlesnake Pub later?"

"Sounds good." Sam breezed out the door. "Text me."

After a quick shower, Rey decided to take a look at the bills. In the two weeks since Carl had vanished, none of them had been paid. Which made sense, because that had always been one of the things that Carl insisted on doing himself.

Sam had been getting the mail and simply stacking the unopened bills in the inbox on Carl's desk. If he'd noticed the pile growing taller, he clearly hadn't thought about mentioning it to Rey. Until this afternoon.

But Rey couldn't just blame his younger brother. The desk sat in plain sight of the living room and kitchen.

The two of them walked past it multiple times a day. Somehow, Rey had also managed to overlook it.

If he didn't get the bills caught up, they wouldn't be able to buy feed or hay or fencing materials, or any of the other numerous things needed to keep the ranch running.

Pulling out the office chair, Rey opened the middle desk drawer in search of his father's checkbook. When he located it, neatly stowed next to Carl's favorite pen, he opened it to check the most recent entries plus the balance of the ranch account.

Satisfied that everything was as it should be, he grabbed the letter opener and settled in to pay bills.

Thirty minutes later, he'd written all the checks, affixed stamps to the envelopes, meticulously recorded each deduction and then calculated the final balance. Once he'd finished, he decided to take everything to the post office. A few of the bills, like the one to settle their account at the feedstore, he planned to hand deliver while in town.

Feeling a sense of accomplishment after having completed such a small task made him shake his head. He did much more complicated and difficult things on a daily basis, so he wasn't sure why paying bills felt so different. Maybe because he felt like he'd done something to help out his still absent father.

Chapter 11

When Willow next opened her eyes, she was pleasantly surprised to realize she'd slept until nearly noon. Since she considered herself a morning person, this was something she never did. At least, she hadn't since college. But clearly, she'd needed the rest.

Stretching, she pushed back the sheets and hopped out of bed. She felt remarkably better, almost as if she hadn't been running around country roads with Rey in the middle of the night.

Remembering, the thought sobered her. All these people disappearing and then a couple of them turning up under strange and mysterious circumstances. She wondered when Rayna would call with more information, but imagined the sheriff would be busy talking to the family of the deceased person and working with the coroner. That meant she wouldn't be calling anyone who wasn't involved anytime soon.

Frustrated, Willow wanted to do something more to help. Though she'd been born and raised in Getaway, since she'd moved away to California, she knew some people considered her an outsider. Which only lasted until they talked with her and realized she was the same person she'd been before she'd left. You can take the girl out of Texas, but you can't take Texas out of the girl.

Though she hadn't actually joined any of the search teams on the sign-up sheets at the meeting, she wanted to get with Rey and see if he'd join her tackling some of the more remote ranches. While technically these places weren't inside the city limits, their mailing addresses were still Getaway.

Since she knew he would be busy most of today, she figured she'd talk with him about this later. Right now, since she'd had a late start, she might as well tidy up around the house and snoop around some more to see if she could find any hints as to her grandmother's illness or where Isla might have gone.

Already having done a thorough search of obvious places, this time she planned to do a deep dive, no matter how intrusive.

Despite previously going through all of Isla's dresser drawers, this time she removed every single item in each one and felt around for a fake bottom. She found nothing.

Finishing up with both dressers and the nightstands, she moved into the master bedroom walk-in closet. She reached into the pockets of pants, cardigans and skirts. She checked inside every single pair of shoes and boots. And Isla apparently collected purses and wallets. There were quite a few, but Willow looked inside each one.

After going through every article of clothing and finding nothing, she removed all the random items Isla had piled on the top shelf above the hanging rack.

There, she found ski gloves, a knee brace, several pairs of compression hose and several boxes of greeting cards that Isla had received over the years. But nothing

referencing her grandmother's medical issues or litera-
ture for an upcoming vacation.

The idea made her shake her head. The fact that she
could still cling to the possibility that Isla and Carl, along
with numerous other people their age, had taken off
for some secret getaway without telling a single family
member seemed ludicrous.

Once satisfied that she'd checked everywhere in the
bedroom, she moved on to the bathroom. Even though
she'd checked twice before, she did so again.

Since over an hour had passed and she'd found nothing, Willow decided to get cleaned up and head into
town. Back when she'd been a teen, whenever she'd had
a problem, she'd gone to Serenity. Talking to the self-
proclaimed psychic always made her feel better. Even
though she'd stopped by a few days ago, she knew Serenity would always welcome her.

Decision made, she took a quick shower, got dressed
and put on her makeup. For convenience's sake, she
scarfed down a bowl of cereal for a meal, even though
it was afternoon. Then she grabbed her keys.

Driving the familiar route downtown, she thought
of how many times she'd traveled this road as a teenager. Back then, she'd owned an old Chevy Impala that
Isla had gotten her as a sixteenth birthday gift. It hadn't
been a pretty, girly car, but Willow had loved it anyway.

Downtown, she found a parking spot right in front
of Serenity's store. Mood improving by the second, she
hopped out and headed inside.

Though she'd expected Serenity to come out and
greet her, the same way she always did, the empty shop
seemed different. For one thing, no incense burned on

the counter, filling the air with the thick scent of patchouli. For another, Serenity hadn't turned on her sound system to play the esoteric, heavy-on-harps soothing music that she always played.

Alarmed, Willow hurried toward the back, calling out Serenity's name.

The back area was empty. Since Serenity and Isla were about the same age, for a heart-stopping moment Willow wondered if Serenity too had gone missing.

Then she noticed the closed bathroom door. Taking a deep breath, she knocked, three hard raps of her knuckles against the wood.

"Just a moment!" Serenity shouted. "Please go wait up front. I'll be out to help you in a few minutes."

Though still alarmed, Willow retreated to the store itself. No longer panicked now that she knew Serenity was alive, she still had to wonder if she was all right.

Five minutes later, Serenity emerged, sweeping through her colorful beaded curtain. "Willow!" she gushed. "I'm so sorry you had to wait."

One side of her face looked swollen, and a large bruise purpled under her left eye.

"What happened to you?" Willow asked, once again concerned.

"Oh, this is nothing." Serenity tried to brush her off. "I tripped over my own two feet and fell."

Willow took her arm and steered her toward the back room. "Are you dizzy? Why don't you sit down and tell me all about it."

The older woman allowed herself to be helped over to a chair. "I am a bit off today," she admitted, once she'd taken a seat. "I felt weak and kind of faint this morning, but figured I could press past it. But right after I opened up for the day, I turned too sharply, and my feet got tangled up and I fell." She gave a rueful smile. "I guess I'm just getting old."

"When was the last time you ate something?" Willow asked.

Serenity shrugged. "I'm not sure. Yesterday?"

Opening the small refrigerator, Willow located a cup of Greek yogurt on the shelf. She retrieved a plastic spoon from one of the drawers and set it down in front of the other woman. "Eat this for now. If you'd like, I can run and get you a burger or something."

"I don't eat meat," Serenity said, smiling slightly. "But I'm sure this yogurt will be just fine."

Willow spotted a new coffee machine on the counter. It had the option to make individual cups or a carafe. Knowing Serenity's fondness for tea, she made a pot of hot water.

"Where do you keep your tea bags?" she asked.

Serenity, having finished her yogurt, smiled. "In the cupboard right above you. I'll take oolong, please. You have whatever you'd like."

After making the tea, Willow carried both cups over to the table. She went back for the small container of sugar and a couple of spoons.

"Do you still feel dizzy?" she asked. "That shiner is getting darker. Do you think maybe we should take you in to let Doc Westmoreland look you over?"

"No, no. I'm fine." Serenity waved Willow's concerns away. "I feel better already. Sit, please. We can drink our tea and chat. I want to know all about how you and Rey Johnson are doing."

Startled, though she supposed she shouldn't have been, Willow sat. "We're fine," she said, blowing on her tea before taking a tiny sip. "He's a nice guy."

Serenity snorted. "I saw the way the two of you looked at each other at the town meeting. I thought you both might burst into flames."

Willow's face heated. "Er, thanks?"

"I take it you don't want to discuss that?" Serenity asked, her color improving with every sip of tea.

Just then, Willow's phone rang, saving her. Even though she didn't recognize the number, she answered.

"It's me," a familiar voice whispered hoarsely. "Willow, it's me."

Stricken, Willow's gaze flashed to Serenity, still sitting across from her. "Isla? Where are you?"

"I'm with Carl. I'm really worried about him. We need help." The older woman's voice sounded shaky. "He's sick. I don't know what's wrong."

"Tell me where you are, and I'll come get you." Heart pounding, Willow stood, gripping her phone hard.

"I don't know where we are," Isla whispered, almost in tears. "Someone's ranch maybe? But we're with—"

Just then, the call either dropped or Isla was forced to end it. Despite suspecting the reason Isla had been whispering was that she didn't want to be overheard, Willow immediately called back. But either the phone had been turned off or destroyed, because it simply rang twice and then went silent. No voice mail, nothing.

Knowing it was useless, she still sent a quick text. Nothing, despite staring intently at her screen.

"What happened, honey?" Serenity asked. "Are you all right?"

Still standing, Willow swayed. Fist to mouth, shaking, she tried to speak but couldn't. After a few failed attempts, she managed to dredge the words up from the depths of her throat. "That was my grandmother. She says she's with Carl, and he's sick. But she didn't know where she was, just that it seemed like a ranch."

Serenity immediately pushed herself up out of her chair. Even with her shakiness, she came over and pulled Willow in for a hug. And that simple gesture of kindness allowed the dam of emotions to break.

Head on the older woman's shoulder, Willow sobbed as she hadn't allowed herself to do in the entire time since Isla had gone missing. Silent and supportive, Serenity kept Willow wrapped in her arms.

Finally, Willow's tears eased up. Slightly embarrassed, Willow stepped back. Serenity grabbed a box of tissues and held it out. Accepting this, Willow wiped her eyes, wishing she'd used waterproof mascara. She blew her nose, took a couple of shaky breaths and grabbed her cup off the table and drained her tea.

"Would you like more?" Serenity asked, the gentleness in her gaze bringing a fresh spate of tears to Willow's eyes.

"No thanks, I'm good."

"Your grandmother is going to be all right," Serenity said. "As is Carl. I can see this."

"If you can see that much, why can't you tell me where they are?" Willow asked, struggling to keep all bitterness from her tone.

"I wish I could," Serenity answered softly. "But my gift doesn't work like that. I can't make it show me whatever I want to see. Sometimes I receive impressions, other times I hear voices from spirits telling me things. Believe me, I've tried. Over the years, I've helped out with several police investigations. Not once was I able to determine what information came to me. But I was sent what apparently was needed. So I can tell you that your grandmother is okay, as is Carl Johnson. But little else. I'm sorry."

Immediately, Willow felt terrible. "I'm sorry. I didn't mean to question you."

After turning to get her tea pot, Serenity refilled both their cups, even though Willow had said she didn't want more. "Sit," she said, gesturing toward the chair. "We can talk some more."

Not sure what else to do, Willow sat.

On her way back to her own chair, Serenity staggered. She cried out once before collapsing.

After dropping off most of the envelopes at the post office, Rey stopped at the Rancher's Supply feedstore, since he figured he might as well pick up the bags of grain and horse feed pellets he'd ordered. After having them added to his account, he loaded everything into the bed of his truck. Then he stopped by the back office to say hello to Jason, the manager and part owner. Since Jason appeared busy, Rey didn't stay long. He simply handed his account invoice and the check over, apologized for it being a few days late and left.

Before heading over to the Rattlesnake, Rey sent Sam a quick text to let him know he was on his way. Sam didn't immediately text back, which didn't surprise him since the noise level inside the pub could get quite loud at times. Happy hour would be well underway, and there was a dedicated group of regulars who stopped by on their way home from work.

Before shifting into Drive, Rey called Willow. The call went directly to voice mail. Odd, but maybe she was busy.

Walking into the Rattlesnake, he located Sam seated with a couple of guys at a four top near the bar. From the empty glasses scattered close to the middle of the table, they were each on their second or third beer.

"Hey!" Spotting him, Sam gestured toward the remaining empty chair. "Take a load off and order you a beer."

Rey dropped into his seat. Without him even asking, the waitress brought him his usual light beer in a frosted mug. "Thanks, Cecilia," he said.

Smiling, she blew him a kiss and hurried off.

"Wow," Sam stared. "How the hell do you do that?"

The question made Rey laugh. "I dated her once. We're still friends. She knows what I drink, and whenever I come in, she makes sure and brings me one."

"Oh." Losing interest, Sam turned to his friends and began describing loudly his idea for a side hustle, where he believed he could rake in tons of dough.

Luckily, Rey's phone vibrated in his pocket, which was a good thing since he hadn't heard it ring. Pulling it out, he smiled when he saw Willow's name on the caller ID. He stood, told his brother he needed to take a call and hurried toward the door, answering as he went.

"Just a second," he said, unable to hear her. "I'm at the Rattlesnake. Let me get outside and away from all this noise."

Once the door swung closed behind him, he took a

deep breath. "Sorry about that. I'm glad you called. Did you want to drive over and join us? We're here celebrating Sam's accomplishment getting record prices for the cattle today."

"I'm in Midland. I had to take Serenity to the hospital. I'm not sure what's wrong," she said instead of reacting to his invitation. "She'd apparently fallen before I got there as she has a huge bruise on her face, almost a black eye."

"Is she going to be all right?"

"I hope so. We lucked out as the ER wasn't busy. We didn't have to wait long before they took her back. My cell phone isn't working great inside there, so I came out to the parking lot to call you."

"Do you need me to come out there?" he asked. "I can leave right now and head that way."

"No, it's okay. There's no need for that. I've got to call Serenity's sister, Velma, next. Serenity gave me her number." She took a deep breath. "Oh, and one more thing. I can't believe I almost forgot to tell you this, but with so much going on, I'm a little scattered. My grandmother called right before Serenity fell. She was whispering and sounded frantic. She said she's all right, that she's with Carl, and she's worried about him because he's ill."

Rey froze, his stomach clenching. "What's wrong with him? Did she say where they were?"

"That's just it." Voice shaky, Willow sounded on the verge of tears. "She said she didn't know where she was, but thought it might be someone's ranch. The call dropped or something before she could say anything else."

"Someone's ranch." Rey thought furiously. "That

could be anywhere. There are a hell of a lot of ranches around here."

"I know." Her defeated tone made his chest ache.

"We need to go look," he said, deciding on the spot. "You and I. First thing tomorrow. I'll come pick you up at eight. If you're up to it, that is."

"I am," Willow answered without hesitation. "I need to go call Velma now. I'll talk to you later."

"Stay safe," he said, ending the call. He stood there a moment, shocked that he'd almost told her he loved her.

When had that happened? He couldn't actually say it had snuck up on him, because he'd been battling his feelings for a while now.

Shaking his head at his own foolishness, he turned around and went back inside to join his brother and his friends.

After finishing his beer, Rey declined to join Sam and the others in the back room for a few games of pool. He considered driving out to the hospital, but since Willow had said he didn't need to, he decided to stop by the sheriff's office instead. Rayna hadn't ever called him about the identity of the person they'd found alongside the road.

But the sheriff wasn't in. So Rey drove back to the ranch, stopping at Bob's on the way home for a takeout meal of a burger and fries.

After eating, he went outside and kept himself busy putting up hay. A new shipment had been delivered while he'd been gone, and he needed to move the bales into the covered storage area. Usually, he had a crew meet the hay truck and offload directly into storage, but with everything that had been going on, he'd gotten his wires crossed, which was unusual.

He'd just moved the last bale when his phone rang. Dragging his sleeve across his eyes to clear the sweat, he pulled it out of his pocket and answered.

"I'm heading back to town," Willow said. "Velma made it up to the hospital, and she's going to sit with Serenity. Would you mind if I stopped by? I don't want to go home to my grandmother's empty house right now. I'm still trying to process the fact that I actually talked to her."

"Of course I don't mind," he answered. "I've been working outside, and I'm all grimy, so I'm about to jump in the shower. I'll see you soon."

"Okay. I think I'll stop by Bob's on the way there. Do you want me to bring you a burger or anything?"

He had to laugh. "No thanks. I grabbed something from there a couple of hours ago."

"Great minds think alike." She tried to laugh along with him but failed. "I keep hoping Isla will call again, but she hasn't. I've called several times, sent a few texts, but nothing."

"Which seems to be the pattern," he said. "But at least you got to hear her voice."

"There's that," she agreed, still sounding sad. "Okay, go shower. I'll see you when I get there."

The hot shower felt amazing. After, he dressed in clean clothes and quickly tidied up the house. Sam still hadn't returned from his early celebration in town, so Rey texted him to make sure he had a designated driver. If not, Rey volunteered to pick him up.

Sam texted back that he'd be staying in town for the night, so Rey didn't need to worry. This made Rey feel better, especially since Sam would have only mocked his concern in the past. Maybe, he thought, his little brother was finally growing up.

When Willow arrived, carrying her empty Bob's Burgers bag, he pulled her in for a big hug. She hugged him back, and they stood that way for a few minutes, simply holding on to each other.

Breathing her scent and wondering how she always smelled like peaches, he placed a gentle kiss on her silky hair.

When she finally moved away, she headed directly for the kitchen and tossed her paper bag in the trash. When she turned to face him, her expression serious, he thought she had to be the most beautiful woman he'd ever known.

"I want to search some of the really remote areas tomorrow," she said. "Isla said she thought they were at a ranch. I can't shake the feeling time is running out and we've got to find them as quickly as possible."

"We can definitely do that," he replied. "If you want to stay the night, we can head out in the morning at first light."

"Thank you." She kissed him. He kissed her back. Tangled together, they stumbled over to the couch. As always, passion immediately set him on fire for her.

"What about Sam?" she gasped, her chest heaving. "What if he walks in?"

"He's staying in town tonight," he told her. "He texted."

"Oh, thank goodness."

They lost themselves in each other, tearing off their clothes and making mad, passionate love. As usual, Rey had the presence of mind to put on a condom.

And after, still inside her, he held her close, while

shudders still rocked her body. As they tapered off, she sighed and wiggled out of his embrace. "I need to get cleaned up," she said.

"Me too." He followed her to the bathroom. "Let me. Please."

Once she nodded, he got a clean washcloth. Using warm water, he gently cleaned her. Eyes wide, she watched him. When he finished, he dried her with a soft towel.

"My turn," she said, her voice husky. And she did the same for him.

Once they'd gotten dressed, they turned on the TV to watch the early evening news.

When his phone rang, Rey went ahead and answered even though he didn't recognize the number on the caller ID.

"Hey, Rey, this is Jason from Rancher's Supply. I hate to bother you, but I stopped by the bank after work to deposit some checks, and they wouldn't honor yours."

"What do you mean?" Confused, Rey tried to make sense of the other man's words. "Since we both use the same bank, they shouldn't have a problem. They just transfer the money from our account into yours."

"Yeah." Jason cleared his throat. "That's just it. They said the funds are insufficient to cover the check."

"There must be some sort of error. Let me go in and talk to the bank in the morning, and I'll get back to you. I'm really sorry about this. I'll stop by tomorrow morning. I promise I'll make this right."

"I believe you." Jason sounded more embarrassed than angry. "But I'm afraid I'm also going to have to ask you to pay the returned check fee they charged me."

"No problem." After apologizing again, Rey ended the call. "Something's not right," he told Willow. He recounted what Jason had said. "My dad is very meticulous with that account. I checked the ledger. Every check he'd written had been diligently recorded and subtracted from the balance, which was still substantial. There's no way this account is overdrawn. It's just not possible."

Eyes huge, she simply stared at him. "I'm thinking I need to check my grandmother's bank accounts. I know she has her social security check direct deposited every month. Most of her bills are on auto-pay, so I haven't even thought about dealing with any of that."

It took a moment for her words to register. "You believe this might be tied to them being missing?"

"I don't know. It could be a bank error. But if I check Isla's balance, and it too has been depleted, then we have to assume it's all related. And we'll have to let Rayna know."

"Are you able to check right now?" he asked, his throat suddenly dry.

"Sure." She pulled out her phone. "I have the app. Isla put my name on her bank accounts so I could handle funds if anything happened to her." Immediately, she looked stricken. "I don't think she meant like this. I always assumed she was talking about falling ill."

He waited while she pulled up the app and logged in. After a moment, she squinted at the screen and shook her head. "This can't be right. I don't keep up with my grandmother's finances, but I know she would never let her bank accounts get this low. There's barely a hundred dollars in her checking account. And her social security check doesn't come for another ten days or so."

"Are you able to pull up transactions?" Rey asked.

"I think so." She touched a few things on her screen. "Here we are." A moment later, she gasped. "She transferred nearly twenty-five thousand from her savings and withdrew it just a few days before I arrived. That's a lot of money."

He nodded. "Yes, it is. Does she still have anything in savings?"

Frowning, Willow scrolled. "Yes. There is still a decent amount left. But this concerns me. What did Isla need twenty-five grand in cash for? What did she buy?"

"Or who did she give the money to?" Feeling sick, Rey pushed to his feet and began pacing. "I don't have an app, but I am on the ranch accounts as a co-signer. I need to call the bank in the morning. Actually, I need to stop by."

"Should we call Rayna?"

"Not yet." He took several deep breaths, trying to calm his racing heart. "I need to make sure that the bank didn't make an error. Though I have a sinking feeling they didn't."

Chapter 12

After a restless night with Rey tossing and turning next to her, Willow rose quietly before sunrise. She left Rey still slumbering in his bed. He'd finally fallen asleep sometime around three, and she figured he needed all the rest he could get. Standing at the side of the bed, she gazed at him, admiring his profile and the way his big body relaxed in sleep.

While she'd slept, she'd been plagued by dreams of Isla calling out for help while Willow struggled, unable to reach her. She was glad that they were going to do something and proactively search. Sitting around and doing nothing but worrying wasn't productive. And since no one else seemed to be able to find any clues, she'd look for them herself.

Moving quietly through the dark and silent house, she made a cup of coffee and carried it back into the living room to drink while she scrolled through social media on her phone.

Once she'd finished, she emerged again, noticed his bedroom light was now on, but his door was closed. Deciding to get ready before having more coffee, she headed toward the bathroom. After brushing her teeth, she took a quick shower, managing to locate clean towels. She found herself wishing the bathroom door would open and Rey would join her, but he didn't.

When she emerged twenty minutes later, she opened the door to the smell of bacon frying. She made her way to the kitchen and found Rey cooking. Judging from the food spread out on the counter, he either was expecting a lot of company or doing some sort of breakfast meal prep.

"Good morning," she said, wondering if she ought to mention she would have welcomed him in the shower.

"Mornin'. I made a pot of coffee," he said, turning. With his early morning stubble and mussed hair, he looked good enough to eat. "I used the good coffee, the one Carl always keeps in the freezer for special occasions."

"What's the occasion and how did you do all this in what, twenty minutes?" She gestured at the array of food. Pancakes and scrambled eggs, bacon and sausage, toast and the fixins for biscuits with gravy were all spread out on the kitchen counter. "It looks like you made more than enough to feed a small army. Are we expecting company?"

With a grim smile, he shrugged. "I figured I'd text the ranch hands to stop by and eat on their way out to work the cattle. They should be getting up right about now."

She sipped her coffee and watched while he got out his phone and sent a text. A moment later, his phone pinged in response. "They'll be stopping by shortly." He smiled. "I know you've never met my ranch hands. I think you'll like them."

"I'm sure I will," she responded. "Now tell me, what's really going on? Are we still going out searching some of the more remote areas?"

"We are, but not this morning." He dragged his hand

through his hair, his expression distracted. "I'm sure you noticed how restless I was during the night."

"I did." She ached to kiss his frown away.

"That's why I made all this," he explained. "I had to keep myself busy until the bank opens at nine, and then I want to go into town. The ranch can't exist with no money in our account." He took a deep breath. "I'm sorry, but I don't have a choice. Are you okay with that?"

Slowly, she nodded. She liked that he even asked how the change in plans made her feel. "I get it. We can go search after, right?"

"Sure, as long as it's not too hot. Since temps are supposed to be in the hundreds all week, it might be better if we tried early tomorrow morning."

Though she didn't want to wait, what he said made sense. Plus, with everything else he had going on, the poor guy needed a break.

"I've been wondering what we're going to do if it turns out the ranch bank account has been emptied," he continued. "The only people with access to it are me and my dad. Which makes me wonder. Did my father have some sort of backup plan? It kills me that I don't have any idea."

She watched as he continued to cook, moving with a lot of grace for such a big man. He continued setting everything up on the counter. He put out a container of orange juice and some plastic cups, stacked paper plates and disposable utensils nearby and stepped back. "I think that'll do it."

"Where will everyone sit?" she asked, furiously trying to blink away a sudden haze of desire. Rey eyed her, apparently unaware. Clearly, she didn't have the same effect on him as he did on her.

"Outside at the picnic table." He turned back toward the spread. "Dad always tried to cook for the guys at least once a month, kind of as a treat."

A moment later, the back door opened and six men trooped inside. They greeted Rey enthusiastically, smiled and nodded at Willow, and went immediately to grab a paper plate and pile it high with food.

One by one, after filling their plates, they trooped back outside to eat, murmuring their thanks as they passed.

"Grab you some breakfast," Rey said, nodding toward the spread. "Get some before it's gone. I guarantee you they'll be back for seconds."

They both got food and sat down across from each other to eat. Sure enough, most of the crew came back, and after making sure no one had missed eating, they loaded up again. As they carried their once again heaping plates back outside, Willow saw that they'd demolished the spread.

"That's also an incentive for asking them to start work without me or Sam this morning," Rey said, beginning to clean up. "I'd like to be at the bank as soon as they open."

She got up and started helping him. Since he'd used paper plates, all that needed to be washed were the pots and pans he'd used to cook and the serving bowls.

"Would it be okay if I go to the bank with you?" she asked, bracing herself for him to refuse. "I understand if you'd rather I didn't, since this is intensely personal."

His gaze met hers. "I'd appreciate the support," he answered quietly. "Because I'm still struggling with this. The ranch finances have always been something Carl insisted on handling himself. Now I regret not insisting to be part of it. I just don't see how this could happen."

She touched his hand. "Try not to jump to conclusions until you've talked to the bank. They might be able to clue you in on the full story."

"Maybe so." But he didn't seem convinced. "All that keeps running through my head is that this has to be some sort of ransom payment."

Shocked, she recoiled. "Has anyone made a ransom request?"

"No. But what else would be urgent enough to make my father do something like this?" he asked, the anguish in his voice making her want to comfort him.

"I don't know. But hopefully, we'll find out."

Later, traveling into town, she made small talk as she could tell Rey felt nervous. While he nodded and made one-word responses, she finally gave up and stared out the window until they made it downtown.

When they walked into the bank, Rey asked to speak to a man named William Bates. "He's our personal banker," Rey said. They were shown immediately to a small office, more like a cubicle really. A short, bald man with wire-rimmed glasses stood as they entered and held out his hand.

"Good to see you, Rey," William said as they shook hands. Rey introduced Willow, who vaguely remembered William from somewhere.

The two men made small talk for a minute before Rey got down to business and asked the banker to pull up the ranch account. "I wrote a check at Rancher's Supply yesterday, and for some reason, this bank wouldn't honor my check. My father usually handles the ranch's finances, but as I'm sure you know, he's missing. But he's always been meticulous about keeping accurate records." Rey slid Carl's checkbook across the desk. "As you can see, there should still be substantial funds."

Keying something into his computer, William didn't even glance at the checkbook. He frowned as he read something on the screen and then looked over his glasses at Rey. "There would be, except your father made a large withdrawal roughly two weeks ago that essentially cleaned out the account. He only left one hundred and fifty dollars, just enough to ensure he isn't charged any banking fees."

"Two weeks ago?" Rey met Willow's gaze. She knew exactly what he was thinking. This would have been right about the time Carl Johnson and Isla went missing.

"Did he happen to say why?" Rey asked.

"No, he did not," William answered promptly. "But then, we're not in the habit of asking people what they intend to do with their money."

Rey took a deep breath. "One last question. I'm guessing you personally handled this, since we're your clients, right?"

"Correct." Sitting back in his chair, the banker crossed his arms.

"Then I need to know, if my father came in person to make the withdrawal, which I'm assuming he did, was he alone or did he have someone with him?"

This made William frown. "I believe he came by himself." He glanced at Willow. "Your grandmother wasn't with him, if that's what you mean."

"Okay," Willow replied.

"But that's not what I meant," Rey said. "I wanted to know if anyone might have been with Carl. Someone who made him withdraw all that money."

William puffed up at that. The question clearly offended

him. "I can assure you that your father was not being co-erced by anyone. Rest assured, he came alone." Clearing his throat, the banker stood. "And before you ask, he didn't appear nervous or out of sorts or anything else. He was fine. I'm not sure what you're insinuating, but nothing out of the ordinary occurred with this transaction."

"Thank you." Rey stood also, so Willow did the same. "I appreciate you taking the time to talk to us."

After leaving the bank, Rey went quiet. Willow couldn't blame him. It was bad enough that her grandmother had removed twenty-five thousand from savings, but to have your father empty the ranch's operating account without knowing why...

"You know what," Rey said as they turned into the ranch drive. "It's still early enough that we could cover some ground before it gets too hot. How about we go out for an hour or two? What we don't get to today, we can start with in the morning."

Since anything was better than sitting around wait-ing for something to happen, she agreed. "Let's do it."

Pulling up in front of the house, he killed the engine. "I need a minute to grab some provisions. You can wait here if you'd like."

"I can come help." She followed him into the house, watching as he loaded up a backpack with bottled water, protein bars and other assorted nonperishables. "I thought we were only going out for a couple of hours," she said.

"We are." He zipped the backpack closed. "But where we're going, it's best to be prepared. I learned that the hard way when I was a teen."

They got back in his truck and drove past the barn,

pulling up in front of a metal storage building. "Here we are," he said, hopping out and going around to open her door. Once she'd joined him, he unlocked the building's huge sliding door and pushed it open.

"Our transportation for the next couple of hours." He made a sweeping gesture toward the interior.

She took a couple of steps and peered inside.

"Four-wheelers?" she asked, surprised despite herself. "It's been forever since I drove one of those."

"It's like riding a bicycle," he said. "Once you get back on, it all comes back to you."

"I don't doubt that." She liked the idea. "Two or one? Are you expecting me to ride on the back of one with you, or do I get my own?"

One brow raised, he appeared surprised by her question. "We have two. You'd be driving one. Unless you don't feel up to it."

"Challenge accepted," she promptly responded, making him laugh. "I actually like the idea, but I have to ask why. Is there a reason we can't just take your truck?"

"We could." He shrugged. "But it would take forever, at least to go to the ranches I have in mind. Their land borders ours, but some of them are so huge that their homestead is in the next county."

"So what, you want to cut across pastures? What about fencing?"

"There are gates. Most of them are fairly easy to find. If we did this, we could cut off a lot of distance," he replied.

"Why not just call them? Wouldn't that be an even better time saver?"

He grimaced and shook his head. "I checked Dad's

contact records, and all he has saved are their landline numbers. If they still have landlines, which they probably do, it'd be hard to catch them at home. Unless we called late at night, and even then it's iffy. I don't know any of their cell phone numbers. And, since we also want to look for clues, calling wouldn't help."

Which made sense, sort of. Since she'd never lived on a ranch and had no idea what it entailed, she hadn't even considered how seldom the people living on the ranch were actually inside the house.

"If you'd rather we take the truck, we can," he said.

"No, four-wheelers are fine. If it turns out to be too difficult, we can always come back, right?"

"Of course." He pulled her in for a quick kiss. "And that may be the case. It's been a long time since I've taken these trails to the other ranches. I haven't done it since I was a teenager. They might be more difficult than I remember."

"I guess we'll find out."

Expression thoughtful, he nodded. "We will. Also, there are a couple of remote areas that I want to check out. Over the years, I know some of the ranchers have found squatters living on their land. One time at least, it was long term. As in, they'd built cabins."

"What? How is that possible? Is it really so vast that they can't keep up with what's going on?"

"It is." He handed her a key. "We keep these gassed up and start them at least once a week to make sure they're running. Are you ready?"

"I am." She climbed aboard, inserted the key and started the engine. It came to life immediately.

Rey pulled away first and she followed him, thrilled that she finally might be doing something constructive.

* * *

Though his first thought shouldn't have been how hot Willow looked driving a four-wheeler, Rey had to grin at himself. He couldn't help but admire her courage and readiness to tackle any situation.

They headed north, still on his family's land, toward the location of the first of several gates separating various pastures. The largest part of his ranch lay to the south, and there were two huge neighboring ranches to the north. Since he'd lived here his entire life, he knew exactly where to find those gates.

Finally, they'd passed through the last hundred acres of Johnson land. Pulling up to the final gate, he hopped off, opened it and motioned her through, just as he had with all the others.

"Now we're on Rafferty land," he told Willow. Pointing northwest, toward a visible rise in the land, he showed her where he wanted to go.

They took off. The slight incline made seeing ahead difficult, but he remembered thinking the view from the top was stunning.

However, this time as they crested the hill, an unfamiliar fence blocked the path. The gate had been locked with a chain and padlock, and there were signs posted.

"No Trespassing?" Rey eyed the bright yellow signs and made a gesture around the gently rolling hills. "This is the RF Ranch. It belongs to Don Rafferty, and it's been in their family for generations. We've always had an easement agreement with them. They can move herds through our back pastures, and we can do the same with theirs."

He dug out his phone and scrolled through contacts. "I went to school with Jeremy Rafferty. I think I have his number here somewhere."

Pulling it up, he pushed the button to make the call. A woman answered. After Rey identified himself, she explained that she was Claire, Jeremy's wife. It turned out each Rafferty child had been gifted one thousand acres of the family land, to do with as they pleased. Jeremy had sold his and used the money to buy himself his dream house on the Gulf Coast. They lived there now, and she had to say life had never been better.

"Do you happen to know who the buyer was?" Rey asked. She apologized, but said she didn't. Jeremy had only said it was some corporation and that they'd promised not to develop the land into condos or retail or a housing development.

Since this parcel sat in the middle of nowhere, without access to paved roads, Rey could see why someone would agree to those conditions. "Any idea what they planned to use it for?" he asked.

"We assume a small ranch," Claire replied. "I'm sorry, but did you need me to have Jeremy call you back? I'm late for an appointment."

Rey left his number, even though he figured she'd already have it. After the call ended, he looked up at Willow and explained the situation. "That's why the no trespassing signs. I'm guessing the new owner doesn't want anyone snooping around."

"Guess so," Willow agreed. "You'd think with the way news travels around Getaway that people would have been talking about this."

"I know. But I didn't hear a word. I honestly had no idea that Jeremy Rafferty sold off a thousand acres." Stunned, Rey removed his cowboy hat and dragged his fingers through his hair where the hat had flattened it.

"The fact that they weren't sure what the buyer intended to do with it is the weirdest part of the entire thing."

"What do you mean?" Willow asked. "I mean, if developers bought it, they'd still have to get permits or something, wouldn't they? And have it rezoned, from agricultural to whatever?"

"They would. But sometimes this kind of thing skates by under the radar. Especially if the developer greases the wheels, if you get what I mean."

"I do," she said. "Unfortunately."

He grimaced. "But Jeremy's wife claimed they got an agreement that the land wouldn't be used for retail or a housing development. She said a corporation bought it and plans to use it for a small ranch."

"Which makes sense, since this is a very remote location."

"I agree." Putting his hat back on, he sat back on the four-wheeler. "But what do we do now? With all these no trespassing signs, we can't legally cut across this property. The new owner would be within his or her rights to shoot at us."

"Can we go around?" Willow asked. "While I'm not familiar with the area, I'm guessing you can tell where the property line ends by the lack of those yellow signs."

"We could, but at this point, it would be quicker to make our way to the road." He struggled to contain his frustration. "It looks like we'd have been better off if we'd taken my truck like you suggested."

The wind picked up, and tiny pieces of grit stung his skin. "That's not good," he said. "Wrong time of the year for something like that."

"Look." She pointed west. "I know it's July, but that sure as heck looks like a dust storm on its way."

Turning, he looked where she pointed. "Damn, you're right. We usually get those in March and April. I don't think we've had one in the summer my entire life."

"We need to take shelter." Panic edged her voice. "And I don't see anywhere we can do that. I've only seen these things from the safety of inside my house. You know as well as I what kind of damage they can do."

"It's going to be okay," he said. "I promise. Like I said, I believe in being prepared. We keep emergency provisions in each four-wheeler. One of these has a small tent. We need to find a place to pitch it and crawl inside until the storm is over." He started rummaging in the storage compartment, hoping Sam hadn't taken the tent out for some reason and forgotten to replace it.

"We'd better hurry." Willow began doing the same thing on her vehicle. "Hey, I think I've found it."

Glancing back at the horizon, he decided the best place would be right below a dip in the land, in the middle of a small grove of twisted trees. Just past all the no trespassing signs.

"There." He pointed. "It's on their land, but I think our safety trumps a sign anytime. Hopefully, no one will even notice we were there."

Leaving the four-wheelers, they climbed over the metal gate, which had been padlocked closed. The wind had picked up, and the sky had turned that particular shade of reddish brown that everyone who'd ever lived in West Texas recognized as an ominous forewarning.

Quickly, he glanced around.

"We don't have too long," he shouted as the wind began to howl. Dirt stung their skin and faces, and he could barely see. "Help me get this tent up."

They struggled against the wind, but somehow managed to put up the two-person tent. "Get inside," he ordered, grabbing his backpack while she crawled in.

Following her, he barely got the zipper closed before the full force of the storm was upon them. Though he'd pitched the tent at an angle that should make it more difficult to blow over, he wasn't sure if it would stand. After all, he'd never actually done this before.

"Me neither," she said, making him realize he'd said his thoughts out loud. She scooched over next to him, and he put his arm around her, tugging her close.

The sides of the small tent billowed and danced, but it held. The wind-driven dust pummeled it, and despite the canvas barrier, some dirt made it inside.

Willow coughed, clearly struggling to breathe.

"Cover your mouth and nose with your shirt," Rey suggested. To demonstrate, he pulled up his shirt.

Instead, she turned to face him and buried her face in his chest. He hoped the low rumble of his laughter, felt rather than heard, comforted her.

Holding tight to each other, time slowed to a crawl. The rise and fall of her chest, the way she relaxed into him, made him feel he could conquer the world. He smoothed her hair, resisting the urge to murmur sweet nothings. Meanwhile, as they huddled together, outside the storm raged, doing its best to annihilate them.

Though he suspected only a few minutes passed, in the moment, it felt like eternity.

One minute, they were being buffeted by wind, and the next, it all suddenly...stopped. Just like that, an eerie silence.

Willow raised her head. "Is it over?"

Kissing her on the forehead, Rey nodded. "Sounds like it. Just a sec and let me check outside."

He crawled the few feet to the entrance and quickly unzipped the zipper to poke his head out. "All clear," he said, glancing back at her. "Looks like our four-wheelers got buried. Once we dig them out, we should be able to make our way home."

When he'd emerged from the tent, he held out his hand to help her up. Simply breathing filled his mouth with grit. "One of the joys of living in West Texas," he mused. "But still, I wouldn't live anywhere else."

Her silence reminded him that not only would she live somewhere else, but she actually did. And as soon as their missing family members were found, she'd no doubt return.

In that moment, he understood how badly that would hurt.

"Help me take this tent down and get it packed," he said, glad of the distraction. "We're going to have to dig out the four-wheelers."

Working together, they made short work of it, folding the canvas into the right shape to slip it back into its storage bag. After going back over the gate, they both got to work uncovering their vehicles. Once done, he got the storage bag stowed back on the four-wheeler, grabbed his backpack and handed her a bottled water.

She drank deeply before passing it back to him.

Once he'd gulped down nearly half, he passed it to her to finish. Then he stowed the empty plastic bottle in the backpack. "Are you ready to go?" he asked, climbing onto his machine.

Nodding, she did the same. As she did, the sharp staccato sound of a gunshot rang out. Then another. Someone was shooting at them.

Chapter 13

"Was that...?" Willow asked, swallowing hard. Her heart rate kicked into overdrive.

"Gunshots. We've got to get out of here, now. Go." Rey shouted, pointing back toward home.

Immediately, she gunned the motor and took off. He stayed right behind her. She appreciated the way he at least tried to shield her and offer some protection from the shooter. It brought a new meaning to the phrase *I've got your back.*

As they crested the ridge, leaving the no trespassing signs and the new fence behind them, Rey finally eased back on his speed. Noticing, Willow did the same.

Finally, Rey stopped. Willow circled around and joined him. "What on earth happened?" she asked, her voice shaky. "Were they shooting at us because we were on their land?"

"Apparently so."

"Which means they either had some sort of shelter close by where we pitched the tent, or they were out in the dust storm," she said. "Which makes no sense."

"Unless they were some sort of patrol, guarding the perimeter of the land."

"Out in the middle of nowhere?" she scoffed. "What would they even be guarding against? They had to have heard us coming. These things aren't exactly quiet."

"I don't know," he replied, his voice as grim as his expression. "But we need to tell Rayna anyway."

She nodded. By mutual agreement, they headed back toward the ranch.

Once they reached the storage building and drove the four-wheelers inside, Willow handed Rey her key. "You know, the fact that someone shot at us for taking shelter on their land makes me even more curious as to what they might be trying to hide."

Rey stared at her for a moment. "I agree," he said slowly. "Especially since anyone from around these parts wouldn't begrudge us taking shelter during a monster dust storm. It's not like we cut down their fence and were joyriding our four-wheelers around on their land."

"Exactly. And this might be taking a giant leap, but I think we need to find out what they're hiding. It might have something to do with all the missing people."

Though he didn't respond, she also noticed he didn't contradict her either. Which was fine. She'd give him some time to think about it before bringing up the subject again.

And if in the end, he didn't agree, she'd figure out a way to go back to that place and conduct a search by herself.

They hopped in his truck and drove back to the main house. When they arrived and parked, he turned to her. "I'm assuming you can ride?"

"A horse?"

"Yes." He nodded.

"Sure," she answered easily. "It's been a few years, but I don't think that's something I would forget. Why?"

"Because next time we go out that way, I think we should go on horseback. It's quieter, though slower." He thought for a moment. "Then again, we might not be safe."

"I'm thinking we should go on foot," she said. "Easier to stay hidden once we climb that fence gate."

He narrowed his gaze. "You are aware that there aren't a lot of places to hide in a wide open pasture like that, right?"

"You have a valid point. But—"

"How did I know there would be a *but*?" he asked, smiling slightly.

"At least think about it," she said, deciding she wouldn't tell him if he didn't agree to accompany her, she planned on going alone.

"I will." He got out of the truck and, as usual, hurried over to her side to open the passenger door. The small courtesy still charmed her as much as it had in the beginning. She wondered how she'd ever go back to dating a guy who hopped out of the vehicle and never looked back.

Oddly enough, the idea of even dating anyone else made her queasy. And since her PTO had almost run out, she would need to ask for an extension or, more realistically, an unpaid, indefinite leave of absence. She didn't really think her company would go for that, so she might have to face the possibility that she could end up unemployed.

To her surprise, the thought brought an immediate sense of relief. She couldn't go back to Cali until Isla had been found, but even after that, she wasn't sure she could ever leave her grandmother again. Something to think about, for sure.

Rey held the back door open, and they walked into the kitchen. Without her asking, he went directly to the fridge and got them tall glasses of iced tea.

Accepting hers gratefully, she dropped into a chair, unable to keep from wondering how it would feel to see Rey every single day. The notion made her positively giddy.

"Are you okay?" Rey asked, taking a seat across from her.

Since her thoughts were getting too deep, she took a long breath and nodded, aware she needed to talk about something else. "I was just wondering if they ever made a determination about the body that was found. Like identity, cause of death, any of that."

"I don't know," he replied. "I'm sure Rayna will call us when she can. I imagine she has a lot on her plate right now." He sighed. "I still want to mention to her the huge withdrawal my father made."

"True." Willow remembered the desperation she'd heard in her grandmother's whisper and grimaced. "I want to keep looking. That dust storm put an unexpected wrench in our plans, but I refuse to give up. Our folks are out there somewhere. We've got to get to them before they're found wandering some dark road."

He nodded. "Stay here tonight, and we can leave at first light in the morning."

Meeting his gaze, she thought about it for a minute. "That sounds like a great idea, but what about Sam?" she asked. "Won't that be a bit uncomfortable?"

"I don't think so, but that's definitely up to you. Sam is aware you and I are seeing each other, and he's clearly moved on."

"I'll think about it," she said. "For now, I guess I need to go on home." Since even thinking about that made her sad, she couldn't keep her voice steady.

"How about we drive some back roads in my truck instead?" he suggested, placing his large hand on her shoulder and squeezing lightly.

Grateful, she turned to face him. "Are you able to take the time away from the ranch?"

"I can arrange it. And when Sam shows up, he should be able to help out where needed."

"Then let's do it. I'll feel much better if I'm actually doing something."

"Me too." His phone rang. Digging it out of his pocket, he glanced at the screen. "It's Rayna. I'll put her on speaker."

Once he'd answered and informed Rayna that Willow could also hear, he placed the call on speaker.

"I'm glad I caught you both," Rayna said, her voice grim. "Because I was about to call Willow next. We've identified the deceased individual and spoken with his family. I'm not sure if either of you know him, but it was Alvin Pottsboro. Though we'll need the coroner to confirm, the ER doctor said it appears he died of starvation."

Horrified, Willow gasped. "Starvation?"

"Yes."

"We've got a few things to tell you as well," Rey said. He filled the sheriff in on the ranch bank account, and Willow mentioned the large withdrawal Isla had also made.

"Interesting," Rayna commented. "That's something I definitely want to discuss with the other families. There's so many now that I think we need to all get together as a group."

"One more thing." Rey asked if she'd known about the Raffertys selling off some of their land. The news appeared to surprise her. "They had a ton of no trespassing signs posted, but we were out when that massive dust storm hit, so we had to take shelter on their land. As we were packing up to leave, someone shot at us."

"What?" Rayna cleared her throat. "Are you serious?"

"I am. Now, I know this is ranching county, and it's not uncommon for some trigger-happy fools to take potshots at intruders, but we're locals and we had good reason."

"I agree. That was a hell of a dust storm," Rayna said. "I think it took most everyone by surprise. Wrong season and all. Maybe the weather people forecast something, but I don't know how many people had any idea it was coming."

"We sure as heck didn't," Willow put it. "Luckily, Rey had a pup tent on his four-wheeler, so we were safe."

"No one was hit?" Rayna asked.

"No ma'am." Rey chuckled. "Obviously, they were only trying to scare us off. Either that, or they're really lousy shots."

Rayna's short bark of laughter made Willow smile. She really liked the sheriff. Everyone in town did.

"I'm just glad you're safe. I'll be in touch about the meeting," Rayna said before ending the call.

"Let's go," Rey told her, reaching for her hand. She

threaded her fingers through his, and together they walked out to his truck.

In a few minutes, they were bouncing along a gravel and dirt road that ran the perimeter of the ranch.

"Are there a lot of deer leases out this way?" she asked as a thought occurred to her. "I have a vague memory from when I was a kid. My daddy used to take me hunting at one of his friend's. They had a couple of old campers on the property, and the only way in was by dirt bike or four-wheeler."

"I'm sure there are," Rey answered, his expression surprised. "But it's not deer season until November, so most of them will be sitting empty. I didn't know you ever knew your father."

"I did." She smiled sadly. "My mother passed when I was a toddler, and my dad tried, but he wasn't really present. For as long as I can remember, Isla's been my only family."

"Tell me about your father," he said. "When did he take you hunting?"

"I was probably around seven. I don't remember a whole lot about him. He died right after Christmas that year. I have no idea why I thought of this now, other than the chance that maybe our missing people are holed up at an empty hunting camp."

"That's a possibility," he said. "Except didn't you say your grandmother said she thought she was at a ranch?"

"I'm not sure she'd know the difference," Willow admitted. "Isla preferred town life. She rarely, if ever, ventured into the countryside. Only if she had to."

His gaze met hers. "Out of curiosity, why do you

call her Isla? I know she raised you. Did you ever think of calling her something else besides her first name?"

"Like Mom?" She sighed, a familiar ache inside her. "I tried once when I was in middle school. She sat me down and told me I only had one mother and she was watching over me from heaven. She told me I could call her Isla or grandmother, and I have ever since."

He coasted to a stop and shifted into Park. Then he leaned over and kissed her, a long, lingering kiss that had her craving more. By the time they broke apart, they were breathing hard.

"What was that for?" she asked, smiling.

"Because I wanted to. You're beautiful, Willow. Do you know that?"

The compliment made her laugh. "You're easy on the eyes yourself." Eyeing him, she decided to speak a little of the truth inside her heart. "I like you, Rey Johnson. A lot."

He leaned over and gave her another lingering kiss. "I feel the same way about you."

Then he straightened, shifted into Drive, and they continued on down the road.

As Rey had expected, they didn't see anything out of the ordinary. Just miles and miles of rugged West Texas ranch land. As always, he found the arid landscape beautiful, making him proud to be able to claim he owned a part of it.

Wide-eyed, Willow searched the horizon but didn't say much. He found himself wondering if she felt at home in the wide-open expanses like he did, or if she still yearned for the palm trees and beaches of California.

Finally, he had to turn the truck around and head back toward the ranch.

"Are you sure you don't want to stay the night?" he asked. "It will save you a trip over here at the crack of dawn."

"You know what? I think I will. But I'd like to stop by my house first so I can grab a change of clothes."

Which made perfect sense. He kept going past the ranch and drove them to her grandmother's place.

Once they went inside, instead of going to grab her things, she asked him if he'd consider simply staying here instead.

"Why?" he asked, even though he suspected he knew.

She grimaced. "Honestly, I don't want to have to deal with Sam glaring at me all night."

He started to laugh, but then he realized she was serious. "He won't. I told you, he and I talked. He gets it."

With her arms crossed, she didn't appear convinced. "Okay, then please call him. See how he reacts when you tell him I'll be spending the night."

"Fine." Pulling out his phone, he hit the button to call Sam's number. Naturally, his brother let the call go to voice mail. "He didn't answer," he said. "But if it makes you uncomfortable, I can stay here. We'll just drive out to the ranch at first light or before."

He hated that his brother made her feel uncomfortable. One more thing he'd need to discuss with Sam. But for right now, he'd do whatever Willow wanted.

"Let me think about it for a minute." Back straight, she walked to the kitchen window, where she stood and stared out at the small, neatly kept backyard.

He waited patiently, trying to figure out a way to

undo his invitation and insist they simply stay at her place. Sleeping separately wasn't an option he wanted to consider. Especially since he'd come to realize how transient their time together was.

When she finally turned to face him, she lifted her chin, a determined spark in her gaze.

"On the one hand, I don't want any drama," she said. "Not now or ever. But on the other, I refuse to let Sam's attitude influence any decisions I make about how I live my life. Staying at the ranch is more convenient, so that's what we should do."

He crossed the room in three steps and kissed her. "As long as you're sure."

Pressing her mouth to his in response, she smiled against his lips. "I'm sure. But I can promise you I'm not going to stand for it if Sam starts any nonsense."

He tried unsuccessfully to hide his grin. "Can't say I blame you."

"Right? Do you mind waiting a few minutes so I can pack an overnight bag?" She took off for her bedroom without waiting for him to answer.

Damned if he didn't love that woman.

Deciding not to think too hard or long about the way the sudden rush of emotion made him feel breathless, he made a slow circle of the living room.

On a bookshelf next to a scented candle, he spotted a framed photograph of his father and Isla. Rey picked it up to study it. Beaming at the camera, Carl had his arm around the diminutive woman's shoulders. She gazed up at him with clear adoration. And Carl's expression, Rey thought, radiated happiness. He looked…the way Rey felt inside when he gazed at Willow. In love.

For whatever reason, this hit him hard. He'd known Carl and Isla were a couple. Hell, they'd all had dinner together too many times to count. But he didn't remember ever seeing this look of adoration in his father's eyes when he gazed at Isla. Or vice versa. But then again, Rey guessed he'd never really paid attention.

It made him wonder if he looked at Willow the same way.

A few minutes later, Willow returned, carrying a small overnight bag. She saw him holding the photo and came over, smiling. "They look good together, don't they? I've stared at that picture a lot since I got here."

Throat tight, he nodded and placed the frame back on the shelf. "Are you ready?" he asked, his voice a bit rusty.

"I am." Studying him, she cocked her head. "Are you all right?"

Slowly, he nodded.

"Okay, then." Hefting her bag, she took his arm with her other. "Let's go."

Rayna called just as they made the turn onto the ranch drive. He pulled over so he could give her his full attention.

"Hey, Rayna. I've got Willow with me, and I'm putting you on speaker."

"Sounds good. That will keep me from having to repeat myself." Rayna took a deep breath. "I'm working on nailing down everything for the next meeting. I've got a time and place. All that remains to be done is to let everyone know."

"That was quick," he commented.

"Yeah, I've had my people working on making calls."

She cleared her throat. "But I decided to call you and Willow myself."

"I appreciate that," he said.

Willow echoed his sentiment. "You said this wasn't going to be another gathering with everyone in town, right?"

"Correct. This time, we're only meeting with all the family members whose loved ones are missing," Rayna replied. "Not the entire town. I want to update everyone on what we've learned so far." She took a deep breath. "Is Saturday morning at ten a good time for you?"

"Sure," he responded. Willow agreed. "I'll mention this to Sam as well."

"Great. I'll mark you and Willow both down. Let me know about Sam, or have him call my office." She paused. "If you don't mind, please inform Sam that this is for family members only, so he can't bring a friend or a date."

Rayna definitely had his brother pegged.

"Will do. Where is this being held?" Rey asked.

"Since there are too many to fit comfortably in my office, Pizza Perfect has agreed to let me use one of their meeting rooms. They won't be open yet, but will let everyone in. And there will be pizza, of course."

"Sounds good," Rey said.

"Definitely," Willow added, brushing her long brown hair back over her shoulder.

Unable to help himself, he reached out and touched one silky strand. Distracted, when Rayna spoke again, it startled him.

"Thank you," Rayna said. "Now, I've got quite a few more calls to make, so I'll let you go. See you Saturday at ten."

After ending the call, he turned to Willow. "She's really on top of things."

"She does work fast." Willow shook her head. "I just wish she'd had better luck getting some leads on where all these people might be."

The frustration in her voice matched his own. Since they were parked, he put his arm around her and pulled her close. Despite the console separating them, she put her head on his shoulder. He wished they could stay that way forever.

"It can't be that easy to hide so many older folks," she continued. "Therefore, they've got to be somewhere remote. That's why I still think we should try going back to that land with all the no trespassing signs."

"And get shot at again," he pointed out. "And while it's not real neighborly, they're well within their rights."

The stubborn set of her mouth told him she wasn't in agreement. But instead of arguing, she simply moved completely back into her own seat.

With a quiet sigh, he shifted into Drive.

She waited until they'd nearly reached the ranch house before talking again. "If we're not going to the no-trespassing place, then where are we going in the morning?"

He gestured toward the horizon. "There are thousands of acres of ranch land that we can explore."

They pulled up to the main house and parked. Sam's truck sat in its usual place, which meant his brother was home.

Noticing this too, Willow quietly groaned. "It may be cowardly, but I was really hoping he had other plans tonight."

As they walked into the house, Rey flipped the switch to turn on a light. A disheveled Sam popped up from the couch, red-faced and looking shocked and horribly embarrassed. A second later, a woman did the same, her hair mussed, holding a discarded shirt in front of her.

"Rey! And Willow." Grimacing, he cleared his throat. "Would you two mind giving us a moment of privacy? We can join you in the kitchen in a few minutes."

"No problem." Grabbing Willow's arm, Rey pulled her down the hallway to his bedroom instead. They made it inside, and he managed to get the door closed before Willow dropped down onto his bed and began laughing.

A moment later, he joined her. They laughed so hard that by the time Willow got a grip on herself, she had tears running down her face.

"I guess I was worried for nothing," she managed, wiping at her eyes. "That poor woman. I bet he told her they'd have the house to themselves tonight."

"Obviously." He grabbed a couple of tissues from his bathroom counter and gave them to her. "I just don't understand why they didn't go to his room."

"You don't?" For whatever reason, this brought on another spate of laughter. She shook her head, dabbing at her eyes. "I mean, it's not like you and I have ever done it on the couch, right?"

He conceded her point with a wry smile.

They waited ten minutes before Rey got up, opened his bedroom door and called out to Sam.

There wasn't an answer. Cautiously, Rey ventured down the hallway into the living room. It was empty, as was the kitchen.

It turned out Sam and his lady friend had taken off. They hadn't even left a note.

"So much for worrying about nothing," Willow mused. "I do feel bad for the woman, whoever she is."

Rey shook his head. "I'd hoped to tell Sam about the meeting with Rayna on Saturday. Not that he's ever showed much interest in the investigation, but you never know."

"True." Placing her phone on the coffee table, Willow sighed. "I just keep hoping Isla will call me again. Or, if she can't do that, send a text."

"I'm worried about Carl now," Rey admitted. "He's always been in good health for a man his age, but if he's ill… I have to wonder what's wrong with him. Hopefully, he's not being starved or something like that."

His words made Willow wince. "Why would someone do that to an older person? Any person actually. I still fail to see the common denominator in everyone's disappearance. Apparently, Rayna hasn't come up with one either, or she'd have better leads."

"It has to be money," he said immediately. "I can't see what else someone would have to gain."

Tucking a strand of hair behind one ear, she nodded. "I sure hope we find something tomorrow morning. I'm tired of feeling like this search is in limbo."

"Me too," he said. And then, since they both clearly needed a distraction, he pulled her close for a kiss.

Chapter 14

For most of her life, Willow had never had to use an alarm. She always simply fixed the time she needed to wake in her mind and went to sleep. But tonight, after a second bout of passionate lovemaking with Rey, she stretched languidly and thought she'd better not risk it. They were in his bed, with the bedroom door closed, since they hadn't wanted to risk Sam and his friend walking in on them.

They reclined against propped-up pillows. She'd pulled the sheet up over her chest while he'd done the same, but only up to his waist.

As she got out her phone, Rey watched her. The tenderness she saw in his gaze made her fluttery inside.

"Are you thinking five a.m.?" she asked, making her voice brisk to mask her rush of emotion. "Or should we get up earlier, like four thirty?"

"You don't need an alarm." His warm smile made her melt. Again. "I always wake right before sunrise. I can get you up if you'd like."

Tongue-tied, she simply nodded. When he leaned over to kiss her, she met his lips with more than simply desire. She wanted this, *him*, for the rest of her life with a fierceness that humbled her and shook her to the core.

When they broke apart, he pushed up out of the bed, stepped into his jeans and, barefoot, went to make sure the house was locked up tight.

Unable to keep from watching him walk away, she shook her head. With Isla and Carl still missing, now wasn't the time to even think about any sort of future with Rey. They'd never discussed it, and for good reason.

Rey returned, got into bed and, after kissing her again, turned out the light. He pulled her close and held her while she drifted off to sleep.

The sound of a cell phone ringing startled her awake. Blinking, she sat up. Next to her, Rey did the same.

"It's mine," Rey said, grabbing his phone. "Rayna, what's up?"

Bleary-eyed, Willow watched him, wondering what kind of emergency would have the sheriff calling at—she peered at her watch—four in the morning. Rey wasn't doing much talking, just listening, and Willow couldn't hear enough of the other end of the conversation to figure out what had happened.

"Thanks for letting us know," Rey finally said. "And I'll fill Willow in, so no need to call her."

Ending the call, he shook his head. "I'm guessing she knows I'm usually up around this time. The Lawson house went up in flames a few hours ago. They think some kind of accelerant was used."

"While that's terrible news, why would Rayna feel the need to inform us about that? I mean, it's a tragedy, but still."

"Because Philip Lawson is one of the missing seniors," Rey said, swallowing hard. "And his sister who lives in San Antonio was staying in his house while he's been missing. Rayna said she was killed in the fire."

"What?" Not entirely comprehending, Willow rubbed her eyes. "Someone died?"

"Unfortunately, yes. And right now, it's looking as if she was murdered."

After such devastating news, going back to sleep for thirty minutes was out of the question. By mutual agreement, they got out of bed. After brushing their teeth side by side, which felt way more intimate than she thought it should have, they went to the kitchen to make coffee.

"I'm glad we have something to do this morning," Willow commented. "Sometimes, I feel like keeping busy is the only way to stay sane."

Though he nodded and tried to smile, his troubled expression negated his attempt. "I think Rayna's wanting to move up the meeting. She said she planned to call each of the families and let them know that this, whatever it might be, is escalating."

Willow almost choked on her coffee. "She thinks we might be in danger?"

"She said she has to consider the possibility that any or all of the families of the missing people are at risk. Her words, not mine."

"But why?" Willow asked, bewildered. "What would anyone have to gain by hurting those of us who are missing our loved ones?"

"I don't know. That's something Rayna is going to have to figure out."

She took a long sip of her coffee. "Are we still going to go out on horseback? I'd really like to continue the search. We should at least have a few hours before she can get the meeting organized, right?"

"Probably. But I'm not sure I want to risk it. What if we're way out there and miss her call? Or can't get back in time to make the meeting?"

Though she didn't like it, he had a valid point.

"I need to try and get a hold of Sam," Rey said. "He'll still be asleep, but if I wake him, maybe he'll actually answer his phone. It's worth a shot."

Watching him while he dialed his brother, his handsome face intent, such a swell of love rose inside her that she had to grip the edge of the kitchen table to keep from going to him.

His strategy must have worked because he gave her a quick thumbs-up before speaking into the phone. "No, Sam. Nobody has died, at least not in our immediate family. Rayna just called me, and I wanted to fill you in on what's—"

Listening, he shook his head. "Sam, please. It's important." A moment later, Rey cursed. "He hung up on me," he said. "Told me not to bother him again unless it was serious. I never even got a chance to tell him about the fire or the Lawson woman's death."

"Or the fact that Rayna feels other family members might be in danger," Willow added, furious at Sam. "Let me try," she said. She grabbed her phone, pulled up Sam in her contacts and called him. After two rings, he forwarded her to voice mail.

"That's pretty much what I expected," Rey said when she told him.

Frustrated, she decided to go home. "There's no point in me hanging out here. You're welcome to come to my place with me. You'll be closer in case Rayna calls a meeting."

She loved that he didn't even try to hide his disappointment. "I think I'll just get started on chores," he replied. "Since obviously Sam has no intention of coming back and helping."

She carried her coffee cup with her into the bedroom. As she got dressed, Rey stood in the doorway and watched her. At one point, when she looked up at him, the naked longing in his gaze stopped her in her tracks.

"Don't do that," she told him. "When you look at me like that, it's almost impossible for me to drag myself away."

Her comment made him grin. "Then don't go."

Instead of replying, she simply walked over to him and pulled him down for a long, soulful kiss. "That'll have to hold us both," she said once she'd broken away.

Though he followed her out to her Bronco, he made no other move to try and stop her. "I guess I'll see you at the meeting, whenever that may be."

"Definitely," she said. "I sure hope Rayna holds it at Pizza Perfect like she'd planned for Saturday. I wouldn't mind a slice or two of pizza."

She got into her SUV and left him standing in his driveway watching her go. Part of her felt like she'd left her heart behind her.

Rayna called right after Willow got out of the shower. "Can you make the meeting around one?" the sheriff asked. "Pizza Perfect has agreed to still let us use one of their meeting rooms and also provide lunch."

"I can be there," Willow replied.

"Great. Please let Rey know," Rayna continued, evidently assuming they were still together. "See you there."

Immediately after ending the call, Willow dialed Rey. She gave him the information, and though he offered to pick her up, she told him she'd just meet him there. He said he was still trying to get a hold of Sam, but he'd definitely attend either way.

Wanting to be early, Willow left for the meeting thirty minutes before she had to.

Since she didn't see Rey's truck in the parking lot, she went on inside. The restaurant was still packed from the lunch rush. An employee directed her to a meeting room in the back of the building. The smell of pizza cooking made her mouth water.

There were already about a dozen people gathered inside, even though the meeting didn't start for half an hour. Willow walked over to a group she knew slightly, greeting them with a friendly smile.

"We were just discussing the possibility that the sheriff's office must have gathered some very good leads," a middle-aged woman with salt-and-pepper hair and tired eyes said. "Otherwise, why would Rayna hold a meeting?"

Though Willow had to wonder if she knew about the house fire, she kept her mouth closed and simply nodded.

"Agreed," someone else said. "This is the first time I've felt hopeful in a long while."

"Looks like there's going to be a PowerPoint presentation," the first woman said, gesturing toward the front of the room where a large portable screen had been set up. "That's got to be a good thing, right?"

Several others agreed, including Willow. Privately,

she wondered what kind of slideshow the sheriff planned to have.

Her back to the door, Willow felt the energy in the room change. She glanced over her shoulder, unsurprised to see Rey had arrived. He met her gaze, and she felt that familiar jolt. As he made his way toward her, she realized she saw no sign of Sam. Relieved, despite feeling he needed to be here, she wondered what had happened. Rey had been so convinced that Sam had turned over a new leaf.

"Hey," Rey said, his arm brushing hers. Even that slightest of touches sent a shudder of longing through her.

"Hey, yourself," she said back. "Do you want to go grab a seat?"

"Sure." He followed her over to two unoccupied chairs in the front row. "I'm sure you noticed, but Sam couldn't make it."

Sitting, she waited until he'd settled in beside her, their hips touching. Again, she felt an inner jolt at the contact. "Was there a problem?" she asked.

He grimaced. "He said he didn't feel like sitting through some boring meeting and wasting his day, especially since I could just fill him in on the details."

Despite his even tone, she could sense his frustration. "I'm sorry," she said.

"Thanks. I just don't understand his thinking. Sometimes, it's like he's still a teenager. It bugs me more than it should, especially since he promised to be more invested."

In the short time they'd been there, more people had arrived and were also taking their seats.

Five minutes before the meeting was due to start, Rayna and two of her deputies entered, all in uniform, a sign to Willow they wanted this to be as official as possible.

"Good morning, everyone," Rayna said, her voice carrying. "Why don't the rest of you get seated, and then we can begin."

She waited a moment while the latest arrivals got settled. "Now, as you all know, despite us diligently working on this case, we've had precious few leads. Finding Mr. Smith appeared to be our first big break, but so far we have not been able to talk to him. The doctors have recently informed me that his health has declined, and they don't expect him to survive the day."

Murmurs went through the audience as everyone digested this news. The bookstore owner had been a well-liked and respected part of the community.

Rayna waited patiently until it was quiet again. "Secondly, there was a devastating house fire earlier this morning. Philip Lawson's house burned to the ground. Since he is one of the missing, his sister had come in from out of town and was staying there. Unfortunately, she lost her life in the fire."

Evidently, not everyone had been notified because the room erupted. People stood, shouting out questions, talking with each other and expressing their shock.

Rey wasn't sure why, but in the chaos of rampant emotions, he felt a strong urge to protect Willow. Without caring who saw, he put his arm around her and pulled her close. She glanced up at him, her mouth parted in surprise, but she nestled into his side.

Finally, Rayna tapped a pen on the microphone and asked for silence. Everyone immediately complied.

"I'll try to answer your questions as best I can," Rayna continued. "Yes, we do think the fire was deliberately set. Our volunteer fire department found traces of an accelerant. We do not know why, or if it was tied to the group of missing individuals. However, we've decided to err on the side of caution and warn each of you to stay vigilant."

This time, instead of simultaneous outbursts, several people raised their hands. "What about insurance?" someone asked.

"I'm sure Mr. Lawson had insurance on the home," Rayna said, answering the first question. "But with him missing, since the policy would pay him, I don't see how that would benefit anyone. The same for his sister's death. Even if she carried a substantial life insurance policy, only her beneficiary can claim that money."

Rey and Willow watched and listened as the sheriff patiently and painstakingly answered every single question and concern. He kept his arm around her shoulder, and she stayed as close as she could while remaining in her own chair. He noticed several people glancing their way, but for the most part, everyone seemed too captivated by the situation at hand to pay them any attention.

Once no more questions related to the fire remained, Rayna moved on. "I have some more news, though unfortunately I'm going to have to keep it vague for now. Our volunteer group that has been canvassing the town brought back several interesting pieces of information that may or may not be connected. Since we don't know for sure, we're not going to discuss this yet. Instead, I want to talk about what we do know."

She looked around the crowd, briefly making eye

contact with Rey among numerous others. He appreciated the sheriff's no-nonsense manner and suspected others felt the same.

"What we have learned from talking to you all, as well as friends and neighbors of those missing, is that many of them were facing serious health concerns. Not everyone, but at least one partner in each couple. But not all of the health issues were similar, or even close. We have one person recently diagnosed with ALS, several with various types of cancer, COPD, kidney failure with congestive heart failure, heart blockages, you get the picture."

Rayna paused, letting all this digest. Rey glanced at Willow, since her grandmother had been diagnosed with some sort of heart issue. Carl had been healthy, at least as far as they knew. Though when Isla had called, she'd said Carl had fallen ill. Worry twisted his gut at the thought. He swallowed hard and returned his attention to the sheriff.

"We've been investigating a few possibilities," Rayna continued. "Beginning with any individuals or groups promising miraculous cures. We're looking into each and every one we can, in order to see if our missing senior citizens were lured away by outlandish claims."

Willow shook her head. Around them, Rey noticed several others do the same. "Isla would never allow herself to be conned by a snake-oil salesman," she said out loud. "She was always on the lookout for scammers."

"My mom was too," someone else said. A couple more people echoed this statement.

"Desperate people do unusual things," Rayna cautioned. "But please remember, this is just a theory." She sighed. "Right now, it's one of the best ones we've got to go on."

The meeting ended on that note.

Most everyone stayed after, helping themselves to the pizza buffet that had been set out on the back table. Rey had lost his appetite, but because Willow made it clear she intended to eat, he followed her over. Since he knew his body needed nourishment, he followed Willow's lead and put a couple of slices on his plate.

They ate quickly and with purpose. When he asked Willow if she wanted to go back for seconds, she shook her head.

"I'd like to go check on Serenity," she said. "I've been worried since she had that episode when I visited her store. I checked with the hospital and they said she was discharged."

"Have you tried to call her?" Rey frowned.

"I did, but she hasn't picked up or returned my call. So I want to stop by."

Shocked, since he'd known Serenity his entire life, he eyed Willow. "If they discharged her, she must be okay, right?"

"Maybe. I don't know. She looked really bad." She shook her head. "Right after all that happened, Isla called, and as you know, there's just been a bunch going on. I should have checked on her sooner."

"Do you mind if I go with you?" he asked. "Now I'm a little worried too."

"Of course. I welcome your support. I'd like to try to convince her to go get checked out by a doctor again, just to make sure."

Her compassion for others was one of the things he

loved about her. *Loved*. There it was again, that word, that emotion. Glancing away, he couldn't help but wonder if she suspected, if she knew. And most importantly, if she felt the same way.

Pushing those thoughts from his head, he knew he needed to focus. "I don't know how much assistance I'll be, but I'll definitely try."

"I don't know about that." Willow smiled. "If she actually does need some help, I suspect Serenity might listen to you better than she does to me."

Her large brown eyes sparkled when she smiled. He had to force himself to look away. How he could be so enthralled by someone while in the middle of a monumental crisis, he'd never understand.

And then there was the fact that she hadn't made any secret of her intention to go back to California when all this was over.

"Let's take my Bronco," she said, jumping to her feet. "We can leave your truck here."

"Why?" he asked.

"You always drive." She shrugged. "I'd like to this time."

Beautiful, he thought. His smile widened. "Makes sense to me. Unless you'd like to walk. It's not that far."

"I'd rather drive," she replied. "Let's go."

Once they were in her SUV, she glanced at him. "You know, I've always considered my vehicle roomy, but you barely seem able to fit."

He shrugged. "I have this problem sometimes. I'm a big guy, which is why I drive my truck."

"You do take up a lot of space," she agreed. "You make the front interior seem much too small."

They pulled up to Serenity's, and she managed to snag a parking space right in front. Stepping out before Rey could come around, she stood a moment peering down Main Street.

"So many memories here," she mused when Rey caught up. "Every year for five years, I rode in the Fourth of July parade with the 4-H Club. And for PE in middle school, coach made us run laps around that church and cemetery."

"You had a horse?" Rey asked, surprised. "I thought you always lived with Isla in town."

"I did." With a rueful smile, she sighed. "But my friend Cindy lived in those five-acre ranchettes out by 36th Street. I'd always wanted my own horse. Finally, Isla bought me an older mare when I was thirteen. Cindy had an extra stall in her barn, so we paid to let Luna stay there. I went every morning before school to feed her and after school to ride her."

Somehow, he suspected Willow had been a natural on horseback. Her petite, athletic build would lend itself well to many athletic endeavors, like surfing.

The vision sobered him. Quickly, he collected his thoughts. "What happened to your horse?"

"We had to sell her when I went away to college." Willow blinked. "I almost didn't go because of that."

He nodded. Were those tears in her eyes? "But you did."

"Yes. As much as I loved that horse and this town and my family and friends, I wanted something different. Something *more*."

Her words cut like a knife to his heart. He could only smile like a simpleton while she continued.

"Back then, restlessness burned like a fire in me. I

spent countless hours poring over information about the West Coast versus the East. All I knew was I wanted to live on the coast. I didn't care which one. I'd known I'd move away to one of those places and live near the ocean, but until the job offer had come in from Cali, I hadn't been entirely sure where I'd live."

When she looked up, Rey met her gaze, hoping his impassive expression hid his churning emotions. "And that's why you moved away after you graduated."

"It is." Apparently weary of the subject, she turned to Serenity's shop. "Are you ready to go inside?"

"After you." He opened the door for her, letting her lead the way. Bells tinkled a cheerful welcome.

Rey looked around. The interior of Serenity's appeared normal. Incense burned on the back counter, the usual soothing music played and a small waterfall had been added to a table over by the front window.

The instant the door closed behind them, Serenity sailed through her colorful beaded curtain, smiling broadly. Judging by Willow's earlier description, he saw that her bruises had faded slightly, and she'd clearly tried to cover them with makeup.

"Rey and Willow! Both of you at the same time!" she exclaimed, hugging Rey first and then Willow. When she finally stepped back, she glanced from one to the other. "Are you here to shop or just to visit?"

"I wanted to check on you," Willow admitted. "How have you been? Any more er…incidents?"

Serenity narrowed her eyes. "By incidents, do you mean falls? If so, I haven't fallen again."

"She's just concerned about you," Rey said, keeping his tone gentle. "We both are."

Just like that, Serenity appeared to deflate. "Thank you. Come on into the back and have some tea, and we'll talk."

As they followed her through the beaded curtain, Willow couldn't help but notice the older woman appeared to lean to one side. Her gait seemed unsteady, and she grabbed a hold of one of the chairs around the table for stability.

"Maybe I should get a cane," she said, half smiling. "I admit I've been having a lot of dizzy spells for no reason. I went to see Doc, but he wanted to order an MRI at the hospital in Midland, and there's no way I'm getting into one of those things." She sighed. "Maybe I should go see that faith healer who sent out the flyers. I just can't seem to find anyone who's used him, so I can't be sure if he's legit."

Once again, Rey found himself glancing at Willow. She'd straightened, her expression suddenly intent.

"What faith healer?" she asked, her tone casual. Waiting to hear the older woman's answer, Rey attempted to match her lack of urgency, despite his racing heart.

Suddenly, Serenity seemed to sense their interest. One perfectly arched brow raised, she looked from one to the other. "You know I attend lectures dealing with metaphysical things. The last one I went to was a month ago in Abilene. There was a group there passing out flyers for some faith healer. I only took some to be polite. Actually, I forgot about them until I fell the other day."

"Do you still have them?" Willow asked.

"I'm sure I do, somewhere," Serenity replied. "I'm not sure why you both find this so fascinating, but I can assure you I was only half serious."

"Did you share the flyers with anyone else?" Rey crossed his arms.

"I put a stack of them on the counter for customers to take, if they were so inclined," Serenity said. "You know I'm not the kind to push things on people. And since there aren't any left on the counter, I'd say quite a few folks grabbed one."

For the first time, Rey thought they might have an actual lead. Rayna had even mentioned investigating medical leads earlier in the meeting. "Did you happen to mention any of this to Rayna?"

"No. Why would I?" Again looking from Willow to Rey and back again, after a second, the confusion in Serenity's gaze vanished. "Do you think this might have something to do with all those missing people? Like Isla and Carl?"

"It definitely could," Rey replied. "It just depends on how badly they needed relief. Desperate people will step outside of their comfort zone. Even you just said you might have to try giving that guy a call."

"True, but I'm hesitant," Serenity said. "Even though this sort of thing aligns with some of my belief system, something about it just seems off for some reason. I can't quite put my finger on it, but I don't get a good vibe."

"Why don't you look and see if you can find any remaining flyers?" Willow suggested. "I'd like to bring one to Rayna and let her take a look."

"Sure. Give me a few minutes. Would you two like some tea while you wait?"

Resisting the urge to insist on helping Serenity search, Willow shook her head. "None for me, thank you."

Rey echoed the sentiment.

222 *Vanished in Texas*

"Okay, then. Wait here." And Serenity disappeared into the public part of her store.

Again, Willow and Rey exchanged glances. "I don't know about you," Rey said. "But I think this could be the break we've been waiting for."

"I agree." Willow swallowed. "Do you think we should go out there and offer to help her? She seems really unsteady on her feet."

Just then, they heard Serenity cry out, followed by a crash.

Chapter 15

Following the ambulance to the hospital, Willow gripped the steering wheel so hard her knuckles were white. Glancing at Rey, she noticed he appeared to be working on unclenching his jaw.

"I swear I've seen more of this hospital these past few weeks than I have in the last several years," he said.

"Me too." Willow felt glum. "And we need to fill Rayna in on what Serenity said about that faith healer."

"It would be better if she'd found the pamphlet." Though Serenity had regained consciousness after the paramedics arrived, her only request had been to ask them to make sure her store was locked up. Naturally, they'd complied, but that also meant they couldn't go back in later and search for it.

"Maybe we can ask Serenity for a key," Rey suggested when she voiced her thoughts. "I'm sure she'd let us go in and look."

"Let me call Rayna. Maybe she can come up with something." She pulled out her phone and put the call on speaker. Rayna picked up almost immediately. "What's up?" she asked, her voice terse.

"We're on our way to the hospital following an ambulance. Serenity fell, and I'm not sure, but she might have had a seizure or stroke."

Rayna cursed. "Has she been ill?"

"We suspect she has." And Willow filled her in on the rest of it, Serenity's black eye, her unsteadiness and the mention of a faith healer.

"A faith healer?" Rayna asked. "Like one of those old-timey revival things were the preacher goes around laying on hands?"

"We don't know," Rey admitted. "She was trying to find a pamphlet when she passed out and fell. The thing is, she said she had a stack of those flyers in her shop and passed them all out to customers. What if this is the missing link?"

"It's a lead," Rayna said firmly. "We don't ever jump to conclusions in law enforcement. But any lead is better than what we have right now, which is next to nothing. Please tell me you got your hands on that leaflet?"

"We did not. And Serenity made us lock up her shop before she'd let the ambulance take her. So we don't have any way to get back in and search for the darn thing."

"If she's okay, please just ask her for her key," Rayna said. "Because based on what you've told me, I don't have a valid reason to break in there just to search."

Disappointed, Willow said they'd try. Privately, she wasn't sure Serenity would allow them to have her key or look through her shop without being present. She honestly didn't seem to understand the possible connection between the faith healer's flyer and the missing people. Hell, even Rey knew it might be a long shot. But it was a hell of a lot more than what they had right now.

They parked. By the time they'd begun walking into

the ER, the paramedics had already taken Serenity inside. Willow had called Velma right after they'd called 911, and Serenity's sister had ridden with her in the ambulance.

"Unfortunately, we can only allow immediate family to go back right now," the triage nurse said. "But you're welcome to wait out here if you'd like."

Since Velma knew they'd made the trip and Willow had given Serenity's sister her cell number, they took seats in the waiting room.

When Willow turned to meet Rey's gaze, the exhaustion in her eyes made him put his arm around her and pull her close. "You can use my shoulder as a pillow if you want," he offered. "Close your eyes and get some rest. I promise to wake you if anything happens."

She gave him a grateful smile and did exactly that.

An hour later, Velma came out. She smiled, appearing relieved. "She's awake and talking. Trying to get them to let her go home. They want to run some more tests and keep her overnight for evaluation. They think she's having TIA's—transient ischemic attacks."

"Oh, no." Willow gripped Rey's arm. "Is she going to be all right?"

"The doctors don't seem too worried." Velma took a deep breath. "I wish I could say the same. I'll let you know if anything changes."

"Thank you," Willow said. Rey echoed the sentiment.

As Velma walked off, she seemed to suddenly remember something. She paused mid-step and spun back around. "Oh, I almost forgot. Serenity tells me you were asking about the faith healer. What did you need to know?"

Willow's heart skipped a beat. "Have you met with him?"

"Oh, no." Velma shook her head, sending her large, dangly earrings swinging. "I just saw the stack of flyers that Serenity had. I even took some for the front counter of my yoga studio."

"Do you have any left?" Willow asked, trying not to sound too eager.

"I'm sure I do. Most of my clients are pretty fit. I only know of a few who took one of those flyers." She met Rey's gaze first before settling on Willow. "I'm pretty sure that Isla was one of them."

Willow's eyes widened. "Hearing that, as far as I'm concerned, that means this faith healer person needs to be looked into. Do you mind if we stop by your studio and grab a flyer?"

"Not at all. I have classes scheduled for this evening, and one of my other instructors will be there teaching them. You can just drop in and get one off the front desk." Velma smiled, gave a quick wave and hurried back to be with her sister.

Willow glanced at Rey, wondering if he could tell her first impulse was to kiss him. "Are you thinking what I'm thinking?"

He stood. "Yes. Let's go. We'll grab a couple of those flyers and hand deliver one to Rayna."

By the time they got back in Getaway and parked outside the yoga studio, dusk had begun to fall. Inside, class had started. Taking care not to disturb anyone, Rey and Willow went to the front desk, saw the stack of flyers and grabbed three.

Back outside, they carried them out to her Bronco

before taking a look at them. To Willow's surprise, they looked professional, with clean, crisp text and colors. There was even a photograph of the supposed healer, a normal-looking man in a well-fitted, navy suit. His name was Jonathan Longtree.

"These seem fairly tame," Rey mused. "I'm not sure what I expected, but maybe some extreme claims about his healing abilities."

"Me too. I thought for sure I'd see something about him healing the blind." She grimaced. "This is way more professional than I expected. It even has his hourly rates."

"Yeah. But one thing it doesn't have is a business address." Rey turned the flyer over and double-checked the other side. "It just says to contact him for an appointment."

"True. But it does say he offers a senior citizen discount." She sighed. "Which definitely would appeal to the older crowd. Still, it's not as much of a huge lead as I'd hoped for."

"Maybe. Maybe not. But I wouldn't entirely dismiss it. Let's get a copy to Rayna. Then we'll grab dinner and head to the ranch. I'd like to make an early start in the morning."

After dropping off the flyer on Rayna's desk—she'd left for the day—they decided to stop for dinner at the Tumbleweed Café. "It's chicken-fried steak night," Rey said. "That's one of my favorite dinners ever."

"You can't get that in California," Willow commented. As they walked into the restaurant, she thought back to all the special occasions she'd celebrated here.

They were shown to a window booth, one where Willow and Isla had sat together many times. Willow sat down across from Rey and sighed. "I'm really missing my grandmother right now. She loves coming here to eat."

He nodded. "So does Carl. From what I understand, he and Isla had a standing Wednesday night date here."

Gazing at him across the table, she realized she wanted all of that with him. Standing dates, making traditions, sharing a history and making a future. She leaned forward, parted her lips to ask him if he wanted the same things and then gave herself a mental shaking. She couldn't ask him something like that. Not when she hadn't even decided her own future.

Her requested PTO was coming to an end, and she'd been putting off calling her boss. She'd either need to request an extension or put in her notice. And as much as the thought of leaving her job pained her, she refused to leave Getaway until Isla had returned home safe.

In fact, right then and there, she knew she wouldn't be leaving at all.

The waitress came over and took their drink orders. They both asked for sweet tea and took a minute to look at the menu. Though Rey opened his, Willow found herself gazing at him again across the table.

"What?" he asked, noticing. "Do I have something on my face?"

This made her smile. "No, not at all. I'm wondering why you're even looking at the menu since you said you were getting chicken-fried steak."

"True." He put the menu down. A few minutes later, they ordered. She went ahead and got chicken-fried steak too.

When their food arrived, they dug in. After they finished eating, Willow grabbed the check before Rey could. "My turn," she said, even though it wasn't.

Though he started to protest, she quickly silenced that by leaning across the table and giving him a kiss. "No debating. Like you said last time, you can get the next one."

"But that's two," he said.

"So? You can get the next two then."

Smiling, he shook his head but gave in.

As they got up to leave, she reached for his hand. They walked out to her Bronco together. "After we get my truck, do you want to take yours home and then ride out to the ranch with me?"

She thought for a moment. "Does that mean you've reconsidered, and we can go out and look around that area tomorrow?"

"No. It means I want to spend the night with you wrapped up in my arms."

How could she say no to that? "I'd like that," she admitted. "But can we at least mention it to Rayna tomorrow?"

"Sure," he answered easily. "As long as she's available, I'd say that's a definite possibility."

Sam strolled in around ten, when Rey and Willow were cuddled on the sofa in the middle of watching an old Western movie. Immediately, Rey hit Pause on the remote and pushed to his feet.

"About time you showed up," he said, keeping his voice level.

"Did you miss me?" Sam grinned, clearly missing the point. "I'm thinking you two welcomed the time alone together."

"I could have used some help with the chores," Rey pointed out. "With Carl missing and it just being the two of us, it takes both of us to keep the ranch running."

Sam's blank stare meant he either didn't get it or didn't care. Rey was betting on the second.

"Sorry," Sam replied. He dropped down into the armchair and changed the subject. "Any news on Dad?"

Right then and there, Rey decided he wouldn't elaborate on anything until they had something concrete. Sam's self-absorption and lack of effort didn't make Rey inclined to share anything with him. "Nope," he said. Willow raised her eyebrows but didn't comment.

"Oh, okay." Sam eyed the TV. "Do you mind if I change the channel?"

"Yes, we do," Rey and Willow answered at once.

"We're enjoying this movie," Willow said.

Sam frowned. "But it's old."

"So?" Rey challenged.

Looking from one to the other, Sam shook his head. "Never mind," he said, standing. "I'll just go watch something in my room."

Once Sam had closed his bedroom door behind him, Rey took the movie off pause and put his arm around Willow. She laid her head on his shoulder, and they watched the rest in a sort of quiet bliss.

This, Rey thought. This sort of domestic evening had never been something he'd thought he wanted. Until Willow. Now, he couldn't even begin to imagine his life without her.

They'd need to talk, and soon. But he knew a conversation about their futures couldn't happen without Isla, Carl and the others being found. He also knew the very real possibility existed that Willow, once she knew her grandmother was safe, would wave goodbye and head back to her home and job in California.

When the movie ended, Willow turned to him and said she wanted to talk. Since this echoed his thoughts, he hid his surprise and nodded. His heart rate picked up as he wondered if she'd actually broach the subject that had been constantly on his mind. Her leaving. Or alternatively, her staying.

"Sure," he managed to say casually. "What's up?"

She took a deep breath and met his gaze. "That area with the no trespassing signs. I know you want to wait and see what Rayna thinks, but I want to go back."

Damn. Hiding his disappointment, he shook his head. "I don't believe it's safe. We've already agreed to mention it to Rayna tomorrow."

She grimaced, clearly reluctant. "I know we agreed to discuss it with her, but I don't really see a need to. She's got her own leads to follow. Why can't we investigate this on our own? I know you feel it's too dangerous, but we can be careful. If we don't have loud four-wheelers, they won't even know we're there."

Persistent, he'd give her that. "Come on, Willow. They shot at us last time. We've been warned. We can't risk it."

"But what if that's where Isla, Carl and the others are being held? I have to think that's a very real possibility."

"Maybe," he allowed. "But we don't have enough reason to get a search warrant. And without something like that, they're within their rights to shoot at us for coming onto their land. This is Texas. The Castle Doctrine says deadly force is justifiable if they believe it's necessary to protect themselves from the unlawful use of force by an intruder."

"But we're not armed. Just trespassing isn't threatening."

"They could claim they didn't know that. It would have to go trial, and that would be too late if they've already shot us."

Though she narrowed her eyes, she finally nodded in agreement. "Fine. We'll talk to Rayna. Maybe she'll have some ideas."

"I'm sure she will. We can run by the sheriff's department first thing in the morning. If I can get Sam to do his fair share of chores. Which might be more difficult than it should be."

Willow laughed, but seemed appeased.

He kissed her then. When they broke apart, he grinned. "How about we continue this in my bedroom?"

She jumped to her feet and grabbed his arm. "Come on. We don't want Sam to walk in on us."

Needing no second urging, he allowed her to pull him along.

Later, as they held on to each other, sated and happy, he kissed the top of her head. Heart pounding, he decided to take a chance and speak his thoughts out loud.

"I could get used to this," he said, quietly.

When she didn't respond, he glanced down at her and realized she'd fallen asleep.

The next morning, Rey managed to get out of bed without disturbing Willow. He headed to the kitchen, where he found Sam finishing up a bowl of cereal. Surprised, he realized his younger brother was already dressed in jeans, work boots and a long-sleeved shirt.

"You slept in?" Sam drawled, taking a long drink of his coffee.

Rey grinned. "Maybe a little," he allowed. "But I'm still up before the sun."

"Truth. I thought I'd get an early start on the chores this morning."

"Good," Rey replied. "I've got to run Willow into town to have a word with the sheriff."

As usual, Sam appeared completely disinterested. He didn't ask a single question or even acknowledge Rey's statement. Instead, he put his bowl and mug in the sink, grabbed his hat off the counter and strode to the door. "See you later," he said.

Once the door had closed behind him, Rey shook his head and went to make himself and Willow a cup of coffee.

After they'd had their breakfast and showered, they hopped in his truck and made the drive into town to see Rayna. Willow had texted to make sure the sheriff would be available. "She says to come on in."

Downtown Getaway still appeared sleepy in the early morning sun. As they drove past the Tumbleweed Café, the usual pickup trucks filled the parking lot, ranchers there for breakfast before heading out to the fields.

When they reached the sheriff's department building, they parked and hurried inside. Talking to the receptionist at the front desk, Rayna looked up and greeted them with a smile. "Come on back," she said.

Once they were settled in her office with fresh cups of coffee, Rey decided to get right to the point. "Willow wants to go back and try to search that area where we were stuck during the dust storm."

Rayna's brows rose. "Where someone shot at you?"

Rey nodded. "I think it's too dangerous."

"But I feel there's a very real possibility we'll find my grandmother and the others there," Willow interjected.

"Based on what?" Rayna wanted to know. She leaned forward, eyeing Willow intently.

Willow shrugged. "Gut instinct. Intuition. Call it what you will, but I can't shake the feeling that they're there."

"Did you discuss this with Serenity at any point?" Rayna asked.

"No." Willow sighed. "If she wasn't still in the hospital, I'd give her a call."

Since Rey wasn't sure why Rayna even brought up Serenity, unless she actually *believed* in her psychic abilities, he kept his mouth shut.

"Well, even if you could ask her about it, that wouldn't be enough." Tone decisive, Rayna sat back in her chair and took a long drink of coffee. "I want you two to promise me you'll stay away from that land," she continued. "They not only have No Trespassing signs posted, but they fired warning shots. They clearly mean business. It's not safe."

"But how else are we going to know if that's where our parents are?" Willow protested.

The long look Rayna gave her spoke volumes. "We don't have a single reason to believe they're there. If I had one, just one valid reason, I could get a search warrant and go in myself."

"What about a drone?" Rey asked. "Don't you law-enforcement types have access to drones? That would be the safest way to find out what's going on."

"I don't have one," Rayna said thoughtfully. "But

I'm sure I could locate one if I made a few phone calls. That's a really good idea."

Rey smiled. "Thanks."

"But they could shoot that down," Willow pointed out.

"Better a drone than a person," Rayna responded. "Let me get working on that. It may turn out to be nothing, but at least we can say we gave it a shot."

"Or," Rey added, touching Willow's shoulder, "a drone might be able to provide exactly the lead we need to bring Carl, Isla and the others home."

Though Willow's disappointed expression revealed her feelings, she simply sighed. "How soon will you know if a drone is available?" she asked.

Rayna shrugged. "This might take some time, but if I can locate one and talk them into letting me borrow it, I should be able to get it by the end of the week."

"That's not soon enough," Willow protested.

"It's the best I can do," Rayna countered. "Now, I'm sorry, but I'm fresh out of time. I'll be in touch as soon as I have something concrete."

After Rayna walked away, Rey took Willow's arm. He could tell she wasn't happy with the solution the sheriff had come up with, but he honestly felt it was a good one. "This is perfect," he said. "Now I don't have to worry about you getting shot."

"But she said it could take a week," Willow protested. "I think we should go in and look around ourselves. If we take precautions, we should be safe."

"Precautions?" He shook his head. "Like wear cammo and try to blend in with the landscape?"

Crossing her arms, she met his gaze. "Why not? It would work."

"I vote we wait for the drone, as Rayna suggested. Not only will that be safer, but we'll get a much better view. Once we have that, we'll see everything there is to see within a matter of minutes. Those things transmit video in real time. It'll be perfect."

Though her expression remained unconvinced, she finally nodded. "Then I guess I'm going to have to go home," she said. "I'm sure you've got work to do around the ranch."

Ruefully, he acknowledged her words. "There's always something that needs doing."

They walked out to his truck. He waited until they were inside before turning to her. "What about you? Any plans for the rest of today?"

After buckling her seat belt, she shrugged. "I'm thinking I might drive back out to the hospital and see if they'll let me talk to Serenity. I'll probably call first, though, because that's a long drive to make if they won't let her have visitors."

"True." He kissed her one more time before starting the engine. Though he couldn't put his finger on it, something felt off. Maybe it had to do with Sam actually doing the chores earlier, rather than the way Willow appeared to be avoiding meeting his gaze.

Chapter 16

After Rey dropped her off at her house, Willow watched him drive away. She knew what she had to do. If she wanted to check out that area quickly, she was going to have to go it alone. Preferably first thing in the morning. No way did she plan on waiting another week to ten days for drones that may or may not be available.

After calling Velma and learning Serenity remained in the ICU—though Velma hoped her condition would soon be upgraded so she could be moved to a regular room—Willow decided she might as well do some housework. It wouldn't do for Isla to come home to a less than tidy house.

She passed the next couple of hours happily cleaning. When she'd finished, she walked around the sparkling house and smiled, imagining Isla's reaction. Though Willow normally didn't enjoy housework (who did?), showing love for her grandmother this way felt good.

Rey didn't call that afternoon. She guessed he'd gotten busy. While she ached to hear his voice, she also had begun to feel guilty about her solo plans for the morning. While she wasn't exactly lying to him, omitting her plans felt wrong. Except for one thing. She knew he'd try to stop her.

They'd never actually had a disagreement. Part of her wondered how he'd handle attempting to convince her not to go. Since she'd begun thinking long-term relationship with him, she knew this would be something she needed to know.

Just not right now. Another time, when the stakes weren't as high.

Though she and Rey had taken to spending every spare moment together, when he FaceTimed her around dinnertime, she claimed she didn't feel well. Which was true. She'd become a mess of nerves. She told him all she wanted to do was get some rest in her own bed. Alone. Which wasn't true.

The hurt that flashed in Rey's eyes wounded her, but she managed to keep herself from offering comfort. He'd be okay for one night. After all, since they'd never discussed her staying, what did he think would happen once she went back to Cali?

Again, she acknowledged she wouldn't be returning. Once she had Isla back safe and sound, she wasn't taking a chance on missing any more time with her. And since her grandmother was growing older and might be facing some health challenges, Willow planned to be by her side to help guide her through them.

Not only that, but she had to admit she couldn't handle the thought of leaving Rey. While they hadn't discussed the future and certainly hadn't made any promises, she realized she wanted to see if what they had now deepened.

That is, if what she planned to do on her own didn't completely tank things between them.

He called her again shortly after nine to ask if she felt

any better. They stayed on the phone for an hour, each of them equally loath to let go of the sound of the other's voice. A couple of times during their conversation, she almost broke down and gave him notice of her plans, but at the last moment, she reined herself in. When they finally said good-night, she decided to turn in early. She knew she'd have a restless night.

Alone in her double bed, she felt Rey's absence so strongly that she almost reached for her phone to call him. Instead, she forced herself to lie still, going over her plans for the morning instead of thinking about him.

Her nerves kept her tossing and turning, and by the time she pushed back the covers and got out of her bed shortly before five, she had serious doubts about her admittedly half-baked plan. For one thing, how hard would it be to find the area with the No Trespassing signs? She didn't have the same familiarity with the land as Rey. To prepare, she'd done some research on the county appraisal district's website and saved a few maps to her phone.

Beyond that, she intended to drive as close to the area as she could, park on the side of the road and go the rest of the way on foot. She would dress in clothing that would hopefully help her blend into the landscape.

She had no concrete plans other than to take photos with her phone if she discovered anything. Unless she caught sight of Isla or Carl, she didn't intend to try to infiltrate any buildings or even get close enough to place herself in any danger.

If Isla, Carl and the others were there, she wanted them out as soon as possible. And if not, then no one would be any the wiser about her investigation.

The pep talk with herself helped. She found some beige, brown and dark green clothing—the closest thing to camouflage she owned—and got dressed. She pulled her hair back into a ponytail and tucked it up under an old baseball cap she'd found in Isla's closet. She also emptied the backpack she'd brought with her from Cali and, following Rey's example, loaded it up with a couple bottles of water and some nonperishable provisions. Just in case.

Once she'd made a cup of coffee to go, she shouldered her backpack and left, too nervous to eat anything. She'd do that once she returned home.

As she left town behind, her headlights swept the empty roads, once again reinforcing how isolated this area truly was. For the first time, it struck home that there'd be no one to help her if she got in trouble. And if the same people who had Isla, Carl and the others grabbed her, no one would have the slightest idea where she'd gone.

She decided she needed to leave a hint or a clue. But what? For the rest of the drive, she considered her options. She could text Rey, but the effect would be too immediate, and if she knew him, he'd head out right away to try and stop her.

A handwritten note might work, but if she was taken, she suspected they'd also move her car. She went over several possibilities before settling on one.

When she reached her destination, she pulled out her phone and searched for Sam's number. If she knew him, he'd be deeply asleep and wouldn't see a text from her for hours.

Sam, it's Willow. I need you to give Rey a message for me. Tell him I went out on my own to the land with the signs. He'll know what that means. Please pass this on to him as soon as you get it, just in case I find myself in trouble.

She reread it and then pushed Send. Satisfied with her solution, she got out of her Bronco, used the key fob to lock the doors and headed in the direction she hoped would lead to the posted land.

Either luck was on her side or she'd somehow retained a good memory, because she'd only been hiking for thirty minutes when she saw the familiar rise in the land that she and Rey had climbed. The sun had just begun to ascend the horizon, and the sky lit up in rose, orange and gold in a West Texas sunrise.

Instantly going on full alert, she headed up the path. When she reached the top, she kept herself close to the large rock and nearby tree, just in case someone might be on the posted land.

To her relief, she saw no one.

So far, so good. She spotted the fence, the gate and the bright yellow No Trespassing signs. And there was the small group of trees where she and Rey had pitched the tent during the dust storm. This brought another twinge of guilt, since she knew Rey wouldn't be happy with what she was doing. But she'd come this far, too far to back out now, even if she wanted. Which she didn't. If nothing came of this, no harm done. And if she did discover something, then everything would change for the better.

Since the posted land sat behind another rise, with

rocky outcroppings dotting the area, she felt certain she'd have numerous places to hide. If they had some sort of regular patrols, she should be able to take shelter and avoid being spotted.

Heart pounding, she shouldered her backpack and sprinted toward the gate. She made it over without incident and, congratulating herself, headed for the small group of trees.

She kept moving, zigzagging between rocks and trees and otherwise trying to stay low to the ground.

Ahead, she saw another slight rise in the land, with two large rock outcroppings that resembled sentries. Since she'd been steadily climbing, she figured things had to level out soon.

As she approached the space between the rocks, out of an abundance of caution, she once again looked around. So far, so good. If whoever owned this land did do regular patrols, they must start later.

In what felt like a safe space, she stood close to the larger of the two boulders and stared. Below, spread out in an area that encompassed at least a couple of acres, sat a sprawling compound. Odd how that word seemed to best describe these buildings, made from a combination of cinderblock and stucco that had been painted the exact color of sand.

What the heck was it? It didn't look like any ranch she'd ever seen. More like a prison or some sort of top-secret, government facility.

Though she hadn't seen any people yet, this would be the exact type of place where she'd expect someone who'd taken hostages to keep them.

Cautioning herself not to get too excited, she plotted the

best way to get closer to the cluster of buildings. Though she still didn't see any movement of people—whether residents or guards—it now made more sense why whoever owned this place would have patrols.

Every nerve ending alive, she kept herself low and kept moving, only stopping long enough to take brief shelter and quickly reassess any possible danger.

The closer she got to the compound, the more suspicious she became. Still, aware of the danger, she continued to take precautions.

At one point, resting behind the trunk of a bent and twisted oak tree, she forced herself to stop and take stock. Beyond seeing the structure, she didn't have a plan. She sure as heck wasn't going to try and break in, especially since she hadn't seen anything concrete that might indicate that Isla, Carl and the other missing townspeople were inside.

She pulled out her phone and began snapping photos. As soon as she had enough, she decided to turn and retrace her route. Though Rey wouldn't be happy, she figured once she showed the pictures to Rayna, the sheriff would want to open an investigation.

Checking the time, she was relieved to see that only a couple of hours had passed. She should be able to get back to her Bronco and be back at the house by lunchtime. By the time Sam saw the text she'd sent and showed it to Rey, there'd be nothing for Rey to say. And she'd have the pictures.

She gave herself a quiet high five and turned to go. Before taking a single step, she once again scanned the entire area for any signs of a patrol.

This time, what she saw made her freeze in her tracks.

Two men, both carrying high-capacity rifles, stood between her and the way she needed to go.

They hadn't seen her yet. Or so she fervently hoped. Neither appeared to be looking her way. Instead, they stood talking, one of them smoking a cigarette, the other continually scanning the area.

If they looked her way, they'd see her.

She didn't dare move. In fact, she had to work hard to control her breathing. If she started hyperventilating and gasping for air, they'd surely hear her.

Move on, move on, she chanted silently. They had a lot of ground to cover. Once they continued their patrol, she could get out of here.

Except they didn't go anywhere. Almost as if they were toying with her. The breeze ruffled the prairie grass, carrying snatches of their conversation to her. *Coffee*, she heard. And the words *target practice*. That last part made her blood run cold.

Afraid to check her smartwatch, she didn't know how long she'd been crouching there, waiting for them to go. It felt like eternity as her legs started cramping. Even worse, she realized that she needed to empty her bladder, which would not be possible right now.

One of the men suddenly pivoted. As his gaze locked on her, she knew she'd been seen. Though every instinct screamed at her to run, she didn't want to take the chance of getting shot in the back.

"Come out with your hands up," the guard ordered, raising his rifle.

As the other man slowly did the same, Willow complied.

* * *

First thing in the morning after he opened his eyes, Rey battled the urge to call Willow, just to say good morning. Not wanting to risk waking her, he forced himself to get up, make coffee and a bowl of oatmeal and eat. The entire time, he kept his phone out on the kitchen table, just in case she texted or called. But she didn't, and he figured she must be sleeping in. He shoved his phone in his back pocket before getting busy doing the morning chores.

Sam hadn't spent the night at home again, which was starting to become a problem. Rey understood how his younger brother might be distancing himself from the ranch, but his desire to do so didn't mean he could skip out on work. Not if he expected the ranch to continue to support him. He guessed he and Sam would be having yet another heart-to-heart discussion very soon.

In the meantime, chores didn't disappear simply because someone didn't show up to do them. Which meant, in addition to his usual tasks, Rey now had Sam's to contend with.

By late morning, he had almost everything done. Glad he hadn't yet showered, he went back to the house and drank a large glass of ice water. Now, he thought, would be a respectable time to call Willow. He couldn't wait to hear her voice.

But instead, he got her voice mail. Disappointed, he left her a quick message, asking her to call him back once she had a chance.

When his phone rang almost immediately after that, he smiled. *That was quick*, he thought. Maybe Willow had been missing him too.

But Rayna's number showed on the screen instead.

"What's up?" Rey asked.

"We've finished checking out that faith healer guy, Jonathan Longtree," she said. "He's a nurse practitioner. Or was, until his APRN license was suspended."

"That can't be good," Rey commented. "So, is he legally allowed to run his healing center?"

"That's where it gets interesting. He played it smart, by labeling his business as religion rather than medical care. There are little to no regulations on churches."

Startled, Rey wished he had the brochure handy. "Is he operating as a church? I don't remember reading that in the pamphlet."

"He doesn't come right out and say that, but it's alluded to. There are several instances where he asks for donations to *keep God's Work going*," Rayna replied. "When you get a chance, take a look at it again."

"I will."

"I reached out to him with the number on the flyer and left a voice mail asking him to call me. I also sent an email. I have a feeling he isn't going to respond."

"Maybe I should try," Rey suggested. "I'm sure he isn't interested in talking with anyone in law enforcement. I can be a regular citizen seeking healing."

"That might work," Rayna said thoughtfully. "Though, I think it would be better if we could get someone older to help us. If this Longtree is our guy, his target appears to be senior citizens."

Which made perfect sense. "Do you have someone in mind who might be willing to help?"

"I'm working on that," Rayna replied. "And I've also

sent out inquiries about borrowing that drone. I'm hoping to hear something back by this afternoon."

"That would be awesome." Rey found himself itching to tell Willow. In fact, he'd give her a call after he finished talking to the sheriff. "Please keep me posted."

"I will. And if you wouldn't mind, pass this info on to Willow for me. I tried to call her, but she didn't answer."

Rey chuckled. "Will do. I'm planning to talk to her as soon as we hang up."

"Sounds great." And Rayna ended the call.

Immediately, Rey punched the contact for Willow. The call went directly to voice mail. He left a quick message to say he'd just gotten off the phone with Rayna and had some news. He asked Willow to call him back when she could.

That done, he tried to understand why his father would trust anyone claiming to be a faith healer. Carl had never been much for church, though he'd started attending with Isla. A pragmatic man, he believed in a power higher than himself, but had little use for anyone claiming to represent that power. Even Serenity, who made no religious claims whatsoever, had been regarded with barely concealed distrust.

Carl was a man of the land. Grounded, he worked with his hands. He understood animals and nature and other people. He had no use for philosophy or esoteric nonsense, as he liked to call it.

If he'd gone to a faith healer, the only reason would have been for Isla. Whether to take care of her health or, if Carl had developed some sort of illness, to please her in trying to take care of his. After all, Carl would do anything for the people he loved.

Damn, Rey missed him. If this faith healer had anything to do with his and the others' disappearance, Rey would be hard pressed not to deck the guy.

Shaking his head, Rey went over a mental list of the remaining tasks that needed to be completed that day. He really should try Sam again and demand his younger brother get his rear home and start pulling his weight.

His phone rang, startling him. *Willow.* The thought of hearing her voice made him smile.

But when he glanced at the caller ID, he saw it was Sam rather than Willow. As if thinking about him had gotten him to call.

Since Sam only phoned when he needed something, Rey took a deep breath. Bracing himself to hear what kind of trouble his brother had gotten into now, he answered the call. "What's up?"

"I'm really worried. I think Willow's in trouble," Sam said, his voice so agitated Rey could barely understand him. Sam then said something about getting a text from her, but he wasn't making any sense.

"Slow down, please," Rey ordered, despite his own now accelerated heart rate. "Read it to me, word for word."

Sam, it's Willow. I need you to give Rey a message for me. Tell him I went out on my own to the land with the signs. He'll know what that means. Please pass this on to him as soon as you get it, just in case I find myself in trouble.

Rey felt like the earth had shifted beneath his feet. He cursed. And then cursed again.

"Do you understand what she means?" Sam asked,

the worry in his voice matching the absolute terror in Rey's heart.

"Unfortunately, I do. How far away from here are you?" Rey asked, his voice grim.

"I'm on the other side of town, at Gia's place," Sam replied. "About thirty-five minutes away."

"Get here as soon as you can. I'm going to take Roscoe and ride out to look for Willow. I need you to take care of the ranch until I get back."

"Take care of...?"

"I don't have time to explain everything to you," Rey said, letting his frustration show in his voice. "I did both my chores and yours this morning. I need you to do the same this afternoon."

He ended the call without waiting to hear Sam's response. Then he took off running for the barn. He saddled Roscoe in record time, climbed on and took off for the far pasture.

Sticking closer to the roads this time, his heart sank when he spotted Willow's empty red Bronco, parked in a ditch. Impressed at her ability to get the area right, he rode on past, heading for the hill where the no trespassing signs were easily visible.

Once he'd ridden to the top, he scouted the area below and on all sides, looking for any sign of Willow. A slender ribbon of water, all that remained of the river that had once cut through this craggy land, shone silver in the distance. Twisted trees, bent sideways from the perpetual wind, dotted the space. They provided only a little shade, though he supposed someone on foot might use them as cover.

Despite searching thoroughly, going over each area in

several sweeps, he saw no sign of Willow. This scared the hell out of him. What if she'd been right, and someone had set up camp here and was actually holding a couple dozen senior citizens hostage? If they caught Willow attempting to sneak up on them, they'd grab her too. And who knows what might happen after that.

A shudder of pure terror lanced through him. Though he knew better than to leap to conclusions, he couldn't help but consider the worst-case scenario.

Why hadn't she waited for the drone? Why take this kind of risk? He wished he knew what the hell she'd been thinking.

Quickly, he ran through his options. He could call Rayna. Should call Rayna, actually. Except Willow had trespassed, and while that didn't give them the right to hold her captive, they could call the sheriff's office and press charges.

Which he supposed most normal people would. Unless they had something to hide. And he suspected whoever had posted the no trespassing signs definitely did.

Was Jonathan Longtree, the so-called faith healer, involved in this? Perhaps here, on this remote acreage in between two huge ranches, had been where he'd built his home or office or whatever he called it.

Right now, Rey needed to figure out his next move.

He could turn Roscoe around and ride back home. He was still on the outside of the boundaries marked by the no trespassing signs.

Or he could ride the perimeter, remaining careful not to break any laws, and try not to be seen by the armed men who evidently patrolled the perimeter. As long as he wasn't on their land, they'd have no reason to shoot at him.

If that worked, he could question them. Maybe they'd answer, maybe they wouldn't. But at least he'd hopefully get some sort of idea what the hell was going on.

And if he didn't encounter anyone? He supposed he might be tempted to investigate further, even if he had to trespass on their land in order to do that.

Decision made, he turned Roscoe in the direction of the incline. He rode to the top, where he had a clear view not only of the posted boundaries, but also of the pastures spread below. In the distance, he saw two large mesas that divided the land. In between them, an opening that appeared large enough to drive a truck through. Though this definitely meant he could ride Roscoe through it, he also noted that once through, if it was blocked, leaving could become problematic.

Instead of trying to open the gate, which he knew from last time would be futile, he rode along the fence line. He didn't really want to trespass, not just yet.

The ride seemed to take forever. Fully alert, some of his nerves communicated themselves to Roscoe. The well-trained and well-seasoned horse had gotten used to just about everything, but having his rider on edge put him there as well. Which meant in addition to keeping watch for armed guards, he had to keep Roscoe under control as well.

Fifteen minutes later, he saw them. Two men, on foot, carrying semiautomatic rifles. They watched him, keeping their distance, though they made sure he could see their weapons.

Deciding to pretend ignorance, he urged Roscoe closer

to the fence and began waving at them. "Excuse me," he hollered. "I need to ask you something."

The guards looked at each other. One shrugged, and then they strode toward Rey. They stopped about twenty feet from the fence. "Are you lost?" one man asked, his tone harsh and unwelcoming.

"Not really," Rey responded, keeping his voice light and casual in contrast. "I own one of the ranches nearby. I haven't been out this way in a good while, but I'm curious about all those no trespassing signs. We neighboring ranchers are a friendly bunch, and we've always given each other free access to each other's land. What's up with all this?"

"Private property," the second man said, taking a few steps closer. "The signs are to make sure it stays that way."

"That's not real friendly," Rey commented, scratching his head as if truly perplexed. "Who's the owner? He must be new. Is there any way I could talk to him, since we're practically neighbors?"

"No." The first man joined the second. In unison, they raised their rifles. "I'd suggest you make your way back to wherever you came from."

Though he could have pointed out the fact that he wasn't on their land, Rey decided not to bother. For now, he'd make a show of leaving. Then he'd return, either with or without Rayna. If they had Willow, he'd need to figure out a way to rescue her.

Chapter 17

Though her heart hammered as if it might pound out of her chest and her legs were shaky, Willow managed to walk as directed toward the compound. Having two large rifles aimed directly at her provided an incentive to follow orders.

For the first time in a while, she wanted to curse. Though she'd known her exploration would be dangerous, she'd honestly believed she wouldn't be caught. Now that she had, what the heck was she going to do?

Since, at the moment, she couldn't do anything, she figured she might as well play it casual until she found out what was going on. After all, it was entirely possible she'd been wrong about this place. Perhaps the owners were extremely private people and just wanted privacy. Maybe they were famous. Or über wealthy eccentrics wanting to live off the grid.

If that turned out to be the case, while she might have wasted her time, she'd also be in a much better position to explain why she'd trespassed on their land. If she played up that California accent she'd heard so many times while living there, maybe they'd buy a story about an overly curious tourist who'd wandered too far off the beaten path. Maybe looking for fossils or arrowheads or something like that.

Because honestly, that was all she could come up with to explain why she'd disregarded the bright yellow signs. If she could convince them she was just some sort of empty-headed female, they might be more inclined to let her go.

Unless of course, Isla and the others turned out to be captives here. That would change everything. While she had no idea what course of action she'd take then, she had to hope she'd come up with something.

When they reached the front of the structure, which she could now see appeared to be a tall, concrete-block wall surrounding the large stucco building, her guards took her around to the side. There, they stopped in front of a metal door with an electronic keypad. One man punched in the code while the other kept his weapon pointed at her.

She briefly considered asking them to let her go, but she equally needed to see what was inside this veritable fortress. Pushing her fear aside, she lifted her chin, took a deep breath and waited.

The first guard pushed the door open, and the second guy motioned for her to go inside.

"Where are you taking me?" she asked, managing to keep her voice steady.

"To see Jonathan," they both answered. "Now, move."

Jonathan. She guessed he must be the owner of all this. Wait. Hadn't the faith healer's name been Jonathan? Yes. She believed it had. Jonathan Longtree. Just like that, her heart rate accelerated. Somehow, she'd managed to stumble upon what she knew deep inside had to be the right place.

They led her to a small, windowless room and left, closing and locking the door behind them. The only furniture inside was a scratched and scarred wooden bench that had been pushed up against one wall. Unusual, even ominous, to say the least.

But then again, maybe she'd simply watched too many true-crime dramas. This guy called himself a faith healer, after all. Healers weren't supposed to hurt people. However, they weren't supposed to hold people against their will either.

As time passed and no one came, she realized they hadn't searched her or taken her cell phone. Almost hyperventilating, she shakily pulled it out. She'd call Rey first, and he could call Rayna.

But though she called his number, nothing happened. That was when she realized she had no signal.

What the...? Not believing it, she tried again. The little icon in the top left corner showed No Service.

Dang it. She tried turning her phone off and then back on. Still nothing. Which meant this building had some kind of cell blocking thing going on. No wonder they hadn't taken her phone.

Still, because she'd read somewhere that 911 would work, she tried that. The call dropped. She tried again with the same result.

At least her smartwatch still kept perfect time.

One hour passed. It had nearly reached two when the door creaked open and a slender man with long brown hair and an equally long, well-trimmed beard came in. He peered at her through his silver, wire-rimmed glasses, expression intense. Though he wore khaki pants and a white button-down shirt, he had a kind of otherworldly presence that she suspected he cultivated deliberately.

"Welcome," he said, his voice soft yet commanding. "My name is Jonathan Longtree."

"Willow Allen," she replied, relieved that he appeared to be relatively normal. "I'm sorry that I wandered onto your property. I promise it won't happen again."

"Oh, I know it won't." He flashed a pleasant smile. "Because I'm not going to let you leave."

Her heart dropped straight to her feet. Not sure how to respond, she simply stared at him.

Finally, deciding she had nothing to lose, she told him the truth. "Look, my grandmother is missing. So are several older people from our town. I came out here looking for them. Have you seen them?"

He blinked. "Guard," he called. Immediately, the door opened, and one of the armed men from earlier stepped inside the room.

"Bring her water and something to eat," Jonathan ordered.

As the man went to comply, Willow wondered how on earth she'd manage to choke down food. She understood that she somehow would have to try. Something about the steely glint in Jonathan's eyes warned her not to cross him, even in the smallest of ways.

A moment later, the guard returned. He brought a large glass of water and a paper plate with carrot sticks, celery and a spoonful of dip on it.

When he handed this to Willow, she accepted it. The moment she did, the guard backed out of the room, closing the door behind him.

"We insist on healthy eating here," Jonathan said, smiling. "Part of the mind-body connection."

She nodded and took a small sip of the water. "What is *here*, exactly?"

"This is the Longtree Wellness Center." His smile widened. "And we specialize in healing people in the older demographic."

For a moment, she could only gape at him. "Does that mean…" she asked, once she'd found her voice.

"That the individuals you've been searching for are here?" His smug smile widened. "The answer to that would be yes."

Time stopped. Her heart skipped a beat or two while she struggled to find the right words. "Would it be possible for me to see them?" she asked, her tone as respectful as she could make it.

He stared at her, eyes hard. "You have to earn favors here. Most people pay money. I know your grandmother did. Her boyfriend too. What sort of skills do you bring to the table?"

Not sure what he meant, she wondered if he meant sexually. Though she tried to remain calm, her eyes filled with tears. "I'm not sure what you mean," she managed, squeaking out the words.

Clearly impatient, he huffed. "What are you good at? What do you do for a living? How are you best able to help us here at the center?"

When she couldn't come up with an immediate response, he shook his head and strode to the door. "I'll leave you here to think about that. Next time we speak, I hope you have an answer."

When he closed the door behind him, she heard the unmistakable sound of a lock sliding into place.

Great. Now what? First, she needed to calm herself. She took several deep breaths, working very hard to slow her heart rate. Then, out of habit, she tried her phone once again, even though she'd already confirmed she had no service. Just in case, she tried sending Rayna a text, but got an error message saying it wasn't able to be delivered. Of course not.

She got up and began pacing the small room, trying to think. If this Jonathan Longtree wanted to play games, she'd better come up with something so he'd let her see her grandmother and the others.

Mentally, she ran over a list of her strengths. She suspected being organized and good with numbers wouldn't fly. Ditto with surfing—they were miles from the nearest ocean. Her cooking skills were limited, though she could make a mean enchilada soup. Maybe she should play up that, since it was the lone thing she could think of that might be of benefit to others.

Once that occurred to her, she started thinking of other stuff she could do to help people, more specifically, seniors. When she'd been a teenager, she'd volunteered in a senior living center. She'd been really good at reading them books, taking on the voices of the various characters. She'd always loved making her audience laugh. She decided to use those two when Jonathan came back. She could only hope they'd be enough.

Alone in the small room, minutes dragged into an hour, then two. She had to tamp down her rising impatience. Knowing she was this close to her grandmother only increased the aching need to see her. Right now!

Waiting felt intolerable, though she suspected he was taking as long as possible as a deliberate way to show her who was boss. As if she had any doubt. This man had clearly made it his life's work to prey on the sick and aging. Why he'd chosen the small town of Getaway, she had no idea. Unless it had something to do with the purchase of this land. Remote enough for nefarious purposes, and in a part of the country where folks weren't inclined to pry into each other's business.

Finally, just as she'd checked her watch for maybe the hundredth time, the door opened and Jonathan sauntered in. "Did I give you long enough to reflect?" he asked, his dulcet tone at odds with the cold glint in his eyes.

Not wanting to seem too eager or do anything to put him off, she meekly nodded. She'd make sure he had no idea that she was seething inside.

"Good. Now tell me, what skills do you bring to the table?"

As his gaze swept over her from top to bottom, for the second time it occurred to her that he really might have meant something sexual. She hid the way this thought made her recoil and forced herself to smile sweetly.

"I can cook," she said. "I'm especially good at baking cakes. And I've also been told I do a good job reading out loud to people. I used to volunteer in a nursing home, and the residents looked forward to attending my reading sessions."

When she finished talking, Jonathan considered her words. He once again appeared expressionless, before bowing his head as if praying.

Once again, her nerves took over. Yet, somehow she

managed to sit completely still, her hands folded tightly in her lap.

"I think that will do," he announced, his beatific smile not fooling her for one second. "Come. I will take you to see the others."

Slowly, she got to her feet, unwilling to let him see her eagerness. Though her pulse had kicked up, she stood quietly, waiting for him to either lead the way or to call for an armed man to escort her. Either way would work, as long as she got to see Isla, Carl and the others.

He opened the door and stepped out. "Follow me," he said without looking back.

As she left the room, two men immediately flanked her. They weren't the two guards who'd escorted her here. She noticed they didn't carry large rifles like the others had. Instead, they both wore pistols, holstered but still within reach.

Silent, they all marched down a long, windowless hallway. When they reached a door and stepped outside, she realized they were leaving one building and going to another.

This second structure, made of the same beige stucco, also appeared to be windowless. Willow frowned, realizing it looked a lot like a prison.

When they reached a metal door, Jonathan entered a series of numbers in a keypad mounted in the wall. The lock made a clicking sound, and the door opened. "This way," he ordered. He strode ahead without looking back.

Willow hurried after him. She had to practically jog to keep up with his long-legged stride.

Down another long hallway, a right turn, then a left, and they finally emerged into what she could only describe as a room resembling a high school cafeteria. Inside, men and women sat at long banquet-style tables, eating.

"You're lucky," Jonathan said, swinging around to eye her. "Looks like you made it just in time for a late lunch."

Too busy scanning the room to pay attention to him, Willow let out a little cry when she spotted a familiar face. "Isla!" she cried out. Then, before anyone could stop her, she launched herself across the room, running toward her beloved grandmother.

As soon as he had cell service again, Rey called the sheriff. Using as few words as possible, he told her about Willow's text to Sam and his experience a few minutes before.

"Semiautomatic rifles?" Rayna asked. "To patrol a pasture? What do they think they're going to be fighting against?"

"No idea." Rey took a deep breath, tamping down his frustration. "But I need help figuring out a way to get Willow out of that place."

"Except you don't know she's in there," Rayna pointed out.

"Where else would she be?" Rey countered. "Come on. I'm asking for your assistance here."

"Without a good reason, I can't ask the judge for a search warrant," Rayna said, her voice heavy with regret. "And while we know Willow planned to go explore that area, we have zero reason to believe they captured her or that she's being held prisoner. Just like we don't know for sure that's where we can find the missing people."

While she had a point, Rey felt obliged to mention he

didn't know what else to do. "What you're telling me is if I want to go in there looking for her, I'm on my own."

"Hold up." Rayna's voice turned stern. "The last thing we need is you disappearing too. Don't you dare go near that property."

"But what if Willow is in there?" he protested. "We don't have time to wait on those drones."

"If she is, I'm sure she'll be fine," Rayna replied. "Go on back home and let me see if I can come up with a plan. I'll call you when I do."

She hung up without waiting for an answer.

Rey seethed. He'd never been the type to sit around and wait for help. If something needed to be done, he did it. And this was Willow, damn it. The woman he loved.

If she needed saving, then that was what he'd do. And once he held her in his arms again, he was never going to let her go. Ever.

Pragmatic, Rey knew better than to try to rush in without a plan. Rayna was right about that. After all, clearly that was what Willow had done, and look what had happened.

For now, he decided to take Rayna's advice and go back to the ranch. Surely, something would come to him if he thought hard enough.

Once he reached the barn, he took the saddle off Roscoe and brushed his horse down. While his hands were occupied, he thought long and hard, looking for an actual course of action. But all he could come up with was what he'd started out with. Steal into the place under cover of darkness, locate Willow and extricate her. But that didn't take into account the very real possibility that all the missing townspeople might be there.

Rayna called as he was walking back to the main house. "I've got an idea," she said, her voice vibrating with excitement. "We were able to verify through the county tax office that Jonathan Longtree, aka the faith healer, is the owner of that land. And I've been talking to a few of my colleagues in Lubbock, and someone suggested that he might be marketing his faith healing as an actual medical facility without a license to do that. I'm having one of my deputies look into that now."

"What does that mean?" Rey asked, impatience cutting his words short.

"It means I can get him on that violation. It's a third-degree felony, punishable by two to ten years in prison and a fine of up to $10,000. Which means we can send a team out there to arrest him. That'll actually give us a legal ability to search the place. And if all those missing people are being held there against their will, that will be even more charges against him."

For the first time since he'd learned Willow had decided to pull this crazy stunt, Rey felt hope. "I want to go with them," he said, his voice fierce.

"No," Rayna immediately replied. "You're a civilian. You can't."

Since he'd guessed she would say that, he clenched his jaw tight and didn't argue. "How long until you know something?"

"I should hear within the hour. We're treating this as urgent, since it is."

Rey thanked her and ended the call. He started to ride back to his ranch, but halfway there, he stopped. Shaking his head, he turned around. If Rayna managed to put together a valid reason to legally go onto the ranch, great for her. But right now, the woman he loved might be in danger. No way was he letting her sit there until the sheriff's office raided the place. That situation could go south really quickly, and he didn't want to take even the slightest chance of letting the woman he loved get hurt.

He'd save her himself. Failure wasn't an option.

Since he'd grown up here and had spent years exploring his family's land and everything surrounding it, Rey figured that was one advantage that he had over anyone else. The no trespassing signs were a new addition, and as kids, he and his friends had roamed all over that land. He knew every cliff, every hiding place, and where to avoid so he wouldn't be exposed and vulnerable. While it might have been years since he'd ridden up that way, even if they'd built a house there, the land wouldn't have changed.

He continued moving forward.

When the low-slung, industrial-looking structure came into view, he sucked in his breath. The damn place, which looked a lot like a prison, appeared impenetrable. From his vantage point, he couldn't tell if the windowless wall was actually part of the structure or a kind of fence designed to keep prying eyes away.

He'd bet on the second.

Since a metal door appeared the only point of entry, unless he could grab somebody going in or out, he wouldn't be getting inside there. He'd have to figure out another way in. Which meant he'd need to circle around to the back of the building.

As he carefully made his way, he spotted a lone guard, on foot, armed with a semiautomatic rifle. The man appeared bored, kicking at the ground and occasionally glancing around at the admittedly monotonous landscape. He continued moving toward Rey, seemingly oblivious to the presence of an interloper.

Luckily, if he moved a few feet, Rey could duck behind a tree. He waited until the guard appeared to be focused on something on the horizon and made his move.

Now partially hidden, he didn't dare try to look to see the guard's progress. He could only go by sound. Luckily, the guy didn't even try to move quietly.

The closer he got, the more Rey's heart pounded. It might be desperate—hell, it *was* desperate—but he knew what he had to do.

He waited until the guard had moved just a few feet from him before coming out from behind the tree. Launching himself at the completely surprised man, Rey knocked him down before he could even get his rifle up. Two quick blows rendered the guard unconscious.

Working quickly, while keeping an eye on his surroundings, Rey dragged the man as close to the shelter of the tree as he could. Then, glad they appeared to be of similar size, he stripped the guard's clothing and put it on. He found a key fob inside the man's pocket, which he hoped could be used to unlock the door into the structure.

Once dressed and armed with the rifle, Rey hustled over to the metal door. No one stopped or even noticed him. He lifted the key fob and pressed the button, holding his breath as he hoped it would unlock the door.

To his infinite relief, the keypad beeped and then made a loud click. He tried the handle, and the door opened.

Now what? Stepping inside, he realized he'd have to play it by ear and hope he didn't get caught.

Strangely enough, the place seemed deserted. As he moved down a long, windowless hallway, he didn't encounter anyone else. Which might be a good thing, but where was Willow?

Finally, he reached an exterior door. This one wasn't locked, so he opened it and exited. Outside, he found himself in a small courtyard, facing another building with a similar door. Maybe inside would be where he'd find Willow.

After gaining entry, he finally heard the sound of voices. Keeping his head down, he hoped if he acted casual, no one would notice him. After all, he wore a guard's uniform, so he should be basically invisible to anyone who didn't work with him.

He passed two men talking. Since neither of them wore any kind of uniform, they didn't even look at him. Perfect.

Ahead, he heard the sound of many voices, which meant a larger group of people. Bracing himself, he continued moving forward. Around one more corner, he stepped into a brightly lit room that resembled a gymnasium or cafeteria. In one corner of the large area, he saw a group of maybe twenty people gathered together.

His heart skipped a beat as he spotted Willow. Then Isla and Carl. All the others who'd gone missing from town appeared to be there as well.

He dug out his phone, meaning to send Rayna a text. But the screen said No Service, so he shoved it back into his pocket.

He realized he couldn't let any of them see him, especially Willow or Carl. If they let on that they knew him, the others would figure out he wasn't supposed to be there, and chaos would ensue.

Alternatively, what now? He didn't have a workable plan for getting everyone out safe and unharmed.

A tall man with long, brown hair, a beard and wire-rimmed glasses strode into the room. This must be Jonathan, Rey realized. Clearly, the faith healer put a lot of time and effort into appearing saintly. He even clasped his hands in front of himself like some kind of yogi.

"Greetings, my friends," he said.

None of the gathered people responded in kind. Some glared at him, others appeared to be pretending he didn't exist. Not exactly the kind of response Rey would have expected, especially if they truly believed he could heal them. Maybe the fact that they were being held against their will had a lot of bearing on that.

Three armed men burst into the room. "We have intruders," one shouted. "A bunch of people from the local sheriff's office are here. They claim they have a search warrant. What do you want us to do?"

Rayna. She'd gotten here even faster than he'd thought she would. Grateful, he began edging toward the captives. He wanted to be prepared to defend them if necessary.

"You!" Jonathan pointed to Rey. "Take these people to the storm cellar."

Careful to keep his face down and expressionless, Rey nodded. As he moved toward the group, he saw Willow's beautiful eyes widen when she noticed him. His father, who appeared very ill, sat next to Isla with his head hanging down and didn't realize his son had come to try and save him.

Several people in the group began grumbling. "We're not going," one white-haired man declared. "If the sheriff is here, she'll take us home. And that's where I want to be."

"Me too," someone else echoed.

Before Rey had time to respond, he heard gunfire coming from outside. This instantly quieted everyone.

Jonathan Longtree, his pale face turning red, spun on his heel and headed away from the door. "Come on," he snapped to Rey and several other armed men who were in the room. "Forget about them. It's time to protect me and earn the salary I pay you."

While the other guards obediently trotted after the healer, Rey didn't move. Neither did Willow or the others.

Apparently used to being obeyed, Jonathan didn't even bother to look back to see if Rey had followed or had begun herding the others to the storm cellar, wherever that might be. Which was good, since Rey had no intention of hiding these people away. And he definitely wasn't about to protect the healer.

More gunshots, some shouting, the words undecipherable. The bedraggled cluster of senior citizens drew closer, some of them voicing their fear.

"It's going to be all right," Willow said, her voice clear and calm in the middle of danger. Though she sent Rey a grateful look, she stayed with her grandmother and the others.

The door burst open, and several armed sheriff's deputies came through, weapons drawn, with Rayna right on their heels. Rey immediately put down his rifle, just as a precaution, and raised his hands. He knew how easily things could deteriorate in tense situations.

Rayna spotted him and hurried over. "Where is he?"

"He and several of his armed guards went out that door," he said, pointing.

With a brusque nod, Rayna motioned to her deputies. "Let's go get him."

Once they'd left, he turned to face the woman he loved, her grandmother and his father. *Safe*, he told himself. They were okay. He couldn't ask for any more than that.

"Rey!" Willow cried. She came rushing over and wrapped her arms around him. "Did you see? Isla, Carl and all the others are here. And safe."

All he could do was pull her close and hold on. Now his knees finally buckled. "I love you," he murmured, smoothing her hair away from her face and kissing her cheek. "But don't you ever scare me like that again."

And then he went to check on his father, still sitting in the same spot, all hunched over. Carl raised his head to meet his son's gaze. "Hey, son," he said, one corner of his mouth raised in the beginning of a smile. "Glad you finally got here."

In response, Rey gently hugged him, shocked by his formerly robust father's new frailty. "I got here as soon as I could," he replied.

Later, after Jonathan Longtree had been marched off in handcuffs and paramedics had checked out all the people who'd been held captive, everyone was taken into town via a couple of school buses for a joyful reunion with their family members. Carl, who'd hacked and wheezed and had apparently come down with pneumonia, allowed Rey to drive him to the medical clinic so a doctor could take a look at him. He flat out refused to go to the hospital.

Isla remained by Carl's side, her expression worried. She kept one arm linked through her granddaughter's. Rey, unable to tear his gaze away from Willow, found himself aching to haul her up against him and kiss her until they both couldn't think.

"Willow," Isla finally said, clearly seeing right through him. "I think your young man would like a word with you in private."

Pink-cheeked, Willow met his gaze. "Is that so?"

Heart in his throat, he slowly nodded and held out his hand.

"Go on," Isla urged. "Carl and I will be right here when you get back."

When Willow slipped her slender fingers into his, he felt like he'd already won the jackpot. And yet, he hadn't. He still had something he desperately needed to say and wasn't sure how she'd receive it.

When they walked away from the others, Willow spoke first. "Earlier, you said you loved me. Did you mean that?"

"More than you could ever imagine," he responded. "And I noticed you didn't say you loved me back."

Her gaze flew to his. "I thought I did. But you know I do."

"Maybe," he allowed. "Though I really need to hear you say it."

"I love you," she immediately said. "More than you could ever imagine."

Satisfied, he kissed her again. When they broke apart, he exhaled. "Next, I need to know if you're still planning to go back to California."

Eyes locked on his, she shook her head. "I've been thinking about that for a while. Now that I have my grandmother back, no way am I leaving her again. I'm going to give my boss notice, but I'm hoping he'll let me work remotely."

He kissed her once more, long and deep and passionately, hoping she could feel every bit of the all-encompassing love he had for her.

When they moved apart, he was stunned to see her eyes shiny with tears.

"What's wrong?" he asked, using his thumb to gently wipe them away.

"I love you so much," she said. "I can't imagine living life without you."

Heart full, he pulled her close. "Same here. Now it looks like we won't have to."

Her tremulous smile brought tears to his own eyes. "I see a great future ahead for us," he said, touching his forehead to hers.

"Me too." She sighed. "And now we can go on double dates with Carl and Isla."

He laughed, happier than he'd been in a long, long time. "Yes, we can."

Then, arm in arm, they turned and went back to join the others, ready to start their new life together among family and friends. There might be some loose ends to tie up, but he knew they'd handle it all together.

* * * * *